LETHAL HOPE

A Hope Allerd Novel

Robert Thornton

Copyright © 2024 Robert Thornton

All rights reserved

The characters and events portrayed in this book are fictitious. Any similarity to real persons, living or dead, is coincidental and not intended by the author.

No part of this book may be reproduced, or stored in a retrieval system, or transmitted in any form or by any means, electronic, mechanical, photocopying, recording, or otherwise, without express written permission of the publisher.

ISBN-13: 9798338225417

Cover design by: Book Cover Zone
Printed in the United States of America

ACKNOWLEDGEMENT

A big thanks to my great beta readers: Jen and NeNe. Couldn't have done it without you!

To Vivi. Make reading a lifelong habit, kid.

When fascism comes to America, it will be wrapped in the flag and carrying a cross.—SINCLAIR LEWIS

The First thing I'm going to tell my successor is to watch the generals...—JOHN F. KENNEDY

LETHAL HOPE

CHAPTER 1

An authentic American lives by the tenets of no compromise and absolute devotion to duty. He embodies unrelenting courage, loyalty, and persistence. And if pursuing those beliefs means committing cold-blooded murder on an industrial scale, then so be it.

This was Brad Trett's mantra. He'd internalized every word, absorbing it into the very fiber of his being. He had no doubts this was what made him the ideal man for the job at hand. And it gave him a feeling of superiority over the brawny Russian facing him. He flashed a half-smile as he compared his muscular six-foot frame and blue-eyed, coiffed blond-haired, rugged John Wayne-handsome complexion to the brutishly massive six-four bald butt-ugly Slavic arms dealer, Lev Petrov.

They stood in an ankle-high verdant field of wheatgrass facing a colossal barn of rotting plank wood. The Russian clutched a duffle bag. Brad thought they might be somewhere in Belarus if his navigational instincts were correct.

He glanced back at the Range Rover sitting on the dirt road a hundred yards behind them, in which they'd driven for four hours.

After agreeing on a price, Petrov had insisted they come here. Not wishing to upset the negotiations, Brad acquiesced. But now, standing in this lonely field, he had his doubts. His prime concern was that this was a good place for an ambush.

Finally, letting his anxiety-fueled curiosity get the better of him, Brad asked, "Why are we here?"

Petrov grinned, his fat crimson-traced lips widening. He wiped his bald head with a handkerchief from the pocket of his khaki pants and squinted at the blazing overhead summer sun. "Demonstration," he said in a thick Russian accent.

"What?"

"You Americans always want demonstration. I arrange."

"You think I don't trust you?" Brad frowned and adjusted the Atlanta Braves ballcap on his head.

"Your late President Reagan once said, 'Trust, but verify.' I give you verification."

Brad sighed. "What, this old barn?"

"You will see. First, we prepare." Petrov released his gray duffle bag, letting it fall into the soft grass. He opened it and removed an orange article of clothing wrapped in cellophane. Handing it to Brad, he said, "Here, put on."

Brad stood holding the bundle, letting the clear enclosure crackle between his fingers. "What is this?"

"Protection. Open and put on. You will need."

Petrov removed another from the duffle bag, opened the cellophane wrapping, and shook it to reveal an orange jumpsuit-type garment. He donned it, pulling the hood over his head. "Hurry," he said, "sun is very hot." A scar running diagonally from his forehead across his left eye and down his nose began to redden as if on cue.

Brad followed suit and, lying his ballcap on the grass, put on the item of clothing. "What's this for?" he asked.

"Like I said, protection. You Americans ask too many questions."

Bristling at the accusation, Brad said, "Look, I paid you

half a million US dollars. I've got a right."

Petrov shook his head. "Rights, rights. Always with rights. Better you listen for a change." He reached into the bag again, withdrew two gas masks, and handed one to Brad.

Petrov put the black mask on and assisted Brad with his.

Feeling claustrophobic, Brad resisted the urge to tear the mask off. Having the mask on took him back to his days in Army basic training. During an exercise when he and his fellow recruits had to don gas masks, enter a building filled with teargas, and then remove the masks. He hated wearing the mask then and he hated wearing it now.

"Are you sure this is going to work?" asked Brad.

"Is Russian made. Best in world," came Petrov's tinny reply from within the gas mask.

Brad detected a hint of sarcasm in the Russian's voice and felt his heart rate quicken.

Petrov completed the procedure by giving Brad a pair of rubber gloves and taking a couple for himself. Grabbing a roll of duct tape from the bag, he rolled the adhesive material around the American's wrists and ankles, sealing the suit. Brad then did the same for Petrov.

Lastly, Petrov removed a small black box with an LED bulb and toggle switch from the bag. He nodded. "We are ready."

The Russian walked toward the barn door. Brad hesitated momentarily, then followed, wondering what lay on the other side of the decaying wooden enclosure.

As they got closer, Brad noticed a breeze blowing through the graying, splintered wooden slats of the barn. This seemed to cause it to squeak and groan in an agonal death rattle as if the structure was ready to collapse at any moment.

Petrov forced the sliding door open and stepped in. Brad, reluctant, stopped at the threshold.

"Is safe," said Petrov, beckoning him to enter.

Brad crossed over the sill. The interior was a vast, empty expanse illuminated by shafts of sunlight shining through spaces formed by missing or uneven vertical boards.

What the American saw next made his gut churn. At least two dozen young women lay around the periphery on a hay-covered dirt floor. They looked to be in their late teens to early twenties with ratty hair and dirt-streaked faces. A few wore party dresses covered in filth, but most wore only a bra and panties.

In the center of the floor were two large buckets filled to the brim. Around the buckets were scattered hundreds of paper wrappers and empty fast food paper cups replete with plastic covers and straws. It took a moment for Brad to realize what the buckets contained. The brownish pulpy mass was their urine and feces.

What was this hell hole? Sickened, Brad turned to Petrov.

The Russian shouted, "Wakey-wakey!"

One by one, the young women opened their eyes. Some stood. Brad could now see that chains bolted to the barn's baseboard bound their ankles, most of which were bloody and raw.

The whole truth hit Brad like a sledgehammer. These women had been kidnapped and kept here in this barn for goodness knows how many days.

He continued to stare at Petrov. A white-hot anger intensified at the Russian's cruelty.

All of the women were now on their feet. They slowly walked toward the two men with arms outstretched. A cacophony of moans and shrieks filled the barn.

Brad took a step back.

"Don't worry," said Petrov in a biting tone. "They won't hurt you. It took Sergei two weeks to collect them. Mostly runaways, prostitutes, orphans."

Some began speaking in what Brad considered to be some Eastern European dialect, articulating phrases repeatedly. But, within the dissonance of voices, he heard something familiar. An American accent pleading, "Help me, help me," came through.

Brad looked to his left. A blonde-haired, blue-eyed waif, no more than twenty, with outstretched arms, in mud-encrusted panties and bra, implored him to aid her.

Heat inflamed his cheeks, and his fingers flexed as Brad's inner storm of indignation mounted. He ached to choke the life out of the Russian then and there.

But the mission. It came first, even above quashing the monstrous depravity standing before him. Brad thought for a moment that maybe he could plead for the American girl's life. However, the reality of the situation called for Petrov to end each of the young lives in that barn. Any survivor talking risked Interpol's wrath.

"Now for demonstration." Petrov raised the device in his hand and flicked the toggle switch. The LED bulb glowed a bright red.

Anticipating some sudden cataclysmic event, Brad flexed his muscles, ready to run. But what happened next was...

...anti-climactic.

The young women continued their extended-arm blathering supplications.

"Well?" shouted Brad.

In a confident timbre, Petrov said, "Wait for it."

Seconds later, their cries dampened. Their arms began to drop to their sides. Eyelids fluttered. Brad looked to his left again. The American girl began to sway. Others dropped to their knees. A minute later, all of them lay in a heap. They'd fallen where they stood, lips and cheeks taking on the pale blue hue of death.

Brad trembled as he took in the enormity of the "demonstration," translating in his head a vision of the plan's awful final results.

A half-hour later, after having removed all their clothing and footwear, scrubbing clean under a portable shower, and dressing in a fresh set of clothes and shoes from a bag in the Range Rover, Brad sat in the passenger seat still contemplating what had just happened and the arrogance of the beast who carried out the so-called "demonstration" as the Russian walked toward the barn holding a metal can.

Petrov doused the structure with gasoline from the can and set it ablaze. He then circled the burning barn several times, holding a shovel to prevent the surrounding field from catching fire. When he returned to the vehicle and started the engine, he locked eyes with the American and asked, "When do you plan to use device? I want to be far, far away."

Brad smirked and said, "Then beware the Ides of March."

CHAPTER 2

Hope Allerd, M.D., smiled at the screaming infant being held by her mother as she inserted the otoscope's funnel-shaped speculum into the child's ear and peered at the swollen red eardrum.

"She's got a middle ear infection," said Hope, removing the otoscope. A gentle sea breeze swirled through the mid-December tropical outdoor setting. Hope inhaled the salt air, content to be back on the island of Mousseux doing what she loved to do: caring for sick patients.

Taking a plastic bottle of pink amoxicillin powder from a bag in the back of the Jeep Renegade, she gave the mother precise instructions on mixing it with water and dosing for her child.

This was the last patient in a long queue of ill and injured villagers on the "poor side" of the resort island. Hope was happy to make house calls at the small enclaves in the hilly landscape above the rock-strewn coast, considered less than ideal beachfront property by the island's developers.

"Thank you, Dr. Allerd," said the grateful mother as she bounced the whimpering child in her arms.

"You're welcome," replied Hope. Looking around, she marveled at the progress made in the area. Homes of cinderblocks and corrugated tin roofs with wood or linoleum floors had replaced huts made of logs, driftwood, and dried grasses with dirt floors. Powerlines ran along the periphery, and multiple water spigots were present among the homes. Outdoor cookfires and makeshift wells were now a thing of the past. A paved road reached the edge of the village.

The improvements were the brainchild of Hope and the President, Marie Dubois, the wife of the late corrupt President Andres Dubois. The money for the recovery project came from an expansion of the tourism trade that included, of all things, a new theme park.

Hope had lobbied for the changes. And since President Dubois considered Hope a national hero of Mousseux for her work in establishing hospitals and clinics for the poor and helping bring the unscrupulous Dubois to justice, she'd consented with pleasure to the doctor's recommendations.

Hope began removing equipment and supplies from the folding table that served as the outdoor clinic. She stowed them into the rear of the Renegade. One of the two soldiers dressed in jungle camo and a black beret helped Hope to fold the table and chair and place them in the vehicle. The other one, an M-4 carbine at the ready, watched the dense tropical forest background for any untoward movement in the foliage.

The two young stone-faced mahogany-skinned guards appointed by President Dubois accompanied Hope everywhere she went on the island. It was not out of concern over some wayward islander plotting harm. On the contrary, Hope was a minor celebrity in Mousseux.

Hope's life, along with those of her brother, Jack, and her fiancé, Clive Andrew, were threatened by a secret international organization bent on overthrowing the U.S. government, EQV. Jack, a computer genius, had stolen twelve million dollars from EQV's offshore account to save Hope. Now, the organization demanded their blood as payment.

Hope tossed the car keys up and down in her hand, grinned, and said, "I'm driving." Her bodyguards piled into the SUV. She looked over the village before getting into the driver's seat. In colorful turbans and white blouses, the women drew water for washing, hung clothing on lines, or chased wayward children darting between houses. The few men busied themselves with woodworking or metalworking, carving intricate statues or fashioning brass trinkets to sell at local bazaars.

As she started the engine, the air became calm. She felt a strange chill. Despite the warm, pastoral scene flowing before her, something was wrong.

Hope's eyes narrowed as she surveyed the jungle foliage for...what? She wasn't sure. Nothing looked out of place.

"Anything wrong, ma'am?" asked one of the guards.

Hope shook her head. She put the Jeep in gear and drove out of the village. A breeze blew through her short goddess braids, washing away her uneasiness.

Instead of driving to the hospital, Hope redirected the Renegade toward the beach. "I feel like a swim," she said.

The guard in the passenger seat said, "Yes, ma'am," and, with a smirk, glanced at his colleague in the back seat.

Hope could read their collective minds. She wore green scrubs and was willing to bet they had mental pictures of her stripping to her birthday suit before running into the surf.

She pulled to a stop along a twenty-foot strip of sparkling beach between two massive rocky outcroppings. After her guards hopped out and surveyed the area, she exited the SUV. With a mischievous grin widening her lips, she began to remove her scrubs. The soldiers stood with their backs to her, but each took a furtive glance at their charge from time to time.

Leaving the scrubs in a pile on the sand, Hope rushed into the surf wearing a modest black one-piece bathing suit she'd donned under the scrubs before leaving her apartment. Taking high steps into the intensifying surf, Hope turned and laughed at the frustrated bodyguards.

With water over her head, Hope began to swim parallel to the shore. Her freestyle form, muscular arm strokes, and kicks propelled her through the salt water like a leopard seal in search of prey.

When she could, Hope swam in the ocean daily. Swimming had become a type of therapy to stave off PTSD. As a teen, she, her parents, and her younger brother, Jack, were surprised by a burglar when they'd come home from dinner. The intruder, LeKeldric Theophilus Johnson, raised a stolen pistol in the dark and shot each in turn. He killed her mother and father, severed Jack's spine, making him a paraplegic, and wounded a seventeen-year-old Hope in the abdomen.

After multiple surgeries, Hope had gone on a crusade to bring Johnson to justice. He was now a lifer at the Holman Correctional Facility in Alabama.

Although the physical wounds had long ago healed, the nightmares, flashbacks, and hypervigilance had continued to plague her. Tiring of the medications and group therapies, Hope had found solace in swimming.

Hope was cleansed, empowered, and created anew each time she entered her watery domain.

And today was no different. She'd gone about a mile in one direction, turned around, and swam toward her starting point.

Feeling the splendid endorphin-stoked fatigue, Hope smiled with each turn of her head to take a breath.

Finally stopping to tread water, she gazed toward the strip of beach. The Jeep sat undisturbed.

But something was wrong.

Her bodyguards! They were nowhere in sight.

She'd been with them long enough to know that although young, they were dedicated professional soldiers—men who would rather die than leave their posts.

She scissors kicked toward the shore, keeping her head on a swivel.

The first shot hit so close she felt the heat of the expanding air. The bullet sent up a four-foot geyser of water next to her ear.

The second hit between her legs.

Hope submerged.

She plunged as deep as possible, knowing the water was now her sanctuary. Ten, twenty feet down, she wasn't sure. She could see the lightning-like cavitations of bullets streaking through the murk above only to slow and fall harmlessly toward the deep.

She was safe, at least for now.

The problem? She had to surface eventually. All the shooter or shooters had to do was wait her out.

Her lungs started to ache. The urge to take a deep breath underwater was becoming unbearable.

Fighting the lust for air, she became dizzy and confused. Was she up or down?

Overcome by a strange serenity compelling her to inhale, Hope had seconds to live.

CHAPTER 3

Bubbles. Hope saw them rise from her nose and mouth.

Something clicked. The thought, *Follow the bubbles*, manifested from somewhere deep in her brain.

She kicked and waggled her arms. Moments later, her head broke the surface. Hope gulped air with an audible gasp. She could see the narrow strip of beach and the Jeep.

Expecting more gunshots, she ducked underwater and swam for cover behind one of the stony outcroppings. After waiting several minutes, Hope decided to check the area. She climbed the jagged rock until her head was even with the sawtoothed top. She peeked over the craggy stone. Two men dressed in black and carrying rifles stalked the beach as they scanned the waters. She could also see the bloody corpses of her two bodyguards near the Jeep.

Trapped. She looked down. Fish undulated beneath the blue waters.

Fish. She had an idea.

Turning sideways, Hope leaped toward deeper waters just as her would-be assassins spotted her. Ducking underwater, she swam out to the open ocean.

After some minutes of swimming and periodically raising only her face out of the water to take quick breaths, Hope was sure she'd lost them.

Now for the second part of her plan. She'd have to hurry

as she felt the tide taking her further out to open waters and certain death.

She now swam with her head out of the water and on a swivel, surveying the undulating deep for…

…a boat. With a faded and chipped red paint job over the hull and no more than fifteen feet in length, it bobbed up and down like a cork in the choppy sea. Its two fishermen wrestled with a net over the side.

Hope swam for the fishing boat, yelling and occasionally waving an arm. She reached the vessel and put a hand on the faded, splintery gunwale as she lifted herself to the edge. One of the surprised fishermen grabbed her arm and pulled her aboard.

Shivering, she whispered, "Thank you." Her muscles aching, she was barely able to stand, so she plopped down on the rear seat.

The rescuing fisherman turned to aid his companion in hauling a catch aboard, then turned to Hope. "Ma'am," he said in the local accent, "Did your boat sink?"

Hope compassionately regarded the two barefoot sepia-skinned men in dirty jeans and T-shirts. She didn't want them mixed up in this assassination attempt. "Yes," she said. "My boat went down. I was the only one aboard."

The fishing boat's bottom was filled with baskets of their catch and reeked of sweat and fish. "Pretty good haul," said Hope, hinting that they could now head for shore.

The men looked at each other and nodded. One stepped to the back of the boat and started the outboard motor. He turned to Hope and said, "We will go in now. You can call someone from shore."

Once the boat was docked, Hope bound onto the wooden structure amid the bustle of a covey of fishermen unloading their catches from boats tied up along the pier. She thanked her rescuers again and asked if one of them had a cell phone that she could borrow.

She made two calls with the borrowed phone. The first was to President Dubois' office to report the killing of the soldiers by her attackers. The second was to her fiancé, Clive Andrew, an investigative reporter.

Selecting a hidden section of the dock, Hope sat, letting her feet dangle over the side as she waited, praying that the two gunmen hadn't followed the boat to shore.

Hope scanned the briny scene. Fishermen unloaded their catches and haggled with buyers from local fish markets who'd arrived in rickety trucks and, upon agreeing upon a price, loaded their catches into the vehicles' ice-laden beds for fists full of U.S. dollars.

She studied the men's faces, hoping to identify the two assailants if they showed up. Her presence garnered salacious grins and wolf-whistles from the rough-hewn seafarers. After all, how many gorgeous black women in bathing suits hung around the pier?

A couple of the truckers approached her with offers of a ride to the nearest town. She politely declined and continued to sit. Then he approached. A young man, dark-complected, muscular, with a tenderhearted face. He wore dark jeans and an open white button-down shirt over a gray undershirt.

He smiled and extended a hand. Hope thoughtlessly returned his grin. "You look like someone needing help," he said in an accent that didn't ring true for an islander.

"Er, I'm fine," said Hope.

"My Bronco is just down the road a bit. I'd be happy to take you wherever you want to go." He stepped closer and leaned forward.

"I'm waiting on someone."

"It's going to be quite a long wait. There was an accident on the only road in and out of here. My Bronco can go off-road and get you anywhere you want to go."

Hope shook her head. "No thanks."

He sat next to her on her right. Almost hip-to-hip. "Last chance. I promise it'll be a comfortable ride."

"I said no." Hope's countenance darkened.

He leaned towards her, and rabbit-quick reached into the back of his shirt with his right hand and produced a small caliber pistol out of the fishermen's sight. He jammed it into her ribs. "Let's take that ride. Open your mouth, and I'll shoot you right here." Gripping her right arm with his free hand, he said, "Let's go."

He and Hope arose and, in lockstep, started away from the dock. She looked around, anxious to make eye contact with one of the men working on the pier.

As they continued to walk, another young man, dressed similarly to her kidnapper, joined them. She noticed a bulge under his shirt.

Up ahead on the rise, a blue Ford Bronco with the top down sat beside the two-lane blacktop. Pickup trucks and SUVs motored along the road at speed.

"The police will be here any second," said Hope.

"Well, let me worry about that," replied the young man with the pistol. His companion did a three-sixty to make sure no one followed.

Hope knew the drill. Get into the car, and you're a dead woman.

They were ten feet away from the Bronco.

She had to do something. Fast.

CHAPTER 4

Her bare feet made going difficult on the uneven ground. A few paces further, an idea bloomed. With the next step, she purposely planted her foot on a large rock, slightly twisting her ankle.

Hope dropped to the ground with a yelp, pulling her kidnapper down with her. "My ankle," she screamed.

He released his grip, letting the pistol hand drop to his side.

She bolted for the road before he could react. Now, in the middle of the road, she frantically waved her hands to flag down a vehicle.

A ramshackle panel truck approached. The driver was a frail geriatric man with an old fedora pulled down on his head and a pipe in his mouth. He hit the brake and clutch, causing the truck to swerve off the road and head-on into the Bronco.

A loud *pop* cut the air. Hope dove for the opposite roadside as the fishermen and buyers on the pier scrambled for cover.

The gunman fired again and sprinted toward the road. His partner drew his weapon and fired a random shot at the pier to ensure no heroes emerged from the gaggle on the water's edge.

Hope ran beside the road using passing vehicles as cover. Looking back, she saw that the gunman had now crossed over to her side of the road and was in pursuit. She saw his companion running parallel to her on the other side between passing cars.

He fired. Hope heard the whine of the bullet whizzing by her ear.

Then, up ahead, she saw the unmistakable black and white paint job of a police car.

Abandoning caution, she charged onto the road toward the oncoming vehicle, hands waving.

The police car pulled over, and the driver activated the lights and siren. Hope ran to the passenger side and pointed at her pursuer.

The uniformed officer on the passenger side exited and pulled his service weapon just as the gunman stormed onto the road, his timing abysmal. A pickup clipped him, sending him sprawling ten feet away.

The companion made for the Bronco. But the collision with the panel truck left it undrivable. The officers, with guns at the ready, approached him from either side, shouting, "Hands! Let me see your hands!"

Seeing no way out, the man drew his pistol and put a round through his brain simultaneously with the officers emptying their magazines into him.

In the aftermath of the gunbattle, a crowd gathered around the scene. Head in hand, Hope perched in the back seat of the police cruiser sideways, facing the open rear door.

With lights flashing and sirens blaring, a half dozen police cruisers and a fire rescue vehicle pulled up to the scene. The police blocked the road and worked crowd control while paramedics tried in vain to resuscitate the gunmen.

One of the two original officers squatted in front of Hope. "Dr. Allerd," he said, "are you all right?"

Hope looked up and nodded. "Yes. Uh, wait, how do you

know me?"

"President Dubois personally sent us. Also, I remember you. You treated my brother's pneumonia."

With a slight smile, Hope nodded again. "Thank you."

Still exhausted from the ordeal, she continued to sit in the back of the cruiser, head down and eyes closed, until…

"Hope?" The voice was familiar, unmistakable.

She looked up to see him and grinned. "Clive," she whispered as she bound from the car into the arms of her fiancé, Clive Andrew. The embrace was magical. She was renewed in his enfolding arms. Looking up at his luscious brown eyes and enchanting smile, she knew this upside-down world would right itself.

Clive pulled back. Gripping her shoulders, he surveyed her body like a jeweler inspecting a fine diamond. "Are you all right?"

Hope nodded. "Yes."

"I came as soon as I could. Had to borrow a car."

"I'm just glad you're here."

"What happened?"

"Two men attacked us while I was swimming. They killed my bodyguards. I escaped on a fishing boat only to have them follow me here. They were EQV."

"How do you know?"

"I just know. I bet they don't have any ID." Hope glanced at the body of the one hit by the panel truck just as paramedics covered him with a sheet.

Clive shook his head. "I brought a set of scrubs like you asked. They're in my car." Hope accompanied him along the road to a rusted 1980s model Toyota Corolla. He removed the green scrubs from the front seat, handed them to Hope, and returned to the crime scene.

"Where are you going?" asked Hope.

"To check on something," said Clive, not bothering to turn around.

Hope watched him approach one of the officers. She then donned the scrubs over her bathing suit.

A moment later, he was back. "You were right," he said. "Neither of them had any identification."

"EQV," said Hope.

"We can't be sure."

"Who else would want to assassinate me?"

"I don't know."

Hope was quiet momentarily, then: "I have an idea. Maybe we could use facial recognition to identify them."

"Does Mousseux's National Police have that kind of technology?"

Hope smiled. "Well, if they don't, I know who does."

Jack Allerd, Hope's younger brother, answered the phone call on the third ring. "Hey, Sis."

"Jack where are you?" asked Hope. She sat in her tiny apartment attached to the hospital built by the John C. and Cora H. Allerd Foundation; a charitable organization Hope started in honor of her deceased parents.

A pause on the other end, then, "Undisclosed location."

"What's wrong?"

"Sis, a black sedan was parked across the street from my

house for two days straight."

"You think it was EQV?"

"Not taking any chances. I see by your number you're using one of the burner phones I gave you."

"Yeah. They tried to kill me today."

"EQV? What happened?

"I was out for a swim, and two gunmen ambushed my bodyguards and pursued me to a pier. The police and a truck driver took them out. They're dead. That's why I'm calling. Can you work your computer magic and use a facial recognition program to ID these guys?"

"Yeah. The FBI has some new software that does a great job."

"You hacking into the FBI computers?"

"They won't even know I was there. You got JPEGs of their faces?"

"Yeah. The police were kind enough to let me take photos with Clive's phone before putting them in body bags. I transferred them over to my burner. I can send you the pics."

Hope sent the pictures, and Jack had the results after ten minutes. "Information's coming to you, Sis," he said.

A moment later, a text notification appeared on her phone. "Thanks, Jack," said Hope.

"Hey, is old Clive there?"

"Yeah. He's been working at the hospital with me."

"Tell him I said to take better care of you, or I'll come down there and kick his English ass."

Hope chuckled. "Will do, Jack. Thanks again. You're the best."

"I'll see you in a week."

"A week?"

"You're still going to the White House, right?"

"Oh, yeah. Almost forgot. I'm still going."

"Sis, getting the Presidential Medal of Freedom is a big deal."

"Been working so hard, guess I just forgot. Are you sure it's safe for you to go?"

"Don't worry. I've ticked off so many corporations and government entities with my computer hacking that I've become an expert in disappearing. Which reminds me, you using the IDs I got you?"

Hope opened her desk drawer to reveal four U.S. passports, a Canadian passport, and five driver's licenses, all with various aliases. "Yeah, Jack."

"OK, just remember to use the forgeries for travel and have your actual IDs for admission to the White House. Also, take a couple of burner phones to use."

"Got it, Jack. I know what to do."

"Don't use any credit cards. Cash-only transactions."

"I know, Jack."

"If you have to use wi-fi, make sure it's public wi-fi. Don't call any friends or relatives besides me. And—"

"Jack."

"—when traveling, wear a hat and sunglasses and avoid eye contact. You don't want anyone getting a good look at your face."

"Jack. I know the drill."

"And have a couple of plausible backstories in case the

police stop you."

In an exasperated tone, Hope said, "I swear, Jack…"

"I guess that about covers it."

"You know, sometimes you can be a real pain."

"Love you too, Sis. Gotta go."

After Jack hung up, Hope glanced at the text with two attachments he'd sent. *Later*, she thought. She turned out the lights and flopped onto the bed.

Nearly being killed was more than enough excitement for one day.

CHAPTER 5

Sleep eluded Hope, and an hour later, she sat at the desk in her apartment, perusing the photos she'd taken of her two deceased attackers and the accompanying IDs from Jack. Clive had come over. He looked over her shoulder and frowned at the two reddish-brown faces on Hope's cell phone. Young men in their twenties, he estimated.

"So," said Hope, "who are Joseph Igwe and Samuel Okeke? And why is further information stamped 'Classified'?"

"The surnames are Nigerian, I think," said Clive.

"It makes no sense. Who in Nigeria would want to kill me?"

Clive shrugged. "Don't know. Could have been hired."

"By EQV?"

"Possible, I guess."

"If we find out the classified information, maybe that would lead us to the people who hired them."

"How would we find that out? Jack couldn't with his hacking."

"No, but I think I know someone who might be able to help." Hope opened her desk drawer and rummaged through the fake IDs and miscellaneous papers for a business card. "Here it is," she said, holding it at eye level, and began to punch in numbers on her cell phone.

Her call was answered on the third ring. "Carter Security, Security Specialist Tina DeLuca speaking. How may I help you?" said the voice on the other end.

"Tina, it's Hope."

"Hey girl, it's been a minute. How you doin'?" said the voice in an unfamiliar tone that seemed to lilt in time to a hip-hop song playing in the background.

"Tina is that you?" asked Hope on hearing the uncharacteristic cadence.

"Yeah, girl, what's happening?"

"Why are you talking like that?" asked Hope. She'd known Tina as a taciturn, no-nonsense special agent in the FBI before taking her current job with a private security company. And not this white girl trying to sound Black.

"Oh, uh, sorry."

"What's going on?" asked Hope.

Hope heard the background music diminish. "It's my new job," said Tina, sounding like her old self. "Mainly, I work as a bodyguard to the big-time rappers and hip-hop artists here in New York. When I'm not on tour with them, I'm hanging with them for half the night in some exclusive nightclub. Guess I just picked up the lingo."

"Yeah, well, I need the hard-as-nails Tina DeLuca who helped me with that serial killer right now."

"Fair enough. What can I do for you, Hope?"

"EQV. They tried to kill me earlier today. Two assassins murdered my Mousseux Army bodyguards and came after me. The police killed one, and the other died in a traffic accident. My brother, Jack, was able to use facial rec to ID them."

"Good old Jack. What'd he do, hack into the FBI's facial rec software?"

Hope was silent momentarily, wondering if calling Tina was a good idea.

"Hope?" said Tina. "You still there?"

"Yeah. I'm here."

"Sorry, please continue."

"Anyway, he got their names. Two Nigerian nationals, Clive and I think. Joseph Igwe and Samuel Okeke. But the rest was classified."

"And you want me to give you the classified part."

"Yeah. At least that way, we could maybe find out if it's EQV and plot our next move."

Tina sighed. "OK, let me see what I can do. I know a couple of special agents who owe me large. I'll call you back. Er, you're probably lying low and using a burner phone. Should I use this number?"

"Oh, yeah, hold on," said Hope. She fumbled through her desk drawer, removed a second burner phone, and turned it on. She gave Tina the number. "Thanks. I appreciate anything you can give us." Hope turned to Clive, who was now pacing. "What do you think are our chances?"

He stopped to gaze at Hope. "Chances for what?"

"Taking down EQV."

He shrugged. "I dunno. I know we pledged to stop them, but it might be more than the three of us can handle."

"Four. Tina will help."

"OK, more than the four of us can handle. Why don't we continue to lay low for a while."

"They didn't send two thugs to kill you."

"I understand, and I—"

"Understand nothing. Clive, we are on their radar. They're going to keep after us until we're all dead."

Clive sidled up behind her and began massaging her shoulders. "I think we're safe here in Mousseux. I say we ride this out."

Shrugging off Clive's hands, Hope bolted from her chair and wagged her index finger in his face. "No! I need to know, are you with me or not?"

Clive raised his hands in a gesture of surrender. "Calm down."

"I'm the one who was nearly shot this afternoon. Don't tell me to calm down. I need to know. Are you going to help me get EQV or not?"

Clive dropped his hands to his side, stepped back, turned, and slinked to the apartment door.

"Where're you going?" demanded Hope.

"Need some air." Clive opened the door and stepped into the night.

"That's right," yelled Hope as she gripped the doorknob. "Run away. It's the only thing you're any good at."

She slammed the apartment door as tears came.

It was past midnight. Hope lay in bed, eyes wide open, expecting Clive to come creeping back in at any moment with an apology on his lips.

As the minutes ticked by, she sank deeper into despair over their engagement and their continued relationship as a couple. The one thing she hated about Clive was that he bolted when a situation became sticky. When the odds put their backs against the wall.

It had happened when she needed his help finding a serial killer. And it was happening again. *Maybe*, she thought, *I should just call the engagement off. I need some space to think this over.*

She rolled over and closed her eyes.

Just as sleep was about to take hold, her cell phone rang.

Hope padded to her desk, and for a moment, she was unsure which of the two burner phones was chiming. Finally picking up the correct one, she answered with a slurred, "Hello?"

"Hey, girl." It was Tina. A funky bass beat throbbed in the background.

"Tina? Where are you?"

"Girl, I'm in the club. Working security for Cherry Mary."

Hope recalled hearing Cherry Mary's hit song, *Mary Is As Mary Does*, once or twice on the radio. "What time is it?"

"I don't know, two thirty, maybe."

Hope sat down at her desk. "What's going on?"

"OK, I contacted Special Agent Renfro and got him to dig into those two would-be assassins. He had to jump through half a dozen hoops at the Justice Department and the Department of Defense."

"Department of Defense?"

"Yeah. Anyway, you were right. Igwe and Okeke were two Nigerian nationals, here on a Green Card. They'd enlisted in the Army, and—"

"What? You can not be a citizen and do that?"

"Apparently so. They became Army Rangers, then wound up in some special ops outfit called Unit-458. I've never heard of it."

"So, what does this Unit-458 do?"

"That's why I had to call you. There was nothing more that Renfro could find. So, I was sitting here in the club talking with Big Reggie. He works with me at Carter Security. I knew he was in the Army, so I asked him about Unit-458. And he told me…. Know what, why don't I let him tell you?"

"Er, OK." Hope heard some whispered conversation. Then…

"Hey, uh, Hope?" said a gruff voice.

"Yeah?"

"Big Reggie here. You wanna know about Unit-458? Man, it's a super secret organization. Only reason I know about it was I applied for the unit. Woulda made it if I didn't break my ankle on a twenty-mile run."

"Sorry to hear that," said Hope.

"Unit-458 is the Delta Force on steroids. Know what I mean? They take on the toughest of the tough assignments. And when they finish, nobody knows they were there. All they know is there's a bunch of dead bodies lying around. Know what I mean?"

"Yeah, I think so."

"Look, they're so secret that ninety-nine percent of the Army brass, hell, even the POTUS don't know about 'em."

"POTUS?" asked Hope.

"Oh, uh, President of the United States."

"Good to know."

"It was like they some secret army within the Army. Know what I mean? Taking orders only from their commanding officer. Last I heard, they were disbanded. But that's the beauty of Unit-458. It was so secret, it could be disbanded on paper and still exist."

"I see," said Hope. She felt her gut starting to burn.

"If you escaped two of 'em out to kill you, Miss Hope, all I can say is you one tough bitch, er, sorry, tough lady. Props to you."

"Thanks. You won't get into trouble telling me this, will you?"

"Naw. Wouldn't care if I did. Army rooked me out of my pension for my injured ankle. Don't owe them no allegiance. Oh, one other thing. When I was applying, guess who the unit's CO was?"

"Don't know."

"None other than the man. General Benjamin Davis Armstrong himself."

Hope heard a faint "Thanks, Reggie" in the background, then Tina's voice. "Sorry about the 'tough bitch' comment. I'm still working on Big Reggie's social skills. But you see why I called you, right?"

"Yeah, thanks. And thank Big Reggie for me, too." Hope hung up.

As she trudged back to bed, Hope wondered if Clive wasn't right. If those two Nigerians were part of this Unit-458 and working for EQV, she was lucky to be drawing breath.

And, maybe laying low wouldn't even be enough to make it out of this alive.

CHAPTER 6

Hope was awakened by a loud rapping on her apartment door. As she opened her eyes, sunlight filtered through gauze window curtains opposite her bed and stabbed her retina like an epee. Still in the scrubs Clive had given her at the crime scene, she stretched and yawned. Finally, annoyed enough by the constant knocking, she arose and opened the door.

Clive, bearing a cardboard drink caddy containing two grande paper cups of coffee, stood on the threshold. A plastic grin widened his face.

"Hey, you," he said in one of those cheery early riser tones.

Hope sneered, padded to her desk and sat.

Clive stepped in and placed the drink caddy on the desk. He lifted one of the coffee cups out of the holder and set it in front of Hope. "Cream, no sugar," he said.

With eyes half closed, Hope took a sip.

"Sorry about last night," he began. "But I thought you needed some space. You know, to decompress."

"Yeah," she said. "Why is it that every time I need your help, you have to run away?"

"Well, I...uh, thought, that is, I didn't run away so much as I wanted you to, to..."

"Yeah, yeah, I know. Have some space. You know, if you're always running off anytime we have a disagreement, I don't see this working out."

"Guess I'm not very good at confrontations."

"Well, you'd better get good at it and fast. Clive, every couple has disagreements. You have to stick around, particularly with EQV out to get us. After all, we're a team. I need you, and you need me. That's how it works."

With a sappy expression, he nodded and sipped his coffee.

Hope rubbed her eyes. "Tina called me back late last night. The two Nigerians were part of a super-secret Army outfit, Unit-458."

Clive lifted the coffee cup to his lips and returned it to the desk. "Unit-458?"

"Yeah. Ever hear of it?"

Clive's expression hardened. "They don't exist, at least not in the Pentagon files. Some claim they were disbanded. I investigated a rebel uprising in an African country years back. Kasongo, their leader, was a real piece of work. He'd torture and kill men in the villages and rape the women until they died. His soldiers were no better. The country's president begged the Americans to help squash Kasongo. Your president wouldn't lift a finger. Then, a month later, Kasongo and his entire rebel band were found killed, and their camp burned to the ground."

"So?" said Hope. "Sounds like they deserved it. Was it Unit-458?"

"No one knows for sure. Your president denied any American involvement. The catch was that the burned and mutilated bodies and the scorched countryside showed signs of the use of weapons outlawed by the U.N., thermobaric and cluster munitions. There were other cases around the globe; they all involved outlawed weapons like nerve gas and biological weapons, as well as thermobaric and cluster munitions. Nothing traceable back to the U.S. Military. Those weapons seem to be the sine qua non of their operations."

"Sounds like they're some type of Robin Hood organization."

Clive shook his head. "Far from it. They're cold-blooded killers. And if those two Nigerians were part of Unit-458 and were working for EQV, then we're up to our eyeballs in trouble."

"How? Those two are dead."

"Unit-458 doesn't allow people to just freelance. If they were in play, they were just a small part of some bigger operation by Unit-458, likely on behalf of EQV."

"A shadow army for a shadow organization. So, what do we do?"

Clive, looking down at the desk, was quiet for a moment. Then he gazed up at Hope. "I was wrong when I said we needed to lay low. You were right. We need to find out what's going on. And we need to do it fast. Our lives are going to depend on it."

◆ ◆ ◆

The Mousseux Air Force field sat beside the large international airport. Hope stepped out of the military Jeep with only a backpack holding two clothing changes. She wore jeans and a simple white blouse. In her pockets were two sets of forged passports and driver's licenses, along with her actual ones and several thousand dollars in cash and prepaid debit cards. Clive, dressed in jeans and a white button-down shirt and carrying a small duffle, also bore the same type of ID and currency on his person. He exited the Jeep and thanked the soldier driver.

After making morning rounds in the hospital, Hope had

followed Clive's recommendation and called President Dubois, informing her of their need for secure transportation off the island.

Standing on the tarmac, Hope surveyed the sum total of the Mousseux Air Force, six A29 Super Tucano light attack planes, and four Cessna 182 Skylanes used to transport military and government officials. She felt underwhelmed on seeing those ten small gray single-engine aircraft parked on the side of the runway.

One of the Cessnas sat with the propeller turning and the left door open. An older man in jungle camo with silver eagles on his collar stood beside the craft.

Clive pointed and said, "That's our plane."

Hope's eyes narrowed as she regarded the little puddle jumper with the fixed tricycle landing gear and overhead wing. Then she gazed up at a sleek 737 rising from the adjacent international airport. "Tell me why we can't take a commercial flight to Washington, D. C."

"I scoped out the commercial airport along with a couple of Mousseux police detectives. We counted half a dozen suspicious-looking actors milling around. We then scrubbed footage of them from cameras around the terminal. Using facial rec from your brother, they all turned out to have classified records just like those two Nigerians."

"When did you do all of this?"

"While you made your rounds in the hospital."

Hope shook her head. "OK, I guess. But will this take us all the way to Washington?"

"No. We go as far as a little airstrip outside of Miami. From there, we take a train to Union Station. I don't think EQV or those Unit-458 goons will be able to figure out the route."

As she approached the plane, the man in camo extended

his hand. "Good morning, Dr. Allerd. I'm Colonel Duval. I'll be your pilot today," said the raven-skinned officer in an island accent.

Hope shook his hand, continuing to inspect the exterior of the small plane.

Colonel Duval grinned. "Dr. Allerd, the Cessna Skylane is perfectly safe. If you're worried about the overwater hop, the plane has a ballistic parachute and a life raft. Just in case."

Hope nodded and stepped into the plane beneath the overhead wing, taking the right rear seat of the four available. She dropped her backpack between her legs.

Clive shook the pilot's hand and climbed in beside Hope. He grasped her hand and flashed a reassuring smile.

Hope leaned back in the plush leather seat and closed her eyes.

The pilot got in the left front seat behind the controls. He put on a headset, turned to Hope and Clive, and said, "We're waiting for my copilot. He's new and still qualifying."

Five minutes later, a smallish dark-skinned man in jungle camo with silver bars on his collar opened the door on the right, boarded the plane, and sat in the copilot's spot. He carried a small bag, which he deposited on the floor between his legs.

"You're late," bellowed Colonel Duval.

"Sorry," said the younger man. His expression was taciturn, and he appeared unfazed by his superior's castigating tone.

They went through a brief checklist and then taxied along the runway. A moment later, they were airborne.

Hope opened her eyes in time to see the island of Mousseux shrink behind her as the plane gained altitude and speed. Clive squeezed her hand and nodded.

She relaxed and again closed her eyes. *Maybe the flight won't be so bad after all*, she thought as she drifted off to sleep.

BAM!

Startled awake, Hope thought, *We're going down.*

The lightning-quick copilot wheeled around, wielding a small caliber pistol.

The barrel pointed at her face.

Clive clasped the pistol with both his hands.

The copilot pummeled Clive's face with his fisted free hand in a rapid series of blows.

Clive's grip held fast. But consciousness waned.

Looking around, Hope saw a small fire extinguisher on the door.

The blows landed at a slower pace.

Clive wavered.

She pulled the device from its mount and swung the cylinder like a club.

The metal contacted the assailant's skull with a loud thump.

The copilot appeared dazed.

Clive, turning the weapon toward the assailant, wrested the pistol from his hand.

But, as he pulled it back, the copilot's finger caught in the trigger guard.

BAM!

The copilot recoiled from the gunshot, hitting center mass.

Save for the sound of the engine, the cockpit was now quiet.

Hope leaned forward in her seat. To her left, the pilot sat dead from a bullet to his brain—the first shot. Beside him, the copilot, holding a hand over his chest wound, slumped over the wheel.

The plane nosedived.

Through the windshield, Hope saw the Caribbean waters rush towards them at a blistering velocity.

CHAPTER 7

Hope gripped the copilot's seat and leaned over his body. She shoved him against the door, grabbed the wheel, and pulled it back.

The plane responded.

They were again at level flight.

She turned to Clive, who appeared to fluctuate in and out of consciousness.

"Parachutes," shouted Hope. "Duval said the plane had parachutes."

"Whaa...." Clive's speech was slurred.

She began shaking him. "Where are the parachutes?"

Something changed.

Hope no longer heard the purr of the engine. Ahead, she saw the propeller slow.

The co-pilot, apparently still alive, had leaned over to the left and cut the engine. With his dying breath, he turned and sneered at Hope.

The plane once more pitched forward toward the deep blue waters.

She again tried pulling back on the wheel. There was little response.

They were going down to a watery grave.

❖ ❖ ❖

Desperate, Hope lunged toward the firewall to get a firmer grip on the wheel of the plummeting plane.

She could see the blue waters grow larger and larger through the windshield.

As she moved forward, the top of her head scraped something irregular overhead. Without thinking, she turned to see what it was.

It was a recessed part of the overhead containing a red T-shaped handle. Beside it was a placard. It simply stated: WARNING-EMERGENCY PARACHUTE. Beneath were instructions on how to pull the handle.

The plane continued to plunge. Hope could now see the details of individual waves through the windshield.

She yanked downward on the handle with both hands.

Immediately, a loud thump followed by a whoosh filled the cabin.

She was jerked back, falling into her seat. The cabin plunged into shadows, and then she felt as if she was floating.

Looking out the side window, she saw the plane upright and drifting towards the ocean below. Overhead, she saw the deployed white and red parachute and whispered a prayer of thanks.

She shook Clive awake. "We're saved," she said.

He nodded and replied with a slurred, "Yeah." Then, after glancing out of his window, said, "How're we getting out of the plane?"

Hope looked down at the slowly widening picture of gently rippling waves below. Off in the distance, a hazy shoreline loomed.

She was struck with the new reality of the situation. When the plane hit the water, it would likely float for a short time, but as water seeped into the cabin, it would begin to sink.

She looked over at her groggy fiancé and mused, *I could swim to shore, but not with Clive in tow. And he'd go under before I could return with help.*

Hope gripped his hand, unwilling to surrender her true love to a watery tomb alone.

As they continued to drift, the shore faded from her view.

◆ ◆ ◆

Resolved to face her fate with an injured Clive, Hope shut her eyes.

It was then that the voice echoed from within her short-term memory.

"...the plane has a ballistic parachute and a life raft. Just in case," the pilot had said.

Life raft.

What did it look like?

Hope searched the cabin, finally fixing on a yellow object in the shape of a large valise behind the rear seats. She removed it from its storage location and perused the instructions printed on the surface. Next, she removed two quart-sized Ziploc bags from her backpack and jammed the burner phones, cash, cards, and IDs they both carried into them. She sealed the bags and stuffed them into her pockets.

Once the plane touched down on the water, it started to sink slowly, going down by the nose. She opened the door and, taking one end of the long tether attached to the life raft, tied it to the door handle. Next, she flung the life raft into the water, letting it float past the parachute, now encasing the stricken plane like a shroud.

A moment later, a loud whoosh occurred, signaling that the life raft had automatically inflated. She shoved Clive out of the plane and jumped into the cold ocean.

Positioning Clive on her hip, she swam with one hand, holding his chin out of the water and doing a sidestroke following the tether to the raft with the other.

Once at the raft, she shoved Clive halfway in, climbed in herself, and then hefted him onto the plastic floor. A protective canopy overarched them. She cut the tether with a safety knife from the raft's pocket.

Hope found a bag labeled "Survival Equipment" and quickly surveyed its contents while Clive lay half-conscious under the covering.

It took only an hour. As she'd suspected, they had gone down just off the coast of Miami, and recreational and fishing boats dotted the waters. They were picked up by a boater and his wife in a sixty-foot cabin cruiser.

Hope gave the boater, a stockbroker from New York, a backstory of their boat sinking and she and Clive barely escaping after Clive had fallen, hitting his head on the deck.

After docking the boat and calling an ambulance for Clive, the boater bid farewell to them and set off. On arrival of the ambulance, Hope discovered they were in a small town outside of Miami.

Clive, in a hospital gown, lay quietly in a hospital bed after being seen in the tiny ER and having the ER physician pronounce that he had suffered a concussion and needed twenty-four-hour observation. Hope sat in an uncomfortable chair next to the bed. She'd "borrowed" a set of blue scrubs as her clothes were soaked when they arrived at the hospital ER.

"Where are we?" asked Clive.

"Red City Beach. Just outside of Miami," said Hope.

"Pilot and copilot?"

"Both dead. The copilot was likely another Unit-458 goon."

Clive nodded.

"How are you feeling?" asked Hope.

"Pounding headache."

"It'll get better. Up to talking?"

"Yeah. I suppose we could contact authorities in Mousseux to get a flight back."

"No," said Hope. "I think we should continue to Washington."

"But our luggage and…"

"Luggage was lost, but I managed to save our burner phones, cash, cards, and IDs in Ziploc bags. Besides, EQV must know that the plane has gone down by now. And I gave the local officials false names and a backstory of a boating accident. So, as far as EQV knows, we went down with the plane."

Clive nodded again.

"We can travel incognito without worrying about EQV, now."

"Suppose you're right," said Clive.

"Besides, I want to attend that medal ceremony. Talk to President Conchrane face to face. Warn her about EQV."

"Yeah. Likely to be our only chance to have that kind of audience."

"I was wondering," said Hope. "When I spoke with Tina, she had a colleague who had applied for Unit-458 while in the

Army. He said that a General Benjamin Davis Armstrong was in charge then. He kind of made a big deal about this Armstrong. Called him, 'the man.' Know anything about him?"

Clive flashed a condescending smile and shook his head. "You don't know?"

"OK, I'll admit I don't keep up with current events that much. I'm too busy taking care of patients. So, who is he?"

"The Chairman of the Joint Chiefs of Staff. The highest-ranking military officer in the United States and adviser to the President."

"Oh," said Hope. She removed her phone from the bag and turned it on.

"I did a story about him last year. He has quite an impressive resume. His Vietnam veteran father named him after Benjamin O. Davis, the first African American general in the U.S. Army. Armstrong graduated from West Point. He served in several command positions. He fought in Afghanistan. He has a Ph.D. from Johns Hopkins in National Security Studies."

"Impressive." Hope perused Armstrong's Wikipedia entry on her phone.

"The guy's brilliant," said Clive. "There has even been talk of him running for President."

"Sounds like someone I'd vote for."

Clive's eyes narrowed. "Doubt it."

"Aw, he's a widower, too," said Hope.

"Where're you going with this, Hope?"

"Jealous?" Grinning, Hope turned her cell phone's screen toward Clive, revealing a picture of Armstrong from the Wikipedia article. It was his chairman's photo.

In the shot, he was sitting. An American flag and a Joint Chiefs of Staff flag were in the background. The raw umber-complected general stared ahead with confident, piercing brown eyes and a self-assured half smile. His military uniform was replete with row upon row of ribbons and several badges. The overall result revealed a man exuding a coolheaded intrepidity.

In a fleeting fit of ardor, Hope thought, *Yeah, I'd follow him into battle.*

"The guy's dangerous," said Clive.

"How so?"

"The rumor is that he was radicalized while serving in Afghanistan some years back by his commanding officer, General Zimmer. Since the recent election, he's been going around to these large rallies sponsored by this Eric Lattimore."

"The shock-jock radio host who ran against Conchrane in the recent election?"

"Yeah. Armstrong has been the featured speaker at these events, preaching that President Conchrane is unfit for office since winning a second term. He's been saying that she will be the country's downfall, leading America down the road to perdition. They've been drawing basketball arenas full of supporters."

"Perdition, huh? Can soldiers do that? Go around making speeches like that?"

"Who's going to stop him? Soldiers traditionally stay away from politics. But the guy has clout."

Hope shrugged.

"And you didn't know about this?"

"Alright, I get an 'F' in current affairs. I see patients all day. And when I'm not seeing patients, I read medical journals and have the occasional cup of coffee with you."

Clive smiled. "And I cherish those moments."

Hope slipped her hand into his and squeezed it. She then scowled, making the apparent connection. "Wait a minute. Could this Armstrong guy be EQV? Maybe the head?"

Clive nodded. "The thought hasn't escaped me. When we get to Washington, we'll meet with Father Jan Mazur. He's my contact in the area who gave me info on EQV that helped me locate Father Agee."

Hope's eyes narrowed. About a year ago, she'd consulted on a serial murder case and discovered that Agee was the mastermind behind the killing of several millionaires. The local police and FBI had a BOLO out on the errant priest and master of disguise. But he'd, so far, eluded capture.

"I'd like to find that Agee and take—"

"Hey," said Clive, raising the hand in Hope's grasp. "You're squeezing the blood out of it."

"Oh, sorry." Hope released her grip. "It's just that every time I think of what that Father Agee did, it makes me so angry."

"You're not alone. But let's focus on Armstrong."

"Right. How do we stop him?"

"Expose him for what he is: a self-righteous demagogue."

"Is he really that bad?"

"You need to attend one of his rallies. Then you'll understand."

"Understand what?"

"That he's an existential threat to America."

CHAPTER 8

The following morning was a cloudless South Florida sunshine-sprinkled beach day. Bright rays of daylight showed through the slanted slats of the window blinds in Clive's room.

Despite the two-hour neuro checks the nurses made on Clive throughout the night, Hope had gotten the best sleep she'd had in the last three days.

As Clive snored softly in his bed, she checked the time on her burner phone. It was six-fifteen a.m. The attending doctor would probably be by around eight to tell them that Clive was doing well and could be discharged.

But she wanted to get a jump on things. One situation that was bound to happen was a visit from the local police about the so-called "boating accident." They had to leave before some small-town deputy, thinking he was Sherlock Holmes, came by asking too many questions.

Their clothing hanging in the closet was dry but retained a lingering briny odor. She quickly dressed, awoke Clive, and assisted him in getting into his clothes. She next went to the hospital's business office and paid Clive's bill in cash as soon as it opened.

On her way back to his room, she plotted a route out of the hospital that would involve being seen by the fewest people.

Back inside the room, she said, "Ready to go?"

Clive, sitting dressed on the side of the bed, nodded. As he hopped onto the floor, he wavered for a moment. "A bit dizzy, still," he said.

Hope put an arm around his waist and guided him to the door. He steadied himself with an arm around her shoulders.

She peeked out the door, watched the nurses' station and waited. At precisely the right time, when all three nurses had their backs turned to the door, they slipped out.

From there, a quick scurry down the hall, a left and a right, took them to a side door. Exiting, they found themselves on the lush green hospital campus. A two-block stroll along the quaint palm-lined downtown street brought them to a mom-and-pop diner. They ducked in. Hope ordered bacon and eggs with coffee for both of them.

One hour and an Uber ride later, they were in the Miami Amtrak station, a single-story building with an interior of patrons sitting in rows of plastic seats or queued up in front of glass-barrier ticket booths. They got in line to pay the fare. Finally, holding a sleeping car ticket for two en route to Washington, D.C., they boarded the Silver Star for the twenty-seven-hour train ride.

The trip to D.C. was uneventful. They took the opportunity to shower for the first time since going into the drink. After that, Clive slept most of the way. Hope continued to monitor him for any lingering brain injury with every two-hour neuro checks.

◆ ◆ ◆

On arrival at Union Station, they disembarked and found the mall area on the second floor. A quick shopping trip to the Express provided them with new clothes and the opportunity to discard the old saltwater-stained duds.

Dressed in fresh jeans, shirts, and shoes and carrying shopping bags with the attire they'd wear to the White House, they exited the station. After calling Father Mazur, Clive insisted they immediately meet him at his church.

A cab ride took them to the seedier part of D.C. Ensconced among tenement high-rise apartments, and brownstones was a small Roman Catholic church.

As they exited the taxi in front of All Saints Church, a rake-thin man in black pants and a jacket with a white clerical collar waved from the top step of the entrance.

Clive bound up the steps and shook his hand. "Father Mazur, good to see you again." He turned and extended a hand toward Hope, who was topping the final step. "This is my fiancée, Hope Allerd."

Mazur smiled. His erudite expression, along with his wire-rimmed glasses, gave Hope the impression that she was meeting a college professor. With just the hint of an Eastern European accent, he said, "Ah, Hope. Clive has told me so much about you."

Hope shook his hand. "I trust it was all good."

"According to Clive, you're the best thing to ever happen to him. Welcome to our neighborhood." Mazur extended his left hand in a sweeping gesture.

Hope took in the scene. Graffiti-covered stone facades were all around them. A gang member in a flannel shirt and do-rag driving a hopped-up sedan that diffused bone-rattling bass beats cruised past. Homeless men lying on makeshift cardboard bedding were scattered along the sidewalks. An older woman, head down and stealing furtive glances, pushed a rusted cart full of groceries past boarded-up storefronts.

"God's people," said Mazur. "Which reminds me, you're just in time to help."

"Help?" asked Hope.

"Yes. We offer food and shelter to our homeless parishioners. Nights are getting too cold to spend on the streets this time of year. And we could use a couple more servers in our cafeteria line."

Hope gazed at Clive and said, "I'm in."

After getting the chance to put their shopping bags down and rest for an hour, Hope and Clive found themselves side-by-side in plastic aprons and gloves and wearing hairnets in the church cafeteria's serving line along with other volunteers. With a long metal spoon, she dished out green beans onto metal trays slid along the railing by disheveled men and women.

Hope tried to maintain a cheerful facade and say an encouraging word as she served them and looked into their dirty faces. Some were a downcast picture of despair, while others held a stoic stare. A few spoke to fouled neurotransmitter demons only they could hear.

The metallic slap of the spoon onto the trays and the "God loves you" greetings she pronounced were becoming rote when it happened.

A diminutive man in a ratty suit jacket, full beard, and wiry brown disheveled hair lingered in front of her a little too long.

"God loves you," said Hope, probably for the hundredth time, as she spooned a portion of beans onto his tray.

His dirt-encrusted face widened into a wry grin. "Indeed, he does, Hope."

"Wait, how…?"

She recognized him. Then, in a flash, he was gone, dissolved into the sea of hungry, tattered men and women seated on benches at long tables in the expansive hall at the back of the church. Hope stood petrified.

She felt an elbow's nudge. "Hope? Hope?"

She looked up at Clive.

"What's wrong," he said, pointing toward a woman in a tattered shawl awaiting her portion of beans.

"I saw him," said Hope. "He was here."

"Who?"

"Agee."

CHAPTER 9

"I tell you, I saw him. He was in line with a tray. He called me by name." Too shaken to continue serving, Hope sat in a small room off the cafeteria with Clive and Father Mazur.

"Who is this Agee?" asked Mazur.

Scowling, Hope said, "He's a priest. Part of EQV. He ran or likely still runs a black-market ring selling rare and expensive stolen ancient Egyptian artifacts to wealthy collectors."

"We may as well tell him the whole story," said Clive.

"Telling the whole truth is always a good thing," said Mazur.

Hope took a ragged breath. "Agee, along with three other priests in the St. Bede's University archaeology department, were involved in time travel. The University's physics department had, believe it or not, invented a Time Machine. At first, the four priests time-traveled back to ancient Egypt to study the civilization firsthand. But then they realized that they were sitting on a gold mine. Pristine artifacts of gold and silver for the taking. Worth a fortune. The money going to EQV. But that wasn't the worst of it. Agee also murdered several multimillionaires whose wills left enormous sums of money to the archaeology department. He's a fugitive from justice."

"Since time travel was so prohibitively expensive, they continued to finance their money-making scheme with those gifts to the department," said Clive. "Also, Hope traveled back to ancient Egypt to pursue the killer. When it was time for her to return, no money was available to pay the power company to energize the Time Machine. We had to take funds from an EQV offshore account to get her back. That's why they're after us."

Mazur was quiet for a moment. Then he said, "This just sounds so fantastic. Why hasn't news of this been in the media? I mean, how can something like this be kept secret."

"Soon after Agee was discovered, the U.S. Government took over the project. The scientists were sworn to secrecy, and nothing more was said about it. I guess their thinking is that the Time Machine will become just another piece of folklore like Bigfoot or UFOs."

"What of the other three priests?"

Hope said, "Two are dead. One other, Father Weir, disappeared."

"But why would Agee come here?" asked Mazur.

Hope shrugged. "I dunno, to taunt me?"

"I first found him," said Clive, "living among the homeless in Birmingham, Alabama, the location of the serial murders. He told us that he was hiding from EQV."

"He played us," said Hope. "He wanted to be found. That homeless act was a way to draw on our sympathy as well as hide from the police. I was a consultant with the serial killer task force, and I think he wanted to find out just how much we knew. Now, he's done it again. He's located us for EQV. Clive, we'd better go. Now!"

"Well, I suppose to be prudent—"

"Prudent, hell. They'll be here any minute with their assault weapons."

"Are you certain it was Agee, my child?" asked Mazur.

"I tell you, it was him. He was wearing a false beard and dressed in worn-out clothing, just like he had done in Birmingham. Father, I'm sorry, but we may have put your life in danger by coming here."

Mazur arose from his seat and put a hand on Hope's shoulder. "Calm yourself, my child. We're safe here."

Hope scanned the tiny room—a simple wooden floor, cracked walls covered with peeling sea green paint, and a creaky table and chairs in the center. The place couldn't have looked more precarious. "But, how...?"

Mazur smiled. It was one of those benighted expressions that Hope took as ignorance of the impending danger. "God is in control," he said. "And he works through the local gangs. Anyone appearing in this neighborhood with assault weapons will have to go through them."

"Well," said Hope, "at least can we search for Agee?"

"As you wish," said Mazur. All three left the room and casually strolled between the tables of hungry, homeless men and women, with Hope leading the way.

Hope became agitated after looking into every male face in the dining hall. Agee was gone. "OK, I...," she began. Then she saw it sitting at the end of one of the tables. She walked over to the table and pointed to a tray loaded with uneaten food.

"Hey," said a gray-bearded, bedraggled African American man who sat in front of it. He gripped the metal edge like it was a million-dollar lottery ticket. "He said I could have his tray."

"Who?" asked Hope.

"Little old white dude. Had kinda red hair and beard."

"Agee," whispered Hope. She scanned the hall again for

the errant priest. "Where did he go?"

"I don't know. He was here when I sat down next to him. He said, 'Ain't hungry. You can have it.' Then he left out that door." The man pointed to the rear exit.

Hope bolted through the door into an alley. An uneven brick wall stood on the other side of a narrow road running the length of the block. Hope stepped into the street. Looking in both directions, she saw no one. She then climbed onto the wall and observed the rear of derelict one and two-story buildings.

Hope returned to the church's rear door and said to Clive and Mazur, standing just outside, "He got away."

They reentered the dining hall. Mazur preached a short homily to the diners on God's unchanging love. Afterward, the diners who wanted to stay were berthed on bunk beds in upstairs rooms.

Hope, too keyed up to sleep, volunteered to help clean up. Wearing a pair of rubber gloves and an apron, she stood over a sink of scalding sudsy water and scrubbed metal trays with a wire brush. Clive, attuned to her enthusiasm, dared not sleep. He stood beside her, taking the handoff of clean, wet trays, drying them with a dishtowel, and stacking them in a wooden strainer.

"Hope," said Clive after depositing a dry tray into a slot, "I was thinking, since we're back on EQV's radar and we've got a few days before the awards ceremony, it might be a good time to take a little side trip."

Hope scowled. "Side trip?"

"Yes. Out of the country."

"What? Are you crazy?"

"Hear me out. Remember that I said that anytime Unit-458 is in play, they use some banned weapon of mass destruction?"

"OK," said Hope.

"Well, we need to find out what type of weapon. That would go a long way in helping us determine what they are up to."

"And how do you propose we do that?"

"We travel to Moldova. I know an arms dealer, Lev Petrov. A few years back, I did a story on the illegal arms sales market, and I got to know him then."

"What, he's just going to spill the beans on Unit-458?"

"No. Lev's more subtle. My story got his chief rival imprisoned for twenty years. He owes me a favor. While you were attending Father Mazer's service, I called him in Moldova, and he's agreed to see us."

"Well, it would be nice to get out from under EQV's nose for a while. Suppose they'd never guess we were in Eastern Europe. OK, let's go."

"Good. I took the liberty of booking us on an Air France flight to Chisinau. If we leave now, we can make the flight with time to spare."

Father Mazur drove them to Washington National Airport in his Volkswagen Bug and left them at the Air France terminal, promising to have something essential regarding EQV on their return.

CHAPTER 10

The hop across the pond, as Clive had termed their flight, was restful, especially since there was no sign of any goons from Unit-458 at the airport or on the plane.

Chisinau, the capital of Moldova, was adorned with numerous churches and monasteries featuring Byzantine-type domes. These were surrounded by clusters of old Soviet-style apartment and administrative buildings that stood like whitewashed monuments to past authoritarian rule. Additionally, modern glass and steel structures rose above the ancient edifices, making the city an amalgam of architectural styles.

Amid a light dusting of snow on the city streets, brightly decorated Christmas trees and strings of colored lights, as well as street markets packed with enthusiastic evening shoppers, imparted a festive holiday mood to the old city.

Hope and Clive, bundled in thick down jackets purchased during their layover in Paris, strolled through one of the markets. They stopped at a kiosk selling colorful ornaments. The tantalizing aroma of sour cabbage pies from a neighboring booth filled the chilled air. An ornately decorated merry-go-round at the end of the street offered rides to kids.

Clive checked his watch. "We'd better go. Lev is probably waiting."

Hope nodded and took his arm as they walked for two blocks. They entered the Gastrobar Tavern on the first floor of an ultramodern high-rise. The lobby was packed with hungry shoppers and holiday revelers in coats, scarves, and hats. The buzz of alcohol-fueled conversations, as well as the aroma of cooking meals, filled the air.

Clive looked over the full dining area and suddenly grinned. He waved. A figure at the corner table waved back. With Hope in tow, he pointed out that they had a table to the maitre d' and plunged into the throng of diners and waiters carrying large trays above their heads.

At the table, a massive man stood. He was brutish with serpentine eyes that darted back and forth as if perpetually searching for someone. His bald head reflected the muted lighting. On seeing Hope, his thick sausage lips widened into a smile. He struck Hope as someone she'd dread meeting on a darkened street after midnight.

"Lev," said Clive. "This is my fiancée, Hope Allerd. Hope, Lev Petrov."

Hope smiled. "Pleased to meet you."

"Clive, you pluck such beautiful angel from heaven," said Petrov in his thick Russian accent. "Please sit."

"Thanks for agreeing to meet us on such short notice," said Clive.

"Happy to do for old friend."

A waiter came with wine glasses, followed by the sommelier with a bottle of red.

"I ordered wine," said Petrov. He spoke to the sommelier in Romanian. The young man then proceeded to open the bottle of wine and pour a small amount into Petrov's glass. The arms dealer tasted it and nodded his approval. After pouring wine for the table and placing the bottle in the center, the sommelier left.

"It's been a long time, Lev," said Clive. "How have you

been?"

"Life is good. When you have health, you have everything. Oh, I also order for us. You will love."

A moment later, a waiter came with a tray of food. He set a dish containing stuffed cabbage rolls in front of Hope. She cut into it and ate. After devouring a morsel, she said, "It's delicious."

"Glad you like."

The Russian stuffed his cloth napkin under his collar and gobbled his meal like a man who hadn't eaten in a week. As they ate and drank, Clive made small talk with Petrov. Hope busied herself with the cabbage rolls stuffed with chicken and rice. The wine was sweet and aromatic.

On finishing his dish and third glass of wine, Petrov put down his knife and fork. His thick lips widened into a smirk. "What makes reporter come all this way?" he said. "For Christmas in Chisinau with fiancée? I think not."

Clive frowned and leaned forward. In a furtive tone, he said, "Unit-458 is active. I know they always use some form of illegal arms to carry out a mission. I need to know what you know."

"My friend, you come here during holidays to talk of illegal arms and secret armies. This is very bad. Better you talk of joy of Christmas."

Hope drained her glass and glared at the Russian. "We need your help. People will die if they carry out their plan."

"Beautiful lady should not worry over such things."

"They tried to kill me twice. I don't have a choice. Are you going to help us or not?" Hope's glare became icy.

Petrov chuckled. "Clive, you will have hands full with this one."

"Are you going to tell us what you know? Or maybe you've lost your touch, and Unit-458 is buying from a rival. Someone with a better inventory."

Petrov's face reddened. He scowled. The table grew quiet for a moment. Finally, the Russian said, "There is no better in all of Europe. You want information?"

"Yes," said Clive. "Whatever you can provide would be immensely helpful."

Petrov reached into his jacket pocket and produced a thick wallet. He opened it, removed several bills, and tossed them onto the table. He then stood and snatched his napkin from under his collar. Dropping it on his plate, he said, "You Americans have such drug problems." He stepped toward the exit, turned, and tapped his watch. "Recommend Tupolev exhibit at National Museum. Was great painter. Must not miss magnum opus."

As Petrov walked out, Hope arose to follow him. Clive gripped her arm and shook his head. She sat back down. "You're just going to let him walk out of here?"

"Hope, we're on his territory. He could have just as easily had us murdered as sitting down to dinner with us. We tried."

She lifted the near-empty wine bottle, poured the dregs into her glass, and downed it. "What was all that talk about 'drug problems' and seeing an art exhibit?"

On leaving the restaurant, they walked to their hotel room. Mindful of Hope's insistence on a platonic relationship before the wedding, Clive had arranged a room with double beds.

Hope, in paisley PJ's, snuggled under the covers. She turned to Clive and said, "Good night."

He lay on top of his bed, eyes open.

Sleep eluded Hope. Something about the Russian's cryptic

parting words kept the tumblers in her brain's mechanisms turning.

An hour later, Hope sat up in bed. "Clive, wake up. We've got to go to that museum tomorrow. I know what Petrov was trying to tell us."

CHAPTER 11

It had snowed overnight. The light dusting of the evening was now two inches of powder covering the streets and sidewalks of Chisinau.

Hope had risen early, showered, and dressed, and now sat on her bed in jeans and a blouse, awaiting Clive to exit the bathroom.

When he finally emerged, dressed and ready to go, Hope said, "Ready, slowpoke?"

Clive stopped for a second. "The term is slowcoach."

"What?"

"That's what we say in the UK."

"OK, slowcoach, let's go." She gave him a peck on the cheek as they started out of the room.

They took the elevator to the first floor and stopped in the hotel's restaurant for breakfast. It was a generic space of pine tables and chairs decorated with Christmas trees draped in colorful blinking lights. Hope ordered the American Breakfast of bacon and eggs, while Clive had an assortment of pastries.

While waiting for their server to return, Clive said, "Just what did Petrov say that made you wake me in the middle of the night?"

Hope grinned. "It's plausible that there could have been spies or undercover police in that restaurant last night."

"I suppose so. Petrov is probably wanted in several European countries."

"Then it's likely that he wouldn't just come out and say, 'I sold arms to so and so.' Right? So, if he would tell us anything, it had to be some cryptic message."

"Like Americans use drugs and to visit a museum?"

"Hey, I didn't say it would be easy."

"OK, what is that brilliant mind of yours concocting?"

"Last night, while you slept, I Googled the artist Tupolev. He was some nineteenth-century realist painter, famous for these massive canvases of historical events."

"So, what was his great work?"

Hope shrugged. "It didn't say. So, we're going to the museum."

After breakfast, Hope and Clive bundled up and trekked through the snow. They first hit a few kiosks in the outdoor market while awaiting the museum's opening. Later, they walked to the National Art Museum of Moldova, an expansive two-story structure of what appeared to be Georgian architecture. They were first in line for the opening. After purchasing tickets, they made a beeline to the Tupolev exhibit.

Traipsing the parquet floors, they marveled at portraits and still lifes hanging on white walls. These were his early works.

Entering a second room, they were taken aback by a floor-to-ceiling painting entitled *Napoleon's Retreat from Moscow*. It depicted a dumpy, nearly life-size Napoleon on horseback looking despondent, surrounded by downtrodden soldiers tramping through foot-deep snow.

There were other paintings just as striking: a Cossack cavalry charge and a Russian Imperial court scene.

Unsure of which painting Petrov had referred to as Tupolev's great work, Hope approached a young man in a blue uniform standing in the center of the room directing spectators. "Sir," she said, "which of these is Tupolev's greatest work?"

"It is there," said the young man, pointing to a large painting on the far wall in the next room.

Hope stepped up to a scene of ancient Rome. Clive followed. Large columns and statues formed the background. Over a dozen agitated men dressed in togas and brandishing bloody short swords stood around one man. He was unarmed. His toga was awash in blood. His face was creased with agony, and his arms extended as if imploring for mercy toward another who, at that moment, had plunged his sword into the dying man's gut.

She immediately recognized it as the assassination of Julius Caesar in the Senate. Hope scanned for the title. To the side on a plaque beneath the Romanian title was the English translation: *The Ides of March.*

Hope, a wry smirk on her face, turned to Clive. "We now know when. We just have to figure out how and where."

"What?" asked Clive.

"March fifteenth, Clive. Unit-458 is going to strike on March fifteenth."

◆ ◆ ◆

The over-ocean leg of the flight back to Washington, with nothing but blue water to see, turned out to be hypnotic. Even so, Hope couldn't sleep. There was still one part of Petrov's ambiguous message she had yet to decipher. The Americans using drugs was a puzzler. Assuming he wasn't just spouting off about the general drug problem in the U.S., she pondered what precisely that portion of his likely code meant.

Looking over at Clive, who reclined in his seat softly snoring, she jabbed him awake with her elbow.

"Wha...," he said, looking irritated.

"I need your help."

"What?" He was now fully roused.

"That part about Americans using drugs. What do you think he meant?"

"Haven't thought much about it."

"Come on, Clive. You must have some idea."

"Well..." He appeared deep in thought for a moment, then said, "I recall reading about your CIA supposedly being responsible for the crack cocaine epidemic in the African American community of South Central Los Angeles in the 1980s."

"Tell me more."

"Supposedly, the CIA wanted to back a group of rebels, the Contras, fighting against a leftist government in Nicaragua. They used profits from the sale of crack to finance the Contras."

Hope frowned. "Sounds draconian."

"Quite so," said Clive. "But I don't think that's Unit-458's style. They have usually pulled off some swift, decisive operation leading to regime change."

"What if they were repeating the CIA playbook, selling cocaine in some low-income community to bankroll an operation?"

Clive shook his head. "From our two failed assassination attempts and assuming your assessment of Petrov's parting words is accurate, I'd say Unit-458 is already active. And one more thing."

"What's that?"

"Those past stories about Unit-458. Once the press picked up on some unusual paramilitary activity in a country, within ten to twelve days, without fail, Unit-458 struck."

"So, what are you saying?"

"I'm saying they aren't going to strike on March fifteenth. That's some two and a half months away."

"So, when?"

"If we're lucky, we may have less than three weeks to stop them."

CHAPTER 12

Hope, in a black round-neck, pleated-skirt sheath dress and matching heels, stood just outside the East Room of the White House along with ten other Presidential Medal of Freedom recipients, awaiting the start of the ceremony. The buzz of conversation from dignitaries and guests milling around the sizable room over the piano etude played by the small orchestra made Hope a bit anxious, even though she had no speaking part in the program.

She could see the slightly raised podium with empty gold-painted hardback chairs lined along the rear for her and the other recipients. A floor-to-ceiling window with closed gold drapes and three American flags formed the background. Several rows of hardback chairs faced the stage area.

A voice from somewhere within the room intoned, "Ladies and Gentlemen, please take your seats. The program will begin shortly." The conversations died down as people sat.

Next, a reedy man in a blue suit with blonde hair and a scholarly expression on his boyish face strode past her. A woman in a sensible dress and heels walked alongside him. Hope immediately recognized him as the Vice President. They stood in the doorway for a beat. Then the announcer said, "Ladies and gentlemen, the Vice President of the United States and Mrs. Cranston." They walked into the room arm in arm and took seats on the first row as the audience stood.

"Ladies and gentlemen, the recipients of the Presidential Medal of Freedom," said the announcer. He then began calling each name. As instructed, the recipient, on hearing their name called, walked to the podium framed by life-sized portraits of George and Martha Washington on the wall behind them and stood in front of their assigned seat. Standing behind a tall man bent with age and using a cane, Hope shuffled along, waiting for her name to be called.

"Dr. Hope Allerd." She treaded between the rows of chairs up to the podium. In passing, she saw Jack in his wheelchair on the first row. Her paraplegic younger brother, the lean, handsome, sepia-skinned man with intelligent brown eyes and an engaging smile, was her spitting image. In the row behind him, Clive stood beaming as he applauded with the other audience members.

Once all the recipients' names were called and were in place, they were allowed to be seated along with the audience.

With everyone sitting, the room settled into an interlude of anticipation.

The announcer, whom Hope could now see, was a young towheaded Marine officer in his dress uniform wearing conspicuous military gold braiding on his right shoulder. He stood at the podium and gave a slight nod to the orchestra.

The musicians struck up *Ruffles and Flourishes,* a short fanfare. After repeating it three times, the orchestra became quiet.

"Ladies and gentlemen, the President of the United States," said the announcer. Everyone stood again. Hope recognized the next piece, *Hail to the Chief,* played by the orchestra.

As if by magic, President Martha Conchrane appeared between the rows of chairs. The most powerful human on the face of the planet gently paced along the parquet floor in a mauve pantsuit and black heels. She had blonde hair with gray roots cut into a bob, a round, age-creased, unassuming face, and blue, downcast eyes that crinkled when she smiled. Her shoulders were stooped as if she were carrying the world's troubles. She seemed a lot smaller to Hope in person than when she had appeared on television.

The complete picture of the President reminded Hope of a doddering substitute teacher about to be consumed by a ravenous class of delinquents.

Taking her place behind the lectern, President Conchrane said in a reedy voice, "Please be seated. Good afternoon, and welcome to the White House."

After some opening remarks about the recipients' general tenor and rambling informal remarks about each recipient's intrepidity, she stepped away from the podium and, assisted by two Navy junior officers in their white dress uniforms and wearing the gold braid, placed a medal around the neck of each recipient in turn while the announcer read their citations.

When it was her turn, Hope took center stage and stood side by side with President Conchrane while the announcer read: "A relentlessly dedicated physician, Dr. Hope Allerd, during the height of the recent megalovirus pandemic, worked tirelessly to find a cure. When confronted with the reality that finding and stopping the initial carrier, patient zero, would help end this scourge, she exhibited selfless courage and commitment by tracking down and confronting this malevolent disease carrier at great personal risk. Her dedicated effort brought an end to this dreaded disease, thus saving millions of lives."

Hope faced away from the President as she took the medal, raised the red, white, blue, and gold award by the blue ribbon, and placed it around Hope's neck.

Hope turned and shook President Conchrane's hand amid the audience's applause. The President placed a hand on Hope's shoulder, leaned in, and whispered into her ear, "Sometimes the worst demons shine in the light."

Taken aback by the statement, Hope mouthed, "What?" But before she could say anything further, the next recipient's name was called, signaling it was time to return to her seat.

The ceremony ended. Hope and the multitude of recipients, dignitaries, and guests gathered in a large hall for a reception. Piqued by her strange, whispered message, Hope scanned the room for President Conchrane. As she plodded through the room, she was suddenly scooped up by a beaming Clive. "I'm so proud of you," he said.

Jack was beside him. Her younger brother nodded and said, "Way to go, Sis." Hope leaned over and hugged him.

Hope, still preoccupied with finding Conchrane, asked, "Have you seen the President?"

Clive shrugged. "I think she left."

"What's wrong, Hope? You need to lecture Conchrane on fiscal policy or foreign relations?" said a grinning Jack.

"No. She said something...."

"What?" asked Clive.

Hope gazed at the floor, flustered, and said, "Oh, nothing. It was just...."

Looking up, she faced a tidal wave of admirers and well-wishers. A white-haired, craggy-faced senator extended his hand. "Dr. Allerd, it's a real pleasure," he said. "I'm Senator Eddie Edelstein. I've followed your career since you started that charity to build hospitals on the island of Mousseux. If there's ever anything I can do for you..."

Hope shook his hand. "Thank you," she muttered, a bit overwhelmed.

And so it went, handshakes and well wishes from relative strangers. Clive and Jack removed themselves to a corner of the room to let the felicitations play themselves out.

After receiving congratulations and shaking hands with a gray-haired woman from HUD, the crush of well-wishers hit low tide. Hope took a step toward Clive and Jack when she was blocked by a tall, muscular man in an Army dress-green uniform. His chest was replete with rows upon rows of ribbons and badges. On each shoulder, four silver stars gleamed in the fluorescent lighting.

He projected a natural air of overwhelming confidence. From look-right-through-you brown eyes to the kindly face and wry smile, the raw-umber African American curly-haired man gave the impression that he'd been at the top of his class, first place in athletics, the one to watch.

He extended his hand. "Ben Armstrong," he said as Hope's eyes focused on the black nametag over his right pocket. It had white block lettering that proclaimed, "ARMSTRONG."

Taking his hand, she immediately recognized him from the photo she'd Googled in that hospital room. "Oh, hello," she said.

"Dr. Allerd, we finally meet," he said, voice lilting a bit.

"You're Chairman of the Joint, er,...."

"Chairman of the Joint Chiefs of Staff. I've wanted to meet you for some time. We have or had a mutual friend."

"Really?" Hope was taken aback, sure she had absolutely zero in common with the General.

"General Norman Carter," said Armstrong.

Hope swallowed. Carter had assembled a team to help eradicate the viral pandemic, and Hope had worked closely with him. So close that she'd developed an infatuation with him. "Oh, yes, General Carter," said a sheepish Hope.

"Norm and I were in the same class at West Point.

Afterwards, we lost touch. He went into aviation, and I chose the infantry. I'm told you were the last to see him alive."

Hope nodded. A spring of grief began welling up from within. Carter, despite being mortally wounded, had flown her two thousand miles to confront the source of that dreaded disease.

"Er, yes. He helped me locate and stop patient zero, the prime cause of that pandemic. He was a courageous man."

"Norman Carter disobeyed a direct order."

"No. You don't understand. That pandemic behaved like a hive mind or a neural network. Once I was able to locate patient zero and neutralize her, the pandemic became easier to control. Without General Carter, I wouldn't have been able to do it, and millions more would have perished. He died a hero."

"Some people think you don't deserve this award," Armstrong said, pointing to the medal around her neck.

"I don't. I accept it on behalf of all of the doctors and nurses who were on the frontlines fighting the pandemic. This medal is as much theirs as it is mine."

"Well put, Dr. Allerd. But what about all of the people displaced, put out of jobs, people who lost their businesses because of that pandemic and the reckless policies of President Conchrane? And worse, what about the people killed by her ill-advised and unprecedented use of a nuclear weapon on a city in the United States?"

"I was in that town before it was bombed. There were very few what I'd call normal people there. It was a desperate attempt to halt the pandemic."

"So, you agree with President Conchrane's policies. A President who barely won this recent election. Some would say she stole this election. There are dozens of electoral votes still contested, you know."

"Look, General, I'm a physician, not a politician."

"The real question is, 'Are you a patriot or a plotter?'"

"I, uh…."

Armstrong smiled as if he were guarding some precious secret. "Aw now, Hope, you know for a fact that Conchrane is bad for the country. You can feel it deep down inside. Deep in your marrow. Come on, you know it."

Hope opened her mouth to reply and then gazed up at him. Those electric brown eyes shimmered with a bewitching scintillation, and his countenance beamed like a shooting star as he spoke.

Armstrong continued: "You know that if she continues her careless programs, America will end up on the trash heap of nations. Hope, you can't let that happen. Join me. Stop the decline."

"Well, I…." Hope felt caught up, like a fly in a spider's web.

"I'll ask you again, Hope, are you a patriot or a plotter?"

"Er, patriot, I guess." It was then that she realized he still clutched her right hand in his.

Armstrong released his grip and said, "Good. We're holding a rally tomorrow night at the First Chamber Center. Eight o'clock. It's nothing like you've ever seen before. Be there."

The General disappeared into the dispersing crowd. Before Hope realized it, Clive and Jack were by her side.

"What was that all about, Sis?" asked Jack.

"I dunno." Hope felt lightheaded like she'd been under the spell of one of those Vegas stage show hypnotists.

Clive frowned and looked over his shoulder. "He certainly was quite chatty."

"He wanted me to attend some rally," said Hope.

"Remember? We talked about that," said Clive.

"Oh, yeah," answered Hope. "If he's involved with that Unit-458, I think I know where they might strike."

"Clive caught me up on things," said Jack. "Is there anything I can do to help find out for sure?"

"I don't know."

"So, what's our next move?" asked Clive.

"We attend Armstrong's rally."

CHAPTER 13

Along with Jack and Clive, Hope continued to mill about the large White House reception room, still packed with numerous members of Congress, Cabinet Officers, White House staffers, and dignitaries. She was immediately whisked away from Jack and Clive by a balding man in a black suit who profusely shook her hand while telling her she was the bravest woman he'd ever met. Afterward, she received more congratulations from several people she'd never met or recognized nor was likely to see again.

One woman approached, who Hope knew all too well. Marta Devin wore a purple knee-length skirt and matching blazer, enhancing her slim hourglass figure. Her dirty blonde hair was pristinely coiffed. Makeup enhanced her high cheekbones, azure blue eyes, and pouty lips, giving her the confident look of a gorgeous woman who owned the room.

Hope began to seethe within. Marta was an old girlfriend of Clive's, and Hope was sure that Marta was here to sink her claws into her fiancé.

She stepped up to Hope, smiled, and extended her hand.

"Marta, it's nice to see you," said Hope in an icy tone. She shook Marta's hand with the limp grip of a superstitious woman loathed to touch a leper.

"Congratulations, Hope. You certainly deserved this award."

"Thank you. But you didn't come here just to see me

receive the Medal, did you?" Hope flashed a wry smile and then scanned the room for Clive.

"I was in a conference with Senator Addison about tariff relief for Lithuania, you know, boring work stuff, when he suggested I come to the ceremony as his guest."

"Oh," said Hope to the lobbyist, "I see." She caught a glimpse of Clive near a corner of the room with her brother Jack.

Marta followed her gaze and, turning to Hope with a delighted grin, said, "Oh, I see that Clive is here, also."

Hope's countenance hardened. "Yes. We're engaged, you know."

"Oh, congratulations. When is the wedding?"

"We haven't set a date yet."

"I'd love to attend."

I bet you would, thought Hope.

"I just must say hello and congratulations to Clive." Marta made a beeline for Clive and Jack.

Hope took a step to follow when she felt a firm tap on her shoulder. Irritated by the interruption, she wheeled about to see one of the young Marine officers standing at attention.

"What?" asked an annoyed Hope.

"Sorry, ma'am," he said, "but the President wants to see you in the Oval Office immediately."

Hope opened her mouth to protest, looked back at Marta nearing Clive across the room, then turned back to the rock-faced Marine. "I…uh…," she stammered.

"We can't keep the President waiting," he said, taking her arm.

With a gentle tug, he pulled her across the floor. Guided

away by the Marine, Hope looked back at Marta and Clive, now in animated conversation.

She cursed under her breath as she played a dreaded scenario in her head: Clive under that witch's spell.

◆ ◆ ◆

Hope walked or, more precisely, marched with the young Marine out of the reception area, across the East Room where the medal ceremony was held, through the residence, and into the West Wing right up to the Oval Office.

Outside the Office, the Marine knocked on the door and then opened it. At the threshold, he announced: "Madame President, Dr. Hope Allerd."

Conchrane, in an executive chair behind the Resolute Desk, a gift from Queen Victoria to President Hayes, faced two men sitting on matching beige couches opposite each other across a mahogany coffee table in the center of the room.

One, perched on the couch with legs crossed, Hope recognized as Vice President Will Cranston, who'd attended the ceremony. The other, a tall, erudite-looking man with a hawk face and precise mannerisms who furiously wrote notes in a folio, she didn't know.

Conchrane looked up. "Hope, come in," she said, not bothering to move from her chair.

As Hope walked onto the sky-blue carpet, both men stood. The Marine took one step back and closed the door.

Conchrane extended a hand to make introductions and said, "Hope, you know Vice President Cranston. And this is my Chief of Staff, Sam Withers. Gentlemen, Dr. Hope Allerd."

Both men nodded their acknowledgment of Hope.

Cranston said, "Nice to see you again, Dr. Allerd."

In a rich announcer's voice, Withers said, "Nice to meet you, Dr. Allerd."

"That'll be all," said Conchrane.

Cranston and Withers exited through a door opposite the one Hope entered.

Once alone with Conchrane, Hope said, "Madame President."

"Take a seat."

Hope sat on the edge of one of the twin couches. Conchrane arose and walked over to perch on the couch opposite her. "I suppose you want to know why I summoned you here."

Wide-eyed, Hope nodded.

"I like you, and I've been following your career ever since that awful pandemic. I saw General Armstrong eyeing you at the beginning of the ceremony. I called you in here to warn you."

"Warn me?"

"Yes. Armstrong is trouble. With a capital T. Did you two talk?"

Hope nodded.

"I suppose he ran that 'Are you a patriot or a plotter?' schtick by you."

Hope nodded again.

"He hates me with a passion. Probably because I beat his lackey, Eric Lattimore, in the recent election. Look, don't let him get under your skin."

"Couldn't you just arrest him or relieve him of his duties?"

"I wish things were that simple. If they were, all of Truman's problems with McArthur would have disappeared when he relieved the General of command of the allied forces in the Korean War."

"Madame President," said Hope, "I think things might be more dire."

"What do you mean?"

"I think General Armstrong may be plotting to overthrow you."

Conchrane was quiet for a moment. After taking a deep breath, she said, "And what makes you think this?"

"Clive Andrew and I found evidence of activity by EQV."

"Hope, EQV is a myth."

"Pardon me, Madame President, but that myth almost killed me."

"You are passionate about this, Hope. I'll give you that."

"Two men attacked me in Mousseux. Later, the co-pilot of the plane Clive and I took to the States tried to crash it in the ocean. Those aren't coincidences. And Clive has seen the work of the military arm of EQV in the past. We've talked with an arms dealer who made a sale of some weapon of mass destruction. Clive is certain that means EQV is about to strike. Soon."

"I see. And do you have any plans to look into this further?"

"General Armstrong asked me to join him. I'm not sure what that entails. But he wanted me to attend one of his rallies. I'm considering going. If I can get close to him, maybe I can obtain more detailed information on what EQV will do."

"Hope, I was serious about General Armstrong being trouble."

"Is that what you meant by, 'Sometimes the worst

demons shine in the light?'"

"I wanted to warn you."

"I'll be careful."

"Don't get too close. Remember, when a light bulb begins to shine too bright, it's about to blow out. And when Armstrong explodes, he'll take you down with him."

CHAPTER 14

Clive sipped his nonalcoholic punch as he surveyed the crowd for Hope.

Jack adjusted himself in his wheelchair and said, "She's probably got some senator's ear about health care or something."

"Yeah, probably so." He took one more sweep of the room and saw her approach.

In a purple suit, Marta Devin strode toward him with that self-assured air he knew all too well meant she desired something.

Something costly.

"Isn't that Hope?" said Jack.

"Huh?" Clive looked past Marta to glimpse Hope disappearing around a corner on the arm of a Marine.

Before he could answer Jack in the affirmative, Marta walked up. Her fetching smile caught both men unprepared.

"Hello, Clive, Jack," she said, her voice lilting with the slightest German accent.

Clive cleared his throat and responded, "Oh, hello, Marta. I'm, uh, surprised to see you."

Jack's eyes narrowed. "Hi Marta," he said, then looked from her to Clive.

"Jack," said Marta, "you must be very proud of your

sister's achievement."

Nodding, Jack said, "She deserved it."

"Yes, well, if you don't mind, I'd like to borrow Clive for a moment." She slid her arm around the reporter's elbow and batted her eyelashes at Hope's brother.

Jack sighed. He exhaled an exasperated "OK" and rolled across the room toward a table serving shrimp.

Once he was out of earshot, Marta turned to face Clive. "Now that we're alone, I need to speak with you about something very critical," she said.

"What?" asked Clive.

"Sophie," Marta spoke their daughter's name like a plea.

"Is she all right?"

"She's fine. But, since George's death, she's needed her father back in her life."

Clive, seized by guilt for not visiting his daughter recently, dropped his head.

"I suppose you're going to tell me things have been complicated over the past few months," said Marta.

"Well, uh, they have. We've been...." Clive decided this was not the time to talk about EQV.

"Yes?"

"Yeah, it's been complicated."

"Well, I was thinking that since Christmas is coming up, it would be ideal for you to spend some time with Sophie."

"Oh, uh,...well, yes, maybe we could get together and..."

"I know she'd be delighted if you could spend Christmas Day with her. She's been talking about spending Christmas with her father for weeks. What do you think?"

"Well, maybe…."

"Good. Why don't you tell her?" Marta removed her cell phone from her purse, looked for an unoccupied space in the large room, and pulled Clive over to the spot to stand beside her.

She tapped the screen several times to establish a video call. "Cassidy," she said, "please put Sophie on."

A moment later, a cute-as-a-button brown-skinned cherub with curly hair pulled into a bun appeared on the screen.

"I have a surprise for you, Sophie," said Marta, handing the phone to Clive.

Clive, struck by the resemblance, smiled at his daughter. "Hello, Sophie."

"Hello, Daddy," she said with an astonishingly precise English accent.

"How have you been?"

"Just smashing. Are you coming for Christmas?"

"Er, yes. That's why I'm calling. I'll be by Christmas Day. Is there a present you want?"

"Mummy has my list for Santa. I'm certain he'll bring everything on it. Why don't you surprise me?"

"OK, I'll do that."

"And you will be here when we open presents?"

"Wouldn't miss it for the world."

"And dinner. You just must stay for dinner."

"Of course."

"Wonderful. This is going to be the best Christmas ever."

Marta took the phone. "OK, Sophie, Mummy and Clive

have to go. I'll see you tonight."

Ending the call, she looked up at Clive. "Now," she said, "that wasn't so bad, was it?"

"No, I guess not. But why is she speaking with an English accent?"

Marta grinned. "You are clueless, aren't you? You haven't heard of the phenomenon. Well, I suppose you wouldn't. It seems that young American girls who watch a certain cartoon show, Peppa Pig, produced in the UK, have been copying the main character's accent. And also, Cassidy, our live-in maid, is from Liverpool."

"Oh," said Clive. "I see. Do you have a recommendation on what I should get her for Christmas?"

"Don't worry. I've already purchased your gift for Sophie. You'll just have to be there to watch her open it."

"What time should I be there?"

"Eight-thirty would be good."

"Very well, eight-thirty Christmas night."

"No, Clive. Eight-thirty a.m. It'll take all my powers to keep her from rising before seven a.m."

Clive nodded. "Eight-thirty a.m."

Marta smiled. She kissed him on the cheek, turned, and faded into the throng of White House guests.

Clive stood pondering over what had just happened.

"What did she want?" said Jack as he rolled up beside the reporter.

"Oh, er, she wanted me to spend Christmas Day with Sophie, my daughter."

"You gonna do it?"

"Yes, I suppose." The more Clive thought about the encounter with Marta, the more it felt like an ambush—an ambush portending something terrible involving Hope and him.

CHAPTER 15

The First Chamber Arena was a circular, expansive structure that looked more like an abstract sculpture than an indoor sports stadium. Rising five stories, it occupied an entire block of downtown D.C. Tiered seating rose to meet skyboxes that circled the interior. The basketball court below was the home turf of the Washington Sharks, a basement team at best.

But, on this night, the Arena was the site of the Glory Road Rally. Red, white, and blue vertical bunting hung from the rooftop near the entrance. The parquet floor court was populated with folding chairs arranged in neat rows facing an elevated stage at the far end. A podium with teleprompters on either side sat centerstage.

Outside, Hope and Clive stood in a snaking line along the sidewalk that ran down the block and around the side of the Arena. Patrons, primarily middle-aged working-class men and women, trudged along the slow-moving queue, talking excitedly about the man of the hour, the only person many would ever stand in line for over an hour to see, Ben Armstrong himself.

But coupled with the anticipation of witnessing the General, Hope sensed a pang of galvanic anxiety rife in the patrons. For not ten feet away, marching in the street were protestors. Young twenty-something black and white men and women faced the queue of rally attendees shouting and chanting, "Down with Armstrong, down with Armstrong!"

Some brandished cardboard signs proclaiming: "Armstrong is a fascist" or "Support President Conchrane."

D.C. police officers in riot gear and holding batons stood on the curb facing the demonstrators.

The longer she waited in line, the more Hope felt like a fish out of water. Her dark camel Michael Kors pantsuit and beige single-notched lapel long coat stood in stark contrast to the jeans, work boots, puff vests, and ballcaps worn by ninety percent of the attendees. These were Armstrong's people—pragmatic men and women who cared little for the niceties of governmental procedures and polity—his base.

A corpulent sixty-ish man with a gray beard in front of them constantly turned his head to take furtive glances at Hope. She could sense his agitation rising with the intensifying chants of the protestors by the burgeoning crimson flush in his thick neck.

Finally, he turned and glared at Hope. "Why are you here?" he challenged.

Hope looked him in the eye and said, "General Armstrong invited me."

Just as the man was about to unleash a tirade of likely expletives, two young men with crewcuts in blue blazers and khaki pants walked up to Hope. Holding up a cell phone next to Hope's face to reveal a photo of her, one of them said, "Are you Dr. Allerd?"

Hope nodded. "Yes."

"Could you please come with us? General Armstrong has arranged seating for you and your guest."

As Hope stepped out of the formation and fell behind the two young men, she looked back and grinned at the apoplectic male Karen in the line.

They walked to the entrance, bypassing the metal

detectors at the door, and boarded an elevator to the left that took them to the top floor. Stepping out onto a carpeted hallway, they walked past several closed doors along the corridor. Finally, stopping at one, the young man said, "This is your suite." He opened the door and extended a hand, indicating that Hope and Clive should enter.

They stepped into the skybox suite, a large semicircular room with a glass wall looking down into the court. Six plush swivel seats afforded excellent views of the stage below.

As Clive settled into one of the chairs, he asked, "Just what did you and Armstrong talk about at that ceremony?"

Hope plopped into the seat next to his and shrugged.

Thirty minutes later, the arena was crammed to capacity. They could hear the buzz of hundreds of conversations through speakers near the ceiling.

"Quite a show," said Hope.

Clive stared at the crowd below. "Could be a story in all of this," he said. "Middle America seeks a new savior."

"Hasn't the media already done enough reports on Armstrong?"

"Hope, look at the stage."

"Yeah? What about it? It's just an empty stage."

"Notice what's in the background." He pointed.

At the back of the stage, three American flags on poles on either side flanked a large white cross in the center illuminated by spotlights in the rafters.

"It's this whole pseudo-religious thing."

"Pseudo-religious?"

"Yes. These people view Armstrong as a messiah, leading them to some political promised land."

"Really?"

"Just watch." Clive crossed his arms, lowered his head, and scowled at the proceedings below.

Suddenly, the crowd erupted in a cacophony of shouts and applause. A tallish, thin man with an unruly mop of blonde hair appeared on stage. His boyish, angular face pinched into a closed-eyed, crooked mouth sneer as he raised both hands to quiet the crowd.

"Who's that?" asked Hope.

"You're kidding, right?"

"OK, Clive, so I'm not up on current events. I've been working in that hospital for sixteen hours a day. No time for politics or anything else for that matter. Remember?"

"Sorry. That's Eric Lattimore, the radio shock-jock. He ran against Conchrane for President."

"That's Lattimore? He looks like a kid."

Lattimore leaned into the microphones. "Ready to take the Glory Road?"

The audience cheered.

"We're taking back our country," shouted Lattimore, voice laced with a thread of venom. "Conchrane and her ilk are not long for this world. That's right. She doesn't know it yet. But she and all of her corrupt cronies are about to take the big fall. We know she stole this election, right?"

Another cheer erupted.

"All right. OK." Lattimore's sneer deepened. "Without further adieu, I give you the man of the hour. The greatest patriot of this generation. The only person who can take back our country and set us on the Glory Road. I give you General Benjamin Davis Armstrong!" He stepped aside and pointed to stage right.

Screams and cheers shattered the previous decibel levels. The audience stood. A canned orchestral recording played *The Battle Hymn of the Republic* over the PA system.

Out walked Armstrong in a blue suit and paisley tie. In the stark fluorescent stage lighting, he appeared angelic, almost gossamer-like, as he approached the podium. He stood, hands tightly clutching the sides of the lectern's reading top, chin up, eyes cast to the ceiling as if communing with some political deity floating just above his head.

His appearance hushed the crowd as if he had just descended from the heavens with a new commandment for his acolytes. Every neck was craned upwards, and every eye focused on the General.

Looking down at the spectacle, Hope felt her breath catch in her throat. Suddenly, seized by the hoopla, she bound to her feet.

The music stopped. In the quiet, the air was pregnant with expectation.

Hope slowly took her seat.

Armstrong cleared his throat and licked his lips. "My fellow Americans," he began in almost a whisper, "we are at a crossroads. We stand at the avenues of the Status Quo and the Greater Future. If we follow Status Quo, we march down the road to a fractured nation, a path to decline, a way to second-class nationhood. During a second term under President Conchrane, we will fall into a depression. You will lose your jobs. For those of you who will still have a job, your income will decline. Costs for goods and services will skyrocket. It will be a veritable hell on earth."

He paused and scanned the audience, then, in a booming voice, he continued to describe a dystopian society under Conchrane's leadership. Starving families wandering through some Mad Max-like dust bowl.

He then went over his take on the recent election in exquisite detail. In a litany of scenarios, he talked of how Conchrane had bribed election officials in swing states, suppressed voting of groups who opposed her in key states, and her toadies rigged voting machines in dozens of districts to switch votes from Lattimore to her. He named names, pinpointed times, and listed locations.

Armstrong concluded this section of his speech with, "You can live with this fallen version of America, this burned-out cinder of our Republic."

He paused again. "Or," he thundered, "you can follow me down that road to a Greater Future. I will reinvigorate this economy. I will grow jobs at a rate never seen before—good American jobs. I will keep our borders secure. I will rebuild our military until it is second to none. I will renew the exploration and utilization of fossil fuels to make America energy independent. Under my leadership, the time is now to tear down the Conchrane Machine. The time is now to take back our country. The time is now to set America back on her Glory Road. Follow me! Follow me!"

The audience, reacting as one, got to their feet, shouting and applauding. This time, the PA system struck up *Onward Christian Soldiers*. The massive cross behind Armstrong, struck by the stage lighting, glowed red, white, and then blue on a rotating basis.

The General stood there, arms folded across his chest, head nodding, soaking up the adulation like a sun-starved perennial.

The whole thing reminded Hope of those early twentieth-century midwestern tent revival meetings she'd read about.

She turned to Clive. "What did you think of it?"

Scowling, the reporter said, "I think your American democracy is in peril."

"Wasn't it exciting?" gushed Hope.

"About as exciting as a root canal."

"You didn't like it?"

"The guy was talking about insurrection. He wants to take over the country."

"No. It's just hyperbole," said Hope.

"Were you listening to the same speech?"

"Clive, really?"

Just then, the suite's door flew open. The two young men in blue jackets and khaki trousers stepped in, taking positions on either side of the doorway.

A grinning Armstrong stepped inside as Hope and Clive turned toward the entrance. "What did you think?" he said.

Clive glared at Hope.

She said, "I'm not sure I'd agree with everything you said, but it was a grand speech."

Armstrong nodded. "I thought so. We're going on a bus tour. Twelve cities in fourteen days. Come with us, Hope. Tell your story."

"My story?"

"Come on, now. You helped save this nation with your pandemic work. You didn't advocate masks, closing businesses, or remote schooling. You went out, found patient zero, and shut that virus down. Without you, this country would have withered on the vine."

"Well," said Hope, glancing at Clive, who shook his head. "Could I give it some thought?"

"Sure, but don't think for too long. We leave for Pittsburg in four days."

With that, Armstrong swept out of the suite with all the vigor of a man on a mission.

◆ ◆ ◆

As they got into the back of a black SUV motoring them away from the rally, Lattimore turned to Armstrong. "I heard you want that Allerd woman to join us on the tour."

"Why not?"

"For one thing, I don't trust her."

"Come on, Eric, what harm could she do?"

"Don't underestimate her. That little woman has been a thorn in our side since she was involved in that serial murder case in Birmingham."

"Maybe it's a reason to keep her nearby. You know the old saying, 'Keep your friends close and your enemies closer.'"

"I don't like it. She and her computer-hacking brother are nothing but trouble." Lattimore's face widened into a sneer.

"Naw, it'll be fun. She can come on before me. Warm up the audience. And you can introduce her."

"What if she refuses to join us?"

Armstrong shrugged.

Or, thought Lattimore, *what if she's found dead in her hotel room?*

CHAPTER 16

Hope and Clive left the arena via the elevator and the front entrance, blending into the exiting crowd. Still energized by Armstrong's speech, they chattered raucously as they stepped into the late evening midtown.

Hope, jostled by the emboldened attendees, listened to snippets of conversations: "...take back our country..." and "...show them libertards whose land this is..."

Once on the sidewalk, Hope was completely hemmed in by the crowd. There was an inflexibility as she was pressed on all sides by dozens of bodies stiffened for an attack. She could feel the white-hot rage build.

She looked for Clive. He was nowhere to be found.

Suddenly, a brick flew overhead in an arc, landing on a woman's shoulder beside her. Shouts reached a crescendo as the mass surged forward into the street.

Like two opposing armies, the attendees and demonstrators clashed. It was a battle waged with fists, signs, and bricks.

The police, helpless to stop the fray, were trampled or shoved aside.

Hope was carried along in the melee like a swimmer caught in a riptide. She struggled to stay upright as a smallish man shoved her from behind.

Over the shouts and screams came commands from a

bullhorn to disperse.

Seeing a break in the crowd, Hope darted for a park across the street from the arena. Just as she made it onto a grassy mound with half a dozen other people, explosions erupted, followed by blinding smoke.

Her eyes filled with tears, and her throat revolted in spasms when she inhaled the fumes. Bodies silhouetted by smoke and flame slowly trudged across the grounds. Hope, blinking, coughing, and spitting, fell in line with the shadowy people.

Suddenly, a sinewy mass slammed into her back. Hope stumbled and, just before falling, felt the keen thwack of a baton strike her head.

Sharp pain.

A blinding flash. Then...

Nothing.

◆ ◆ ◆

Hope opened her eyes. They burned. Her head throbbed. She lay in cold, wet grass. It took several moments before she could rise to a standing position and recall that she was in a park across from the arena.

She touched the back of her head. Her hair was encrusted in dried blood.

She knew it was nighttime, yet it was lit like high noon. A blast of febrile air lashed her cheeks and forehead like she'd opened a hot oven.

As the scene came into focus, Hope realized that storefronts were in flames up and down on both sides of the street as far as she could see. Several cars in the center of the street burned, sending acrid smoke skyward. Firetrucks and police cruisers sat at one end, blue lights strobing.

Dozens of people ran willy-nilly through the streets, many carrying boxes of varying sizes. As the light of the fires briefly illuminated the parcels, Hope realized these were looters absconding with TVs, computers, and other store items.

Taking a few steps, Hope felt the world spin like a tilt-a-whirl. She found a park bench and flopped down on the end next to a confused older man in blood-stained jeans.

Burying her head in her hands, she sat and waited, wondering what had happened to Clive.

Time ticked by. Hope was unsure how much. But sharp reds, oranges, and yellows of sunrise cut through the pall of smoke that hung over the scene. It was a warzone. Shattered glass of storefronts, debris, and burned-out cars filled the streets. A few people wandered through the rubble.

"Ma'am, are you all right?" said someone standing near her.

Hope looked up to see a paramedic; the woman held a case. Dropping it to the ground, she kneeled and removed some items from within. Immediately, Hope felt the sting of the woman dabbing a gauze bandage against her head wound.

"Might need some stitches," said the paramedic. "Can you walk?"

Hope stood on wobbly legs, holding the gauze to her head, and assisted by the paramedic, lumbered to the rear of an ambulance.

She sat down on a stretcher just inside the open door. Someone in green scrubs, a medical resident, she thought, did a quick neuro exam, then prepped her head and began stitching her wound.

He asked Hope, "Did you lose consciousness?"

"Er, yeah."

"How long?"

"I dunno."

"You have a concussion. Likely will need to be admitted for observation, but..."

"Yeah?" asked Hope.

"But hospitals all over the city are full. Fractured skulls, gunshot wounds, broken long bones, folks with internal injuries from being trampled. You name it."

"It's OK. I'm a physician. I can have my fiancé do neuro checks. I promise he'll take me to a hospital if I don't respond appropriately."

Just as the resident put in the last stitch and placed a dressing over the wound, Hope heard a familiar voice calling her name.

Looking up, she saw Clive stagger towards her. His face was caked with dried blood, which had flowed in dark red stripes onto his jacket and white shirt.

She arose and embraced him. "Are you all right?" she asked.

"I'm OK. Thank God, I found you. I was looking for you all night. Let's go."

"Where?"

"Back to the hotel. I called Jack as soon as I thought it was safe. He came with his van. It's parked a few blocks away."

◆ ◆ ◆

Hope lay in her plush hotel room bed, watching a local TV news station recap the riot. Ten blocks of Downtown D.C. were devastated by the clash, and remnants of fires still smoldered within the rubble.

Clive sat in a chair beside her bed. Although conked in the head by a flying brick during the riot, he hadn't lost consciousness and wandered the streets in search of Hope. After she had schooled him on doing a basic neuro check, he'd stayed by her side diligently performing the exam on her every two hours.

Jack sat at the room's desk, clacking away on his laptop. "I'm getting conflicting reports on who started the riot," he said.

"Conflicting?" asked Hope.

"Yeah, depending on the news outlet, it was the radical Marxist demonstrators or the ultraconservative idiots following Armstrong."

Clive glared at Hope. "Can we please talk about the elephant in the room?" he said.

"Elephant? What elephant?" asked Jack. He turned his wheelchair and rolled towards the bed.

"Armstrong invited Hope to go on his Glory Road Tour."

"What?" Jack turned his attention to Hope. "Of course, you said, 'No'."

Hope looked from one to the other. "Well...."

"Come on, Hope," said Jack. "You're not seriously considering going with that General on some speaking tour. Clive, I think she's still concussed."

"I'm fine," said Hope. "Hear me out. First of all, I think Armstrong would protect me. With that Presidential Medal of Freedom, I'm kind of a celebrity. It wouldn't look good for him and his movement if something happened to me on that tour."

"Oh, yeah, he'll protect you all right, like keeping you from getting caught up in a riot, being conked on the head, and nearly killed," said Jack, his voice dripping with sarcasm.

"No. If I were with the tour, we'd likely be out of town as soon as the program was over. Before anything like that could happen."

"Talk to your bride-to-be, Clive."

"Listen," said Hope. "Time is running out. You said so yourself, Clive. What, we may have less than three weeks before Unit-458 strikes? This may be the only way I can get inside and discover what Armstrong is doing, the only way to stop him."

Clive nodded. "I suppose. But you're walking into the lion's den. EQV is still out to kill us."

"With God's help, Daniel survived the lion's den." Hope flashed a confident smile.

The reporter shrugged. "Yeah. But remember those two Nigerian operatives and that crazy co-pilot made attempts on your life. Even if it's in his best interest to keep you alive, EQV might overrule Armstrong and decide you must die."

Hope buried her face in her hands. A moment later, she looked up. "There's one other reason I think Armstrong will keep me safe."

"What's that?" asked Jack.

"I think he's falling for me."

"What?" shouted Clive.

"Sis, you're crazy."

"You two didn't see how he looked at me when we met after that Medal Ceremony. It was something in the way he acted, the way he held my hand. A woman can sense these things."

Clive arose and began pacing. Jack rolled closer to Hope's

bed.

Hope looked from one to the other. "OK, let's recap. We know Unit-458 is active. Armstrong is likely in command. He hates President Conchrane, and by the tenor of that speech last night, he wants to get her out of office very soon."

"She just won a second term," said Jack.

"Yeah, but I think that's what he's up to. Clive, could that Unit-458 do something here, carry out some regime change like in one of those third-world countries?"

"Possible."

"You've got to be kidding," said Jack.

"Jack, think about it," said Hope. "He's got a growing rabid base following him. Conchrane won by the slimmest of margins. Armstrong just needs the slightest pretense—evidence that Conchrane somehow cheated in the election. I dunno, maybe Conchrane has some radical un-American agenda in the works."

"That still doesn't preclude you from being killed by EQV," said Clive.

"What if I play along? Pretend that I'm interested in him."

"You wouldn't sleep with him," said Clive. He stopped pacing.

"No! I'd act like I'm attracted to him. That should keep me safe."

"And what happens when he makes a move, and you rebuff him?" asked Clive.

"Look, I'll find out what I can about Armstrong's plans and pretend to fall ill before things get serious. I can fake a severe migraine or appendicitis and leave the tour. After all, I am a physician. Oh, and Jack, don't you have some computer magic you can work to monitor my moves? Maybe implant a bug or something? That way, you two wouldn't worry so much."

"Well, I suppose I could do something to monitor your location twenty-four-seven," said her brother.

"I don't like it," said Clive.

"We don't have much time. The clock is ticking. Do you have a better plan?"

Clive glanced at Jack, who just hung his head.

"We only need to learn one fact to stop Armstrong," said Hope.

"What's that?" asked Clive.

"How do you overthrow the President of the United States?"

CHAPTER 17

By the afternoon, Hope was headache-free. The laceration on the back of her head was less tender to touch. *Stitches out in a week*, she thought as she scanned her light application of makeup in the hotel bathroom mirror.

She wore jeans and a red blouse purchased at the hotel's shop, appropriate clothing for another evening working in Father Mazur's kitchen. The cleric had contacted her earlier that afternoon, inviting her and Clive to volunteer again to feed the hungry with an inducement that he had some vital news to share.

She stepped out of the bathroom and said, "Let's go, Clive."

The reporter sat at the room's desk, perusing an article on his laptop. "You know that Glory Road Tour is going to Pittsburg, Chicago, St. Louis, Oklahoma City, Dallas, Jackson, Birmingham, Charlotte, Nashville, Louisville, Columbus, and Detroit," said Clive.

"I know. Twelve cities in fourteen days. That's what Ben said."

"Oh, so now it's Ben."

"Please, Clive, it's just a speaking tour. I promise I'll only say a few words and then retire for the evening. Alone."

Clive arose. "Alone," he repeated as if giving a command.

◆ ◆ ◆

They took an Uber to All Saints Church. Father Mazur met them in the foyer. He was wearing a plastic apron over his clerical garb. Beads of sweat covered his forehead. "Thank you for coming," he said, shaking their hands. "The temperature is dropping fast, so I'm afraid tonight will be very busy."

Moments later, Hope was standing in the serving line dishing out spoonfuls of creamed corn while Clive, holding tongs, distributed a dinner roll on each person's tray.

Disheveled with faces etched with dirt and angst, the homeless men and women moved along the line with trays of food, as before, to sit at the long tables in the adjoining room.

It was past midnight when Hope had finished serving dinner and washing the trays. Holding a dish towel as before, Clive completed drying the final tray and flexed his hands.

Father Mazur stepped between them and put an arm around each of them. "Thank you again for volunteering," he said. "Let's go into my rectory to talk."

The rectory was a small upstairs apartment attached to the church. They sat on a worn leather couch while Father Mazur prepared coffee in the kitchen.

He emerged with a tray containing a carafe, bowls of sugar and cream, three cups, and saucers. He placed the tray on the coffee table in front of them and sat in a straight-back chair opposite them.

As they helped themselves to coffee, the Father said, "I know it's late for coffee, but I want you to be wide awake for what I'm about to tell you. And, if you are willing, what we are about to do."

"What is it?" asked Hope.

"Members of EQV are meeting tonight. My source tells me this is an important gathering. Only the top officers."

"What's this about?" asked Clive.

"They're initiating a new head of the organization, which makes it all the more dangerous for us to try and infiltrate this meeting. Security will be even tighter than when you and I slipped into that meeting, Clive."

"Who is it?" asked Hope.

"It's a secret. No one knows except for the initiate and those performing the ceremony. Of course, I must be there. I swore an oath to monitor their activities and pray diligently for their repentance."

"Watch the watchers," said Clive.

"Yes. But you two. There's no need for you to be there."

"I'll go," said Hope. "I need to know what I'm up against."

"I don't understand," said Mazur.

"Father," said Clive, "Hope was invited by General Armstrong to accompany him on his Glory Road speaking tour. We suspect that Armstrong may be plotting to overthrow the government. And Hope thinks she can find out exactly what he's up to by joining the tour."

Hope glared at her fiancé. "Yes, and the more I know about Armstrong's EQV connection, the better I'll understand what he's up to."

Father Mazur sat back, removed his glasses, and wiped them on his shirt. "Well, I can see your point. But I could go alone and report back to you."

"Excellent idea," said Clive. "Also, tell her how much danger she'd be in by going on that speaking tour."

Hope took a deep breath. "I want to go tonight. Look, Clive, I've got to see their faces. The individuals at that meeting in case they show up during the tour. It'll give me an idea of the organization's hierarchy and who's giving orders."

"I don't like it," said Clive.

"It's like a crime family," said Hope. "If we only identify the low-level soldiers and stop them, the lieutenants and boss get away scot-free and continue their nefarious activities."

"She does have a point," said Mazur.

Clive gazed into Hope's eyes. "What if the Father and I go and take photos of the ceremony?"

Mazur looked pained for a moment. "I'm sorry, Clive. The lighting they used in the ceremony is very low. You can identify faces. But once I tried recording a meeting, I only managed to get photos and videos of shadowy forms."

Hope got to her feet and checked her watch. "Then it's settled. Father, when do we go?"

◆ ◆ ◆

It was nearly three a.m. Taking Father Mazur's VW Bug, they drove to the warehouse district. On the drive over, Clive told the Father about him and Hope meeting Petrov in Moldova.

Mazur parked on the street lined with two-story concrete frame buildings appearing to have been constructed in the nineteen twenties and thirties. A smattering of panel trucks with back ends facing loading docks were parked along the street. Soaring in the distance were high-rise apartment buildings and construction cranes—an indication of the growing gentrification of the area.

As she exited the car, Hope caught a glimpse of the Capitol dome rising just beyond the top floor of a pale gray high rise. Seeing that cupola lit like a remote beacon of freedom energized her with renewed purpose.

Father Mazur got out of the Bug and started across the street. "Follow me," he said. Hope, with Clive in tow, trotted across the deserted street.

They hiked past several storefronts before turning down an unlit alley. As she walked between the towering, faded red brick walls, Hope felt like she was at the bottom of some remote canyon.

Taking a right and then a left, they came upon a nondescript warehouse loading dock. "Here," whispered Mazer. He climbed onto the elevated loading area and walked over to a door on the left side. Kneeling, he removed a set of burglar's tools from his coat pocket. Turning to Hope and Clive, who stood behind him, he grinned and said, "Detritus of a misspent youth."

Unlocking the door with the tools, he entered. They followed. The party walked along a narrow concrete landing. Below was a spacious floor littered with shards of lumber, broken and rusted machinery, and shattered bricks. The opposite wall contained a series of floor-to-ceiling windows.

At the far end of the warehouse was another door. Mazur put his finger to his lips and then opened it. Inside was a nearly pitch-black area. At least Hope thought it was until her eyes began to adjust to the ambient light.

Before her was a slit in the brick wall wide enough to accommodate the three of them. A faint flickering light glowed.

Hope looked into the narrow space. There was a basement area below. Standing in two columns were figures in long robes with attached hoods covering their heads. They each held a long candle, the flames dancing in the musty air. At the far end of the aisle they created was some sort of alter. It must have been covered with a hundred lit candles. Like undulating waves frozen in time, dried wax caked the top. Behind the altar arose a wooden throne. Erect with an imperious posture, another robed and hooded figure perched on the ceremonial chair, pale hands gripping the armrests.

Slow and officious organ music began to play. The standing figures holding the candles started to sing. The musical composition sounded like some medieval choral piece. From the baritone and tenor voices, Hope knew that they were all men.

The robed figure on the throne arose and picked up something on the floor at his feet. He held it in front of him with two hands by a long hilt. A long, broad blade extended from it, reflecting the candlelight. Hope recognized it as an English broadsword based on old movies and photos she'd seen in the past.

Keeping the sword at eye level, the imperious figure walked around the altar to stand before the table. Taking one hand, he lowered his hood.

In the flickering candlelight, Hope recognized the salt and pepper hair crowned, age-etched, jowly face of Reese Winters, the CEO of Winters Madison. Owning subsidiaries of luxury car companies, upscale department stores, cosmetic manufacturing concerns, and half a dozen others, it was the largest conglomerate on the planet. And Reese Winters was rumored to have recently become the wealthiest man alive.

What happened next shocked Hope to the very center of her being.

From the opposite end of the human corridor, flanked by a robed figure on either side, plodded General Armstrong, holding a leather strap bound around his wrists. He was naked except for a pristine white loincloth. Bloody lacerations covered his back. A coarse weave of branches with long thorns crowned his head, points dug into his flesh. His palms and feet dripped blood from fresh wounds.

Looking to the heavens, his blood-smeared face was a mask of agony.

Hope glanced at Father Mazur, who stared at the scene

with an enraged expression.

Armstrong and his party stopped within a foot of Winters. The General then dropped to his knees, extending his arms to his side.

The singing stopped. In a decrescendo, the organ began a dirge.

Winters touched the sword to Armstrong's left shoulder and intoned, "Benjamin Davis Armstrong, do you believe in EQV and all of its holy tenets?"

"I do," said Armstrong.

Lifting the sword over the General's head and placing the blade against his right shoulder, Winter asked, "Will you live by the tenets of EQV for the remainder of your natural life?"

"I will."

Winters once again touched the sword to Armstrong's left shoulder. "Do you swear to give your life in defense of EQV and all of its tenets?"

"I swear."

The CEO again brought the sword in front of his face. "Arise, Lord Benjamin, Master, and Defender of the Sovereign State and Assurance of the Ultimate Victory."

As he stood, one of the men at Armstrong's side produced a robe and placed it on the General. Winters then handed Armstrong the sword and stepped to the right side of the throne. The chant started again as the General, holding the sword in his right hand, walked around the altar to take his seat on the throne.

"We've seen enough," whispered Mazer and turned to go. Hope and Clive followed.

Mazur drove back to his church in silence. Seeing the indignation on the cleric's face, neither Hope nor Clive dared say a word.

Mazur paced in the narthex as Hope and Clive looked on. He mumbled, "Pure sacrilege. The whole thing was blasphemy."

Venturing the courage to break their silence, Hope asked, "What did we just witness?"

"A man making himself to be God," said Mazur, spitting out the words as a bitter invective.

"You mean…?"

"Armstrong has ascended to the head of EQV."

CHAPTER 18

After resting in their room for a few hours, Hope and Clive were joined by Jack for a late breakfast in the hotel's restaurant.

On hearing their description of Armstrong's initiation, Jack said, "Sounds kinda cheesy."

Hope shrugged. "Yeah, and sinister, too. But the guy now runs the show. He's head of the whole organization."

"So, what does it mean?" asked Jack.

"He can do anything he damn well pleases with impunity," said Clive.

"Like overthrowing the President?" said Jack.

Hope took a deep breath. "Yeah, and setting himself up as king, emperor, president for life, or whatever he wants to call himself."

"Which brings me to the point," said Clive. "Going on that tour with Armstrong is now out of the question."

Hope smiled. "I thought you would bring it up. Don't you see, Clive? The change in Armstrong's status means I'm safer than ever."

Jack leaned forward in his wheelchair. "Sis, what have you been smoking?"

"Jack, hear me out. If Armstrong is now head of EQV and still wants me on this tour, there's no way he'd let me be harmed. He wants me to speak on how I helped stop this recent pandemic. He thinks my actions in tracking down patient zero confirm his stance against vaccines, masking, closing businesses, and remote learning."

"You're not against those actions, are you?" asked Clive.

"No. They're all prudent public health measures. But, if I stick to a script outlining my actions during the pandemic at each rally, I think he'll be satisfied and wouldn't want any harm to come to me. And most importantly, I'll be able to find out what he's up to."

"It's still too dangerous," said Clive.

"I agree," added Jack.

"So, what, I'm outvoted two to one?"

Jack nodded.

"Yes, that's correct," said Clive. "So, no more talk of going on tour with Armstrong."

Hope sat back and folded her arms. Eyes slit like a snake about to strike, she scrutinized her brother and fiancé in turn.

In a meek voice, Clive said, "It's for the best, Hope."

The waitress came with their orders on a large tray. After placing the plates on the table and topping off their cups of coffee, she left. Hope momentarily stared at her steaming hot omelet, then slid out of the booth.

"Where are you going?" asked Clive.

"I've lost my appetite." She stalked out of the restaurant.

◆ ◆ ◆

Still angry, Hope took the elevator up to her room. *Who do they think I am?* She fumed as the car stopped on her floor, *some weak little woman that they could boss around.*

Taking her keycard from her purse, she opened the door. Inside, she noticed that the beds were made. She stepped into the bathroom. Fresh towels were on the racks. The floor, shower door, and sink were pristine.

She stood in front of the sink to splash water on her face. As she leaned over, she noticed it.

On the cleaner-than-clean counter, all by itself, lay a solitary square of toilet paper.

Without thinking, she reached down to pick it up and toss it into the basket on the bathroom floor. But, as a finger touched the paper, she thought better of it. Pulling off a section of the roll near the toilet, she picked up the square with it and deposited the clump into the waste basket.

As a precaution, she washed her hands with the scented hand soap by the sink, wondering why the housekeeper was so precise in cleaning the room yet left toilet paper on the counter.

She leaned over and splashed water on her face. On standing, instead of feeling the refreshing chill of cold water on her skin, Hope felt just the opposite.

Weak all over. It was the only way to describe it. She suddenly just wanted to lie down and sleep for a thousand years. The room whirled. Nausea rolled in like high tide. Barely able to breathe, she gripped the sink to steady herself.

Then...

...nothingness.

CHAPTER 19

Clive and Jack quickly pursued Hope out of the restaurant. At the elevators, they took the next car up.

"She was really ticked," said Jack as they passed the sixth floor.

"Can't be helped," said Clive. "We can't let her go on that tour."

The door opened on the eighth floor. Room 834 was halfway down the corridor. Clive arrived at the front door first. He knocked and yelled through the door, "Hope. We need to talk."

No response.

"Just go on in," said Jack, now beside him.

Taking his keycard from his pocket, he tapped it against the electronic lock. The tumblers clicked, and he pressed the handle. The door gave only slightly.

"She must have turned the deadbolt," he said, then called again through the narrow space, "Hope, we need to talk."

Facing Jack, he said, "I know she can hear me."

Jack rolled up to the door. "Hope, it's Jack. Let us in."

A maid emerged from the adjacent room and shut the door. She started down the corridor away from them, pushing her cart.

Clive took a step towards her. "Excuse me," he said. "Could

you help us?"

The young woman turned with a look of sheer terror on her face. She shoved the cart at Clive and bolted for the emergency exit.

He turned to Jack. "I don't like this."

"Way ahead of you," said Jack, holding his cell phone. "I'm dialing 9-1-1."

Police and fire-rescue response was less than ten minutes. After police officers battering down the door, two paramedics entered with their stretcher between them. They found Hope lying face up on the bathroom floor, barely breathing.

Kneeling around her lifeless body, the paramedics set their cases containing medications and equipment and a defibrillator on the tile floor.

Following their protocol, they gave her oxygen, started an IV, pushed an ampule of glucose, and then jammed a spring-loaded syringe of Narcan into her thigh.

After the Narcan, her eyes fluttered, and she took a deep breath.

"Hope," yelled Clive, standing at the bathroom doorway.

She mouthed something, then promptly resumed her somnambulant state.

Another syringe of Narcan.

She awakened only to drop back off to sleep.

After a third syringe and the same brief response, one of the paramedics said to Clive, "How long has she been doing narcotics?"

In an offended tone, he replied, "She doesn't!"

The paramedic gave a fourth syringe while his partner began preparing an IV bag of Narcan. He raised it, letting the narcotic antagonist solution flow continuously into her vein.

Hope began to rouse. They placed her on the stretcher and wheeled her, with IVs hanging and oxygen flowing via a cannula in her nose, to the elevator.

On passing Clive, the paramedic said, "You two gotta get drug counseling."

"Is she gonna be alright?" Clive, near tears, looked frazzled.

They learned that Hope was going to D.C. Metropolitan Hospital. One of the police officers who responded to the 9-1-1 call stopped Clive and Jack from leaving the hotel room. He began questioning them. His partner started a visual search of the room. Looking for drug paraphernalia, surmised Clive.

"You can scour the room," said Clive. "You won't find any drugs."

Jack said, "Find that maid. She acted suspiciously when we asked her to help us."

"How so?" said the officer.

"She shoved her cart at Clive and ran to the fire exit."

"You got a description?" said the officer.

Clive closed his eyes for a moment, then said, "Caucasian, about five-four, brown hair, brown eyes, round face. Kind of plain looking. Had a tattoo of a letter or symbol on her left forearm."

"You're pretty specific," said the policeman.

"I'm a reporter," said Clive.

The second policeman, holding the room phone's handset to his ear, put his hand over the microphone and looked at Clive. "You sure about that description?"

"Yes," said Clive.

"Cause I'm on the line with the manager. The person working this floor is an older Hispanic gentleman by the name of Jose."

◆ ◆ ◆

Due to their police interrogation and downtown D.C. traffic, it took Clive and Jack three hours to get to D.C. Metropolitan Hospital.

Plastic-molded chairs were arranged in rows against the puke-green walls and along the center of the ER waiting area. All of them were occupied by mothers holding screaming infants, older men and women in tattered clothing, staring at the beige tiled floor with faces masked in despair. There were also a few young black men, some in blood-soaked bandages or slings, who regarded everyone with intense gazes while others sat hunched over, nodding off only to jerk awake suddenly.

Clive stood facing the nurses' desk. "For the twentieth time, Hope Allerd is her name," he said to a nurse sitting behind a computer terminal. "She was brought in from the Capitol Hotel. It was an accidental drug overdose."

"And for the twentieth time," said the nurse, looking up from her terminal, "I don't see any Hope Allerd admitted. You need to try Washington General or maybe Mercy Hospital."

"But they said she was coming here."

"Look, mister, step away from the desk. Other people are waiting."

Clive glanced back at a snaking queue that had formed behind him.

Jack looked up. "Let's go. I'll find her. I just need my laptop."

Clive reluctantly started for the exit with Jack when one of the nurses working behind the desk, a middle-aged black woman, called, "Hey, you said you were looking for a Hope Allerd?"

Clive bolted back over to the desk. "Yes. Can you tell me if she's here?"

"I recall about an hour ago, they brought a drug overdose in. Dressed kinda nice. Like she had money, don't usually see many of those here. They usually go to some private hospital like St. Jerome's in Arlington. But I think that's the name she came in under."

"Yes. Do you know where she is?"

"Well, funny thing happened. We were doing intake on her when, out of the blue, these soldiers showed up."

"Soldiers?"

"Yeah. They wore that, what's it called? That camo uniform. Put her on a stretcher. Took her to a waiting ambulance outside."

"Where did they take her?" asked Jack.

"Your guess is as good as mine. But I dunno, if they were Army, then maybe to Walter Reed?"

◆ ◆ ◆

Clive and Jack waited at Bethesda's visitor control center at Gate 1. A polite man with a buzz cut and a pleasant face in a blue blazer and khaki trousers told them that nongovernmental employed civilians aren't admitted to Walter Reed and that they should leave.

Beneath the young man's mannered rebuff, Clive sensed something else. Maybe it was in his ramrod posture, his precise gestures, or the staccato rhythm of his voice. But the veiled threat of extreme violence if they didn't comply seemed to linger in the air.

"Let's go," said Jack. He began rolling back to the parking area.

"But...." Clive reluctantly followed.

"I just need my laptop."

"But we've got to find Hope."

"And we will." At the car, Jack wheeled about to face the reporter. "Look, Clive, the military always keeps meticulous records, if nothing else. I just need a little time to do some hacking. Believe me, we'll find her."

Back at the hotel, Jack worked on his laptop at the room's desk while Clive crashed on the bed.

Clive awoke with the sunrise. Seeing Jack still clacking away at his keyboard, he showered, dressed, and ordered room service.

"Any luck?" asked Clive, looking over Jack's shoulder.

Jack's face pruned as he shook his head. "They've initiated some new encryption software."

"You've been at it all night?"

"Yeah." Jack, looking dog-tired, backed away from the desk.

There was a knock on the door. Clive checked the peephole and opened the door, letting a uniformed hotel employee enter with a cart containing the room service order.

"Jack, why don't you get something to eat and then get some rest? Like you said, we'll find her," said Clive.

They ate in silence, and afterward, a defeated Jack rolled down the corridor to his accessible room for a much-needed shower and nap.

Clive paced back and forth in the room, trying to devise some plan, some ruse to find Hope. But each mental tactical track he went down always led to one individual—Armstrong.

As he walked to the window for seemingly the millionth time, he began formulating some way of confronting the General, like conning him into sitting down for an interview; the room's door clicked and opened.

Preparing to confront the intruder, Clive tensed and wheeled about.

CHAPTER 20

Clive gasped, then whispered, "Hope?"

Standing in the doorway, dressed in green scrubs and holding a plastic bag, was Hope. Her mouth widening into a crooked smile, she softly purred, "Hey, you."

He kissed his fiancée, scooped her into his arms, and lifted her off the carpet. He spun her in a circle like a carousel. Putting her down, he said, "Hope, where have you been?"

She shrugged and answered, "I'm not sure."

"Do you need to lie down?" Clive gripped her shoulders, eyes scrunched in a concerned look.

"No. I feel OK."

"But where were you? Jack and I went to the D.C. Metropolitan Hospital. That's where the paramedics said they were taking you. Oh, I'd better call Jack." Clive picked up the room phone and dialed Jack's room number.

Two minutes later, Jack rapped on the door. As Clive opened it, he wheeled past the reporter to confront his big sister. "Hope, where were you?" he asked. His tone was plaintive, eyes red and glistening.

"Jack, I really don't know." She sat in the desk chair.

"What's that you're holding?" asked Clive.

She looked at the clear plastic bag in her hand for the first time. Inside was a sheaf of papers.

Clive took it from her and removed the papers. He perused the sheets. "These are discharge papers from D.C. Metropolitan Hospital dated today."

"But," said Jack, "they said some soldiers took you away. We tried to find out if you were in Walter Reed Hospital but were turned away. I tried hacking into their computer system but couldn't get in."

Hope shrugged again. "All I recall is lying in a hospital bed for, I dunno, a day or two, then being wheeled out to a waiting car. An Uber, I think. When I arrived here, I stopped at the front desk, and they gave me a new keycard."

Clive brandished the first sheet. "Says here your discharge diagnosis is dehydration."

"Let me see those papers." Hope took the discharge papers, placed them on the desk, and reviewed them page by page.

"Sis, got another question. Where are your clothes?"

Hope looked down at her scrubs and up at Jack with an embarrassed expression. "I dunno. I was in a hospital gown during my stay, and when I was ready for discharge, the nurse gave me this set of scrubs."

"You didn't ask about your clothes?"

"Gee, it was all such a blur. I guess I didn't. Or, at least, I don't recall asking about them."

"Well," said Clive. "I don't believe that diagnosis of dehydration."

"Neither do I," said Hope. "The discharge lab work shows a normal BUN and creatinine. But I suppose if I was dehydrated and they gave me IV fluids during my stay, those numbers would go down to normal. Still, things don't add up. I mean, nothing I did over the past few days would cause me to become dehydrated."

"What do you remember just before you were taken to the hospital?" asked Clive.

Hope closed her eyes and rubbed her temples. She looked up at Clive with a pinched-eye stare. "We were in the restaurant downstairs. We had a fight about me going on that tour with Armstrong."

Clive and Jack both nodded.

"I left and took the elevator up to the room. Uh, I went into the bathroom to splash some water on my face, to cool down and...."

"And what?" asked Clive.

Hope got up and walked to the bathroom. Clive followed her. She stood before the sink, staring at her reflection in the mirror. She then looked down at the sink and turned on the faucet. The room was silent except for the sound of running water.

Clive looked over his shoulder at Jack.

Hope turned the water off. She then brushed her hand over the counter.

"What is it?" asked Clive.

"I'm not sure. There was something.... Er, something out of place."

"What?"

"I don't know. The next thing I recall was waking up in that hospital room."

"The paramedics claimed you were doing drugs," said Clive.

"What?" Hope turned to glare at her fiancé.

"Jack and I came up to the room. The deadbolt was engaged, so we called 9-1-1, and the police and paramedics came. When they got in, we found you unconscious on the bathroom floor."

Hope looked down at the counter and continued brushing her hand over a spot. "What did the paramedics do?" she asked.

"They started an IV, then injected something into your thigh. You kind of woke up but then went back to sleep."

"Yeah," said Jack. They did it about three more times; each time, you woke up and went back to sleep."

Hope rubbed her thigh. "Narcan," she said.

"What's that?" asked Clive.

"A medication to counter the effects of a narcotic. It's usually packaged as an easy-to-administer syringe and needle. And you say they gave me four of them?"

"Yeah," said Clive.

Jack nodded. "That's right."

"But I'd have to have taken a serious overdose to have...."

Clive looked more concerned. "And I think they put more of that Narcan in the IV."

"Oh, almost forgot," said Jack. "We tried to get what we thought was a housekeeper to open your door. This young woman in a hotel housekeeping uniform just ran away. Turned out she didn't work for the hotel."

Hope didn't respond. She again brushed her hand over a spot on the counter.

Neither Clive nor Jack said anything. They just stared at Hope as she stood at the sink, focused on the small counter space to her left.

A rap on the room door shattered the tranquility.

Clive went over to the door and looked through the

peephole. He suddenly turned to face Jack with a look of utter rage.

"Who is it, Clive?" asked Hope.

He walked into the bathroom and whispered, "Armstrong."

"Who's at the door?" asked Jack.

Hope walked past her brother to the door and said, "General Armstrong."

"What's he want?" demanded Jack.

"One way to find out," said Hope, opening the door.

Standing ramrod straight in the doorway wearing his dress uniform, service cap tucked under one arm, was Ben Armstrong. He had the look of a man fighting back broken heartedness. Swallowing once, he clenched his teeth and uttered, "Dr. Allerd, are you all right?"

Hope nodded. "Yes, I'm fine. Would you like to come in?" She opened the door wider. Looking back, she saw Jack and Clive whispering, "No."

Armstrong waited a beat, then stepped into the room. The heels of his black spit-shined shoes clicked together as if he marched on a parade ground when he stopped just inside the door.

A smile of relief widened his lips. "I heard you were hospitalized and then discharged. I came as soon as I could."

"Thank you, General," said Hope.

"You trying to tell us that you didn't transfer her to Walter Reed?" challenged Clive.

"What?" Armstrong looked genuinely baffled. "Walter Reed? I don't understand."

"Jack and I followed her to D.C. Metropolitan Hospital,"

said Clive. "When we got there, a nurse said some soldiers took her away."

Armstrong slowly shook his head. "I don't know anything about that."

"Sure, you don't," said Jack.

Hope glared at her brother, then turned to Armstrong. "I'm sorry, General, this whole affair has been upsetting for my brother."

"I understand. Please, if there is anything I can do, don't hesitate to ask."

With a fist to mouth, Jack coughed out, "Leave."

Armstrong again clenched his teeth. He then smiled at Hope. "I trust this little incident won't prevent you from joining me on our speaking tour. Our bus will stop here for you in the morning. Eight a.m., sharp." Turning on his heels with military bearing, he walked out of the room.

Hope closed the door and turned to her brother and fiancé. Wagging her finger like an exasperated teacher, she asked, "What will I do with you two? That was so immature. I swear, sometimes you're nothing but a couple of...of petulant schoolboys."

Jack and Clive dropped their heads and pursed their lips, ashamed to look Hope in the eye.

After a moment of tense silence, Clive said, "You aren't still going on that tour, are you?"

Hope started for the door.

"Where are you going?" asked Jack.

"I'm going to apologize to General Armstrong for your knuckleheaded behavior. And, yes, I'm still going on that tour."

She stormed out, slamming the door behind her.

CHAPTER 21

Ten minutes later, Hope returned to the hotel room. Jack and Clive stared at her like two petrified gazelles about to be attacked by a hungry lioness.

"He'd already gone," said Hope. "And, yes, I'm still going on that tour tomorrow. So, no more talk about it."

"Sis, what about your hospitalization?" asked Jack.

"Yeah, and this possible overdose?" said Clive.

Hope stepped into the bathroom again and wheeled about. "I think I know what happened. I came up here after our argument. That so-called maid apparently left something laced with some narcotic in the bathroom. I...I must have inhaled it." She looked at the roll of toilet paper next to the commode. "It was a square," she said.

"What?" said Clive.

"I remember. It was a single square of toilet paper on the counter here." She touched the spot with her fingers. "I think I took a wad of tissue and removed it." She then looked in the waste receptacle. It was empty.

"So, you touched it, and it got into your system," said Jack.

"No. I must have inhaled it." She walked out of the bathroom. "That maid probably came back later and emptied the waste basket. The only narcotic that powerful I can think of is fentanyl."

"So, someone tried to murder you with fentanyl,"

concluded Jack.

Clive took a deep breath. "A good reason for us all to leave. Right now."

"No," said Hope. "Don't you see? Whoever tried to kill me tried to cover their tracks when you called the paramedics. That's likely why my clothes eventually went missing. They were concerned that someone would find traces of the fentanyl on my clothing."

"And you still don't think Armstrong's behind all of this?" asked Clive.

"It's complicated," said Hope.

"Come on, Sis. Clive is right. We need to leave."

"I don't think Armstrong wants to kill me. It's more likely one of his associates did this. Which solves one piece of the puzzle."

"What's that?" asked Clive.

"Remember when we talked with that arms dealer, Petrov? He said something about Americans having drug problems."

"Yeah," said Clive.

"I think it was his way of telling us what he sold to Unit-458."

"Fentanyl?" said Clive. "How would you weaponize a narcotic? It would take months to distribute it. And to whom? We know that Unit-458 is going to strike soon."

Hope gazed at the crook of her elbow. "First, we've got to be sure it's fentanyl."

"And how do we do that?" asked Clive.

"Jack," said Hope. "How are your hacking skills these days?"

"Good as ever."

"Get your computer. We need to hack into D.C. Metropolitan Hospital's computer system. I've got to get them to run a test."

Three hours later, they stared at Jack's laptop screen to confirm Hope's theory. It was obvious that when she arrived at D.C. Metropolitan, the ER staff ran blood tests. What Hope banked on was a little-known fact: hospitals keep a small sample of blood on hand for a few days after they run tests in case there are erroneous results and tests have to be repeated.

Jack had hacked into the hospital's system and created a stat order for a test on Hope's stored blood.

Now, they watched and waited.

"It's ready," shouted Jack.

The screen flashed "Lab results ready."

"Well, pull it up." Clive looked anxious.

Jack hit a few keys. The lab results appeared on the screen. Both Clive and Jack looked at Hope with a puzzled expression.

Hope began to visibly shake. She stepped back from the screen, face frozen in terror. "My God," she whispered, "I know exactly what Unit-458 is going to do."

◆ ◆ ◆

"Mass murder," said Hope. "They're going to commit mass murder."

"What's carfentanil?" asked Jack, staring at Hope's lab results on the screen.

"An analog of fentanyl. It's used to tranquilize large animals like elephants and bears, and it's a hundred times more potent than fentanyl. That's why it took so much Narcan to rouse me."

"But how can someone use it to commit mass murder?" asked Jack.

"Unit-458 is going to use an aerosolized form. They can kill hundreds of people in a matter of minutes within a closed space. Clive, remember that hostage situation in a theater in Russia?"

"Yes. Chechen terrorists took hundreds of theatergoers in Moscow hostage. The Russian authorities pumped this gas into the theater to thwart the terrorists. They killed the terrorists all right, along with a hundred and twenty-five hostages."

"The gas they used was an aerosolized form of carfentanil," said Hope. "The only problem was that they forgot to alert the emergency personnel that they were using carfentanil, so no one thought to administer Narcan right away."

"So, what's next?" asked Jack.

Hope said, "We know the how. We've just got to figure out the where and when."

Jack's eyes narrowed. "Sis, I still think going on that tour is too dangerous."

"Don't you see? It's more important than ever that I go on that tour now. I've got to find out when and where Unit-458 will strike and stop them." She looked from Jack to Clive. "Otherwise, we let hundreds of people die. And none of us wants to live with that on our conscience."

"OK," said Jack. "We'll go with you."

Hope glared at her younger brother. "The way you two acted around General Armstrong? Not on your life."

◆ ◆ ◆

At six a.m. Clive shook Hope awake. "Hey, sleepy head. It's time to get up. You've got a big day ahead of you."

Hope opened her eyes. "Wha…. What time is it?" She sat up.

"Six o'clock." He shoved a steaming cup of coffee in her face. "Cream, no sugar."

She took the paper cup and sipped the hot brew through the slit in the lid. "Why are you so cheerful? You know I'm leaving on that tour in a couple of hours, right?"

Clive smiled and nodded.

"OK, something's up. What is it, Clive?"

"Well, you said you didn't want me or Jack to go with you, but…."

"What did you do?"

Clive produced a business card from his pocket. "You didn't say anything about someone else going along. So, when you went to sleep, I went through your belongings and found this."

"I don't appreciate you going through my things, but go on."

"It's Tina DeLuca's card. I called her and told her what you were doing."

"Clive, you didn't."

"You said Tina would help us. Remember? Anyway, she insisted on driving down from New York to accompany you on that tour. She's waiting outside the room with a colleague. I believe she said his name is Big Reggie Frazier."

Hope lifted the bedcovers to shield her decolletage and said, "OK, don't keep them waiting outside."

Clive opened the room door. In stepped Tina DeLuca.

Hope immediately recognized the diminutive, fiery, no-nonsense, green-eyed, brown-haired ex-FBI special agent. The disconnect came with her dress—baggy camo jogger pants, sneakers, and a T-shirt.

Hope opened her mouth to comment on Tina's hip-hop appearance, thought better of it, and said, "Tina, good to see you."

"Hey, girl," said the ex-special agent. She turned to her left and nodded. "This is my colleague, Big Reggie Frazier. Remember, you talked with him on the phone about that Unit-458 a few days ago."

Beside her was a giant of a man in loose-fitting jeans and a hoodie. His round, dark brown face was as composed as a monk's with joyless eyes that perpetually appeared half closed. His large lips unremittingly downturned and puckered as if always sucking on a lemon.

Big Reggie nodded and muttered, "S'up."

Hope looked from one to the other. "Guys, thanks for coming. I really appreciate what you're doing."

"Hope, I dropped everything when Clive here called and said you needed me. Big Reggie volunteered to accompany me."

"Yeah, heard you gonna take on Unit-458. They did me wrong. And I wanna piece of 'em."

Hope's eyes narrowed. "But how are you going to come with me?"

Tina smiled. "We drove down in Big Reggie's Escalade. Clive said it's going to be a bus tour, so we'll just follow you. I promise you; they won't know we're there. Reggie and I will be down in the lobby."

After Tina and Big Reggie left, Clive said, "Still not too late to change your mind."

Hope glared at him.

"OK, I'll be in the lobby." Clive exited the room.

Now, all alone in the room for the first time, Hope began to have doubts about taking this bus tour with a man who, in all likelihood, was planning to commit mass murder in order to become the most powerful human on the planet.

CHAPTER 22

At precisely seven forty-two a.m. Hope exited the elevator into the hotel lobby, pulling her suitcase behind her.

The area was a beehive of activity. Men and women dressed in business attire stood in line to check in or check out at the desk. Patrons sat on couches and chairs, reading papers or engaging in animated conversation while mothers chased unruly children across the floor.

Clive met her in the elevator corridor. "Hey, you," he said.

"I'll miss you," said Hope.

"Fourteen days is a long time."

"I know. I'll call you every night."

"Be careful."

"I will. Got my two guardian angels with me, remember?"

Clive nodded. They kissed. Clive pulled back and touched his forehead to hers. "Come back to me," he whispered.

"I will. I promise." Hope stepped back and turned to go.

Halfway through the lobby, she saw Jack rolling towards her. She walked over to her brother.

"You weren't leaving without saying goodbye, were you?" he asked.

"Not on your life. I was about to call your room."

"Got something for you." Jack lifted a plastic bag from his lap and gave it to Hope.

"What's this?"

"Couple of burner phones. Got special GPS trackers on 'em. Just keep one on you at all times. And call me if anything happens."

Hope nodded and put them into her suitcase. She leaned over and hugged Jack. "See you in a couple of weeks," she said.

A large tour bus, motor running, sat conspicuously in the hotel's porte-cochere. Hope started for the exit. Passing Tina and Big Reggie seated on a couch, she gave them a tacit nod.

As soon as she stepped outside the hotel on the sunny, crisp Washington winter morning, a young man in khaki pants and a blue blazer approached her. He took her suitcase and said, "I'll store this for you, ma'am."

Before boarding, she watched him approach the open luggage compartment at the bottom of the vehicle and gingerly place it among a myriad of suitcases, trunks, and backpacks.

At the bus's top step, Hope hesitated. The plush leather seats ran the length of the aisle, with two on each side. About half were occupied by serious-looking men and women either talking on cell phones or clacking away on laptops. But in the row behind the driver, a plastic table with a mahogany finish divided the first two rows, with the seats just behind the driver facing backward.

In the far seat on the side facing Hope sat General Armstrong in blue trousers, a white shirt with the top button open, and an askew red tie. He talked on a cell phone, gesturing as he spoke as if giving commands to armies in battle. Beside him sat a young woman in the same khaki trousers and blue blazer uniform as the man who took her suitcase. She typed away on a laptop computer on the table.

Armstrong ended his call, looked up at Hope, and smiled. He turned to the young woman beside him and said, "That'll be all for now." She closed her laptop, got up, and moved to a seat at the bus's rear. The General patted the now empty seat beside him and said, "Hope, glad to see you. Please sit here."

Hope sat next to him. Across the table, draped in his seat like an old blanket, was Eric Lattimore. He ran a hand through his unruly blonde hair and smirked at Hope. "So, you made it. I guess we can finally start this tour now," he said, not bothering to hide the sarcasm in his voice.

Through clenched teeth, Hope mumbled, "Good to see you, too."

"Don't pay any attention to him," said Armstrong. "He's always grumpy in the morning." He slid a folder before Hope from a stack of papers he'd been perusing. "Our itinerary and a few talking points for your speeches."

Hope opened the folder and looked over the papers inside. Their first stop was Pittsburg. Armstrong had written recommendations that she adhere to a straight narrative of how she helped bring the pandemic under control. She was specifically not to mention wearing masks, getting vaccines, or social distancing as part of her talks. Although she considered these valid public health measures, her activities in finding and stopping patient zero didn't involve any of them. So, she was OK with sticking to a straightforward account of her actions.

"The suggestions about what I should say look fairly reasonable," said Hope.

"Well, I'm glad m'lady approves," said Lattimore.

Hope closed the folder by slapping her hand down on the stack. "What is your problem? Have I done something to offend you?"

The former talk show host sat upright in his chair. "Well, well, Miss Prissy has a temper."

"If you want me to leave, I'll get off this bus right now."

"Now, Eric," said Armstrong, "we talked about this."

Lattimore draped a leg over an arm of the seat and leaned back. His face widened into a caustic grin.

Armstrong touched Hope's wrist as she shot daggers in Lattimore's direction. "It's gonna be a long trip," he said, "Let's all try to get along."

Hope glared at the General.

Lattimore sat up straight again and extended a hand towards Hope.

After a beat, she shook his hand.

"Truce," said Lattimore, his grin widened even more.

The bus driver boarded and took his seat. Turning around, he said, "Ready to go, General?"

Armstrong gave the order, and they were off. Hope reclined her seat and closed her eyes. As she tried to get some sleep, she wondered if Clive wasn't right about going on this speaking tour.

CHAPTER 23

The tour started out well enough. The Pittsburg arena was packed. Hope, introduced by Lattimore in his usual smirk-ladened energetic adolescent style, spoke for less than twenty minutes discussing how the pandemic virus behaved liked a hive mind or neural network and that her key to helping stop the disease's spread was to locate and neutralize patient zero. She didn't mention masks, vaccines, or social distancing.

On his way to the podium, Armstrong gave her a thumbs-up. Taking this as a sign of approval, she sat and watched him repeat his animated, gesticulating rant against Conchrane and all she stood for. His talk ended, followed by that disturbing musical and light show interlude of the flags, and flashing cross at the back of the stage. The audience responded as one with applause and cheering. Vociferous chants of "Jail Conchrane, jail Conchrane" erupted at the end.

Armstrong placed a hand on Hope's lower back as she boarded the bus at the rear of the arena bound for their hotel. She turned to see him grinning.

"Great job, Hope," he said. "I think we're gonna be a winning team."

Sitting beside Armstrong, Hope watched Lattimore board and walk down the aisle, giving her a tight-lipped, acid-laced glare as he passed.

Finally, in her room, Hope changed into a pair of pajamas

and snuggled under the covers. Taking one of the burner phones from her suitcase, she called Clive.

"Hey, you," she said when he answered.

"Are you all right?" he asked.

"Yeah, I'm fine. I'm in bed in my hotel room. The rally went well. I just talked about how—"

"Hope," he interrupted. "You don't know?"

"Know what?"

"Turn on your TV."

Hope grabbed the remote on the bedside table and turned on the flatscreen TV on the credenza. Clicking past the hotel's advertisement channel, she settled on a local news channel. An unsteady camera feed revealed a street scene with burning store and office facades on either side of a mob of people in the middle of a boulevard engaged in what could only be called hand-to-hand combat. Police in riot gear were trampled. A news anchor's voice-over said, "...unable to stop the violent clash of protestors and counter-protestors. Downtown Pittsburg looks like a war zone."

"Do you see it?" asked Clive.

"Yeah." Hope got out of bed and walked over to the floor-to-ceiling glass window. Parting the curtain with one hand, she looked outside. Several blocks down the street, she could see the distant light of flames shooting skyward. Closer in, she saw lines of police cars blocking the street and dozens of officers charging toward the riot.

"Hope, are you there?"

"Yeah. I can see burning buildings in the distance. I don't think the riot will get to where I am."

"What did you say in that rally?" Clive's voice sounded strained.

"What do you mean?"

"All the news networks are saying that Armstrong's rally started the riots."

"Clive, I just discussed the pandemic and how we stopped patient zero. I tried to make it sound as bland as possible. Armstrong ranted on about Conchrane like he did in that rally we saw in D.C."

"And they rioted in D.C. Remember?"

"You don't have to remind me. I'm still having headaches from that police baton to the back of my head."

"I don't like this. Maybe you should fly back to D.C. in the morning."

"I'll be fine. I'm staying in a hotel with everyone else on the tour. I'm sure Armstrong's people will alert me if there's any danger. Besides, our bus is leaving at eight a.m. sharp."

"OK, I just wish you'd change your mind."

"Clive, I'll be fine. I'm gonna try to get some sleep. Love you."

"Love you," parroted Clive.

She pressed the "end" button on the phone, pulled a chair up to the window, and sat. She peeked between the curtains at the conflagration a few blocks away.

Staring at the mounting blaze in the distance, Hope realized she had lied to Clive. There was no way she was getting a wink of sleep.

◆ ◆ ◆

In jeans and a puffer vest, Brad Trett sat on a wooden stool near a workbench at Ralph's Paint and Body Shop. The air was redolent with the mothball-like odor of auto-body spray paint.

The shop, ordinarily alive with shouts and the clanking of machinery, was quiet. It was after midnight, and only he and Ralph Marone, the owner, were present.

Ralph pulled the panel truck to a stop in front of Brad and got out. The garrulous gray-haired man with a large nose and friendly expression in paint-stained overalls looked puzzled. "Here she is," said Ralph, "Fresh outta the paint booth."

Brad hopped off his stool to inspect the work up close.

"Hey Brad," said Ralph, "How long have we known each other? Two, three years?"

"I dunno," he answered.

"Well, all the time I've known you, you never mentioned going to school."

"What's your point?" said Brad.

"I mean, I had a cousin, Santino. He wanted to get into the business. Went to school, flunked out three times before he finally passed and got his diploma."

"Well, maybe Santino was just stupid."

"We're talking ten, twelve months of hard work and studying. Know what I mean? And Santino was not stupid."

Brad shrugged. "Detail's pretty good," he said as he walked around the truck's rear.

"And it's pretty expensive. Cost Santino north of a couple of thousand for classes."

"If you want the best, you've gotta pay for it."

"There's another thing," said Ralph. "How come I had to do this off the books? And at night when everyone's gone home."

"You object to getting cash?"

"No. No. I mean, I appreciate getting twice my usual price

for the work. It's just a little strange."

"Maybe I just didn't want anyone else to see your wonderful artistic work and steal you away before you finished."

Ralph chuckled. "No, seriously, how come all the secrecy?"

Brad shrugged again. "Maybe I'm doing it for a friend. And he wants to keep it quiet."

Beads of sweat appeared on Ralph's forehead. "I hate to say it, Brad, but things just don't add up."

"What do you mean?"

"Well, you haven't been to school. You have me do a custom paint job in secret, and you insist on the work being off the books. I don't know; it just doesn't add up."

"So, what are you saying?"

"Well, if I didn't know you, I'd guess you were up to no good."

Brad finished circumnavigating the panel truck and walked over to Ralph. He put a hand on the auto-body man's shoulder and smiled. "Ralph, did you ever think that maybe I went to HVAC school long before we met? And that I wanted to keep things quiet because I didn't want competition to know that I was starting a new business? It's cutthroat out there."

Ralph emitted a nervous titter. "Oh, uh...I guess I didn't think about that."

Brad nodded and took two steps back. He brought his right hand behind his back under his vest. "Ralph, we've always been friends, so it really pains me to do this."

"What are you talking about?" Ralph looked puzzled.

Brad whipped his right hand from behind his back,

holding a 9 mm pistol with a silencer. Before the auto paint and body man could utter another word, he pumped three rounds into Ralph Marone's chest.

After making sure Ralph was dead, Brad got into the freshly painted panel truck and drove out of the auto paint and body shop.

In the dead of night, few people driving on Washington's streets noticed the detailed paintwork on the sides of the blue truck, which showed a sunrise breaking through clouds over a pristine lake, with lettering proclaiming: New Capitol HVAC Services.

◆ ◆ ◆

Bleary-eyed, Hope boarded the bus bound for Chicago, the next city on the tour. As usual, Armstrong sat beside her in the front. She waited for Lattimore to walk by and swear or say something disparaging on his way to a seat. But the bus started without him.

"Where's Lattimore?" asked Hope.

"Oh," said Armstrong, "he decided to ride in one of the escorting vehicles. Said he liked the quiet of sitting in a back seat alone or something like that."

Although sleep tugged at her brain, Hope had to know. Looking at Armstrong, she asked, "Did you see that riot last night?"

Grinning, Armstrong nodded. "Yeah, wasn't it great?"

"Great? I saw buildings burning. I'm sure people were injured, maybe even killed."

"Hope. Those people deserved to express themselves."

"Yeah, but not like that."

"Thomas Jefferson said, '…a little rebellion now and then

is a good thing, and as necessary in the political world as storms in the physical.'"

"But what about those who might have been hurt?"

"Again, quoting Jefferson, 'The tree of liberty must be refreshed from time to time with the blood of patriots and tyrants.'"

Hope shook her head.

"I asked you before, and I'll ask you again. Hope, are you a patriot or a plotter?"

Hope glared at him. "Is this going to happen at every stop of this tour? Are we going to have people rioting in the streets? Tearing each other apart over whether they like or dislike President Conchrane?"

"What if it does? My followers are passionate people."

"OK, I've got a quote for you from Benjamin Franklin: 'When passion rules, she never rules wisely.'"

Armstrong leaned back in the seat, grinning. "Touché, Hope. We can agree to disagree on how my people should act following our little presentation. I say let them express their full emotions. And you, well, you want them more reserved. Sitting there nodding quietly."

"You gin them up with your rhetoric, and that sound and light show at the end. It's absolutely...."

"Absolutely what?"

"I dunno."

"You want me to tone down my speeches."

"You could be a little less demonstrative."

"And what's wrong with our 'sound and light show,' as you call it? People love the cross and the flag. It's...it's America?"

"I have no problem with displaying the flags."

"Oh, it's the cross. What's the matter, Hope? Don't believe in God?"

"I believe in God. You've been quoting Jefferson. Let me quote the Bible. It says, 'Cursed is everyone that hangs on a tree,' meaning cross; it also says, 'He who knew no sin became sin for us.' Christ died on the cross for our sins. That cross you like to display represents God's unconditional love for sinners, His work in redeeming His people. He bestowed His unmerited favor on us by sending His sinless Son to die there as our substitute. By displaying it at those rallies, you're using the cross as nothing more than a punchline."

Armstrong sighed. "Well, like I said, we can agree to disagree." He got up.

"Where are you going?" asked Hope.

"I just remembered; I need to speak with Eric about something." He removed his cell phone from his pocket and walked to the back of the bus.

CHAPTER 24

Standing behind the Resolute desk in the Oval Office in her teal pantsuit with her hands behind her back, President Martha Conchrane looked out at the view of the White House South Lawn. The grass was covered with a light dusting of snow. The oaks and maple trees bristling with bare branches stood like stalwart sentinels in the early morning sunlight and as a metaphor for what soured her mood this late December day.

The door opened, and Conchrane turned to glance at the clock on her desk. Eight-thirty. *Right on time,* she thought.

Looking up, she saw her Chief of Staff, Sam Withers, breeze into the Oval Office and sit on one of the two couches facing the Resolute desk.

The lanky hawk-faced man moved with a reptilian grace as he sat, crossed one leg over the other, and opened the dark blue portfolio he seemed to always have in his hand.

"Good morning, Madame President," he said.

"What's so good about it?"

"Well, uh...."

"Sam, have you seen my poll numbers?" She walked to the front of her desk, lifted a sheet of paper from it, and gave it to him.

Perusing the page, Sam nodded. "I've seen this."

"How could I just be reelected and have my polling

numbers tanking?"

"Well...."

"I'll tell you how. It's that damn General Armstrong. The man's a traitor, Sam."

"I wouldn't go that far, Madame President."

"Oh, how far would you go? At this moment, the guy's touring the country claiming that I want America to 'march to the tune of the Marxists.'"

"Just political rhetoric."

"Political rhetoric? Really? Everywhere he goes, there's rioting in the streets. And the media is blaming it all on me." She held up newspaper after newspaper from a stack on her desk. "Have you seen these headlines? The Times: 'America Out Of Control.' The Post: 'Anarchy Reigns Under Conchrane.' Oh, and my personal favorite from The Daily: 'Conchrane Fiddles While America Burns.'"

"I admit they are a little over the top."

"Over the top? They are all basically claiming that I'm singlehandedly destroying the Country."

"Well, it was a close election. You've got to expect your opponents to blow off some steam." Withers grinned a bit.

"This is more than blowing off steam. I'm hearing that a group in the House is talking about impeachment. Impeachment, Sam."

"Madame President, almost without fail, a bunch of Representatives start talks of impeachment with each new election. It's nothing new."

"Sam, just whose side are you on?"

"Madame President, I'm on your side."

"Oh, really? I want Armstrong fired."

"I wouldn't be too hasty—"

"I need a Chairman of the Joint Chiefs of Staff that I can trust. Someone who"—she pointed to the oaks and maples outside the window— "who is as stalwart as those trees. Someone who has my back."

"But firing Armstrong would—"

"And don't tell me I can't. Truman fired McArthur."

"Different circumstances."

"McArthur was insubordinate. And Armstrong is insubordinate to me."

Withers raised his hands in a gesture of surrender. "May I suggest a different strategy?"

Conchrane walked back behind her desk and sat. "OK, what do you suggest?"

"Ignore Armstrong. Ignore the headlines and the polls. If you fire him, it'll just make him a martyr to his supporters."

"But—"

"Continue to tout your campaign promises."

"But—"

"Go on as if Armstrong hasn't said a word. I guarantee all of this will begin to blow over in a few weeks." He opened his portfolio and began writing.

Conchrane sat, hands under her chin, studying her Chief of Staff. After a few moments, she exhaled loudly. "All right, Sam, we'll try it your way. For now."

Withers nodded. "OK, Madame President, let's review your schedule for today."

Conchrane picked up the daily schedule on her desk and pretended to scan the appointments, all the while thinking, *I'll bide my time. For now. But, that son-of-a-bitch Armstrong is a dead man.*

❖ ❖ ❖

The Chicago rally went off like the others. But, conspicuous by its absence on stage was the giant cross. Hope smiled on seeing the changed background and gave Armstrong a nod of approval as they sat on stage, awaiting their respective turns to speak.

After the rally, fighting broke out between Armstrong's followers and protesters who had marched in front of the arena. Police, alert to the possibility of clashes, were present in tremendous numbers. The rioting was quelled with minimal injury and loss of property.

Back in her hotel room, Hope called Clive and reported the "minor" riot as a kind of victory based on her discussion with Armstrong.

Before hanging up, Clive said to her, "Gee, I trust you know what you're doing."

Feeling empowered and heartened by the change at the rally, Hope decided to see Armstrong and thank him for listening to her. Still, in her green pantsuit, she stepped out of her room and strolled down the hall four doors away.

She knocked, leaned close to the door, and said, "General Armstrong, it's Hope."

There was some rustling, and then the door opened. Armstrong stood there in pajamas and a bathrobe, holding a bundle of papers. He grinned. "Hope, come in." He stood aside.

Hope stepped into his room. The luxury space had been turned into a command post. Two laptop computers were open on his desk. A large dry-erase board lay on his bed with rows of percentages written beside a column of city names.

Also, on the bed were sheaves of stacked papers. The flat-screen television was on. A war movie was playing with the volume turned down.

She looked around the room. "Wow, looks like you're planning an invasion or something."

"Just some prep work for the coming rallies and other things. "What can I do for you?"

"I wanted to thank you for listening to me."

"What?" Armstrong seemed suddenly mesmerized by the TV screen.

"About the cross."

"Uh, oh, yeah."

Hope noticed that, accompanied by explosions and whizzing bullets, the hero in the movie was running and crawling on a beach. Around him were men being shot or blown apart via ultra-real special effects. Turning to Armstrong, she saw that he was crouched in front of the flat screen, mouth agape, eyes wide open fixed on some, she assumed, imagined objective; arms moved as if he was directing some imaginary soldiers. Sweat blossomed on his brow. His breathing was rapid and labored.

Armstrong began to speak in a voice quivering with adrenaline. He initially mumbled something unintelligible, then, in a clear tone, said, "Immediate suppression. Er...er grid 242971. Authentication is...is tango uniform. Over."

At that moment, Hope realized he was having a flashback.

Hope immediately found the remote and turned off the TV. She then placed herself in front of the screen. "General Armstrong, Ben, it's Hope. What's happening is a flashback. It's not real. We're in your hotel room."

The General continued to stare straight ahead. His

breathing quickened. "No, no," he shouted, "immediate suppression, grid 242971...."

"Ben, Ben," said Hope, "look at me. Look at me. It's OK, you're safe."

Armstrong's eyes flickered for a second. Hope was sure he looked directly at her. He seemed to slow his breathing.

Feeling he was coming out of it, she did the one thing she knew in her heart of heart no one should do to a person having a flashback: Hope touched his cheek.

Armstrong, wide-eyed, shouted, "Get 'em off me!"

Balling his fist, he swung.

◆ ◆ ◆

Hope awakened. She lay on the carpeted floor of Armstrong's hotel room. The left side of her face throbbed and was cold. Taking in a full grasp of her surroundings, she realized a hand towel full of ice was pressed against her pain-seared jaw. Armstrong held it, squatting over her.

"Hope," he said, "are you OK?"

"Er, yeah." She sat upright.

"What happened? I was talking to you, and the next thing I saw, you were lying on the floor. Your jaw looked swollen, so I put ice on it."

"You had a flashback. And I—"

"Oh, no, did I hit you? Hope I'm so sorry."

"No, it's my fault. I shouldn't have touched you. I know better." She walked over to the floor-length mirror on the closet door and checked her jaw. "It'll be all right."

Armstrong put the dry-erase board on the floor and sat on the edge of his bed. Hope took the makeshift ice pack, placed it back on her cheek, and joined him there.

Sitting with face buried in his hands, Armstrong sighed. "I'm so sorry, Hope," he repeated.

"How long have you had PTSD?"

He shrugged. "I dunno. A few years."

"Did you seek therapy?"

Armstrong shook his head.

"You should, you know. It does help."

"Is that your medical opinion?"

"No. Personal experience. When I was seventeen, my parents, brother, and I came home from dinner at a restaurant. The house was dark. We surprised a burglar. He shot and killed my parents. Shot Jack, my brother, and me. Jack developed paraplegia. I underwent what seemed like a gazillion rounds of abdominal surgeries. I still see those muzzle flashes, hear those awful dying moans, and feel that poker-hot stab of that bullet. I got treated for PTSD. It helped some, but I found swimming helps me more now."

Armstrong looked at her. His eyes were reddened, and his face was tear-stained. He opened his mouth to say something but, looking puzzled, just stared straight ahead.

"It's OK," said Hope. "Why don't you get some rest? If you like, I can sit with you for a while."

He smiled and nodded.

Hope closed the two laptops, cleared the comforter of the stacks of papers, and pulled a chair up beside the bed. Armstrong lay on top of the covers as Hope cut off the overhead light and left the bathroom light on as a nightlight.

She settled back in the chair and closed her eyes. As she drifted off to sleep, she began to see Armstrong, not as that stern, square-jawed martinet who questioned her at the medal ceremony but as a kindred soul needing kindness and compassion.

CHAPTER 25

Christmas morning at the Watergate Apartments was quiet. There was little automobile traffic around the complex and even less foot traffic. A chill had ensnared the crisp air overnight, and barely half an inch of snow lay on the walks.

Clive, in jeans, a white button-down shirt, and a wool jacket, approached the doorman, a middle-aged, balding man in uniform, and stated his business for appearing at such an early hour. He checked his watch, eight-twenty-five. Nodding approvingly at his punctuality, he awaited the doorman's return.

The man opened the double glass doors for Clive and, grinning, announced, "Third floor, apartment 357. Ms. Devan and Miss Sophie are expecting you."

He took the elevator to the third floor, found 357, and knocked. He heard a commotion on the other side of the door in the form of footsteps and a muffled scream.

The door opened. Marta stood there in curlers, a full-length nightgown, and a robe, holding a mug of coffee. Sophie, in pajamas covered with some cartoon character Clive didn't recognize, jumped up and down, squealing, "He's here, he's here."

"Clive, please come in," said Marta.

"Hello, Daddy," said Sophie as she clutched his hand.

Clive surveyed the apartment. It was populated with

expensive contemporary furniture. A priceless Ming vase sat on a pedestal in a corner near the door. A seven-foot spruce Christmas tree rose like a monolith near the opposite side of the door. It was decorated with various ornaments and garlands and topped with an angel. Tiny white bulbs illuminated the spruce plant. Over two dozen wrapped presents sat under the tree. Several boxes and a pile of crumpled wrapping paper sat off to the side. A dollhouse about an inch taller than Sophie sat in the center of the room. Next to the dollhouse, four dolls reclined in plastic chairs around a table. Beside them was a toy tea set.

"I noticed you two are still in your sleepwear. Am I too early?" asked Clive.

"Are you kidding?" said Marta. "We've been up since six-forty. Sophie insisted on opening a few presents. Would you like a cup of coffee?"

"That would be delightful."

Sophie pulled him over to the dollhouse. "You simply must see what Santa brought."

Marta disappeared into the kitchen as Clive knelt before the exquisitely detailed dollhouse. Going room by room, Sophie gave him a comprehensive tour of the tiny mansion.

Marta returned from the kitchen with a mug of coffee for Clive. "Sophie, dear, why don't you let Daddy sit for a moment and drink his coffee?"

"All right, Mummy. Can I open more presents now?"

Marta nodded and motioned for Clive to sit with her on the couch. They watched Sophie tear into present after present with the zeal of a bird of prey ripping into her quarry.

On examining each one, she squealed in delight and said, "It's just what I asked Santa for."

Clive inhaled a magical aroma of cinnamon and brown

sugar wafting from the kitchen as he sat. Marta stood. "The cinnamon buns should be about ready," she said.

They moved to the kitchen table and ate the cinnamon buns. Clive had a second cup of coffee. Being sated and fully caffeinated, a strange sensation overcame him. It felt as though he belonged in this Yuletide scenario.

After breakfast, Sophie was back under the tree, opening more presents. Clive sat again with Marta on the couch, watching.

His daughter came to a large, wrapped box in the shape of an apparel container. She picked it up, shook it, and read the tag. "It's from you, Daddy."

Sophie opened it, revealing a lavish pleated skirt and matching top. "Oh, Daddy, it's wonderful." She darted into his arms and kissed him on the cheek.

Marta gave him a wink.

Clive leaned back on the couch, basking in his daughter's adoration.

Sophie began rooting under the tree and produced a small, wrapped box. Charging back into his arms, she handed it to him. "This is for you, Daddy."

"For me?" said Clive, removing the wrapping. It was a felt gift box. He opened it to reveal a silver keychain. An inscription was on the metal plate.

Marta said, "Sophie composed the inscription."

"Read it, Daddy."

Clive moved the plate back and forth to bring the engraved letters into focus. "From Sophie and Mummy, please always remember us."

Clive cleared his throat as tears welled in his eyes.

"What's the matter, Daddy? Don't you like it?"

"Er, no, Sophie. It's about the best gift I've ever received."

◆ ◆ ◆

St. Louis was unseasonably mild—sweater weather. Hope appreciated the climate as she entered the rear door of the arena an hour before the rally.

A couple of the young men in their typical khaki trousers and blue blazers were checking the sound equipment. One of them, a slightly plump, fuzzy-haired man with acne, stood at a mixing console and adjusted some levers. The other, a thinner man, looked over his shoulder, nodded, and said, "Ides of March."

The plump one also nodded and replied, "Ides of March."

Hope, overhearing the exchange, was reminded of the dinner she and Clive had with that Russian arms dealer, Petrov, and his insistence they attend the art museum exhibit of the works of the painter Tupolev. His magnum opus, a painting entitled "The Ides of March," was supposed to be a clue as to when Unit-458 would strike. But the discrepancy persisted: Clive was sure something would happen in the next few days, yet March fifteenth was over two and a half months away.

Well, now was as good a time as any to find out. She approached the plump man and asked, "What does 'Ides of March' mean?"

He looked perplexed like he'd been caught by a teacher's question about a topic he had not studied. "Er...nothing, ma'am," he said, "Just an expression."

Hope turned to his companion. The thinner man shook his head and walked off.

"Wait," said Hope. She began to pursue the young man. A couple of feet from him, she put a hand on his shoulder. He wheeled around and slapped her hand away. His forehead was dappled with drops of sweat.

Raising her hands in a gesture of surrender, Hope said, "Whoa, sorry, I just wanted to ask you a question."

His face pinched in what looked like rage to Hope. He took a step back, turned, and walked away.

"Harassing the help?" came a voice from behind her. Hope turned to see Eric Lattimore standing less than a yard away.

"I was just asking him a question," said Hope. Her tone sounded defensive.

"I'm sure you were."

"Look, maybe you can help me. I've been hearing people say, 'Ides of March' to each other, and I was just curious to know what it meant."

Lattimore smirked. "Right. Why do you want to know?"

"I was just wondering."

"Sure. And you are with us on this crusade of ours because you love America so much that you want to see her rescued from Conchrane and her ilk."

"I'm here because Ben invited me to speak."

"Oh, it's Ben now."

Hope began to feel the heat of outrage smolder in her cheeks as she balled her fists. "What is your problem?"

"My problem is that I don't like you influencing how we conduct our rallies. How you made General Armstrong remove that cross. How his speeches have been less intense since you've been here."

"Those were his choices. Not mine. I just made a suggestion."

"Your influence is not appreciated. You don't understand,

do you? We're at war. This is not the time to be gentle and kind."

"War? What are you talking about?"

"Dr. Allerd, go home. You don't understand what's going on here. And I, for one, will not let you screw things up."

"What things?"

"Just go home."

"Ben invited me."

"Well, I'm uninviting you. Consider this a warning."

"Warning? Are you threatening me?"

"Take it however you'd like. Just know this: go now, or you won't live to see the end of this tour."

Lattimore turned and stalked away.

CHAPTER 26

The St. Louis rally concluded like the one in Chicago. The crowd was enthusiastic but not as rabid as she'd seen in Washington and Pittsburg. *Maybe*, she thought, *I have been a positive influence on Ben. Or perhaps it's because it's Christmas Day, and people are filled more with goodwill than political fervor.*

Back in her room, Hope remained troubled by Lattimore's threat of violence and had to know how serious the radio shock-jock was about her not living out the remainder of the tour.

Changing out of her pantsuit into a comfortable pair of jeans and a blouse, she strolled to Ben's room and knocked.

He opened the door dressed as before in pajamas and a robe. "Hope, come in. This is a pleasant surprise. Merry Christmas, by the way. Thought you'd be sound asleep by now since you were up babysitting me last night. Heck of a way to spend Christmas Eve."

Hope stepped into the room, which was decked out with laptops, a dry-erase board, and stacks of papers like the one in Chicago.

Armstrong gestured toward the TV. "See, it's off."

She nodded. "Merry Christmas. I did want to see how you were doing, but I also had a disturbing encounter with Lattimore just before the rally."

Armstrong shook his head. "OK, what did Eric do this

time?"

"He threatened me when I asked him about that expression I've been hearing. You know, 'Ides of March.' I think he's jealous or something. He thinks you've been unduly influenced by my presence here."

Armstrong chuckled, "Eric is a hothead. Look, I'll talk to him. And, by the way, no TV whatsoever tonight. I'll be fine."

"OK, but I'm just down the hall if you need someone to talk to."

The General put a hand on Hope's shoulder. "You're a good friend, Hope."

"Thanks, Ben. May I call you Ben?"

"I wouldn't have it any other way."

She turned to go and stopped at the door. Looking back at Armstrong, she asked, "Just what does 'Ides of March' mean?"

He looked down momentarily as if trying to formulate a plausible reply. From what she could see, his face looked like he was in the throes of fury. But, looking up with a benign countenance, he said, "Well, you know that we've been focused on President Conchrane's broken administration. Based on her performance, we predict she'll be impeached, tried, and found guilty by the Senate by March fifteenth. Thus, the Ides of March. Kind of a rallying cry."

Maybe it was his initial hesitation or the somewhat convoluted answer itself. Still, on her way back to her room, despite his overall genial demeanor and soothing response to her question, Hope remained troubled by what might be the real meaning of Ides of March.

Her stomach churned as she tried to shake the unsettling thought that the Ides of March was already upon them.

◆ ◆ ◆

Clive and Sophie spent the rest of the morning and early afternoon playing tea party and arranging furniture in the dollhouse. Marta used the time to shower, dress, and prepare dinner.

They ate roast beef, mashed potatoes, and asparagus for Christmas dinner. Afterward, they sat together on the couch and watched the black-and-white version of *It's a Wonderful Life* on Marta's flat-screen TV. Sophie fell asleep halfway through the movie.

After putting Sophie to bed, Marta curled up with Clive on the couch and talked of old times over cocktails well into the late evening. Hope never came up in the conversation.

Looking at her watch, Marta suddenly arose and said, "Oh my, it's eleven-thirty. Perhaps you'd—"

Clive got to his feet. "Sorry, you're right. I'd better go."

She touched his lips with her index finger. "No, silly, I was going to say, 'You'd better stay.' You won't get a cab this late at night."

"Oh." Clive was taken aback.

She walked through the living room toward the hallway leading to the bedrooms. "You can stay in the spare room. Or...."

"Or...?" asked Clive.

"We can share mine." With one hand on the wall and the other on her hip, Marta struck a seductive pose in the evening light. "Oh, and in the interest of full disclosure, I've been recently sleeping in the nude."

CHAPTER 27

The fourth stop on the tour was Oklahoma City. She had to admit the rally was more raucous than St. Louis. A riot broke out afterward. This one resulted in three people being killed.

Heartbroken, Hope sat in her hotel room watching the late evening news reports of the post-rally melee. After viewing the footage of burning storefronts and rabid crowds, she opened one of her burner phones and called Clive.

"Hey, you," he said. "Happy Boxing Day."

"Hey, you. What's Boxing Day?"

"It's a holiday in the UK. It's the day after Christmas Day. It started as a day when people gave donations to people experiencing poverty. But now it's a day when people descend on malls and department stores to shop for sales."

"OK, good to know. Did you see the late evening news?"

"More riots?"

"Yeah. Three people were killed."

"Where are you?"

"Oklahoma City."

"I suppose it would do no good to say, 'come back.'"

Hope, recalling Lattimore's threat, was quiet for a moment.

"What is it?" Clive's voice quivered with concern.

"That radio shock-jock, Eric Lattimore, threatened to kill me."

"All the more reason to leave that tour."

"One more thing. Ben told me what Ides of March means."

"Oh?" said Clive, tone hardening. "Ben told you?"

"Yeah. He said it represented the date by which he predicts President Conchrane will be impeached."

"Oh, really?"

"Yeah. What's wrong?"

"You stay away from...Ben. That guy's nothing but trouble."

"Actually, he's really a nice man."

"Yeah, right. You be careful."

"Sounds like someone is jealous."

"I'm just concerned about you. Remember that guy is the new head of EQV."

"Don't worry. Ben and I are just friends. We kinda bonded. He suffers from PTSD, too."

"I don't care if he has ADHD. He's still trouble. And I still say that Ides of March thing is not two months away. If Unit-458 is active, and we know it is, they're going to strike in a matter of days, not months. Another reason to leave that tour now."

"Look, if that's the case, then me staying with the tour could be the only way we find out what day the Ides of March refers to."

"No, Hope. It's too dangerous. You need to leave. Jack and I can work on when they'll strike. You need to get back here. Now!"

"I'm staying. You know I'm right. I'll find out the date Ides of March refers to, inform President Conchrane that carfentanil gas is likely going to be used in a terrorist attack on that date, and get the heck back to you. But there's one missing piece to the puzzle."

"And what's that?"

"The location. We don't know the location of their attack."

"And just how do you propose to find that out?"

"I dunno. I'll keep snooping around. I'm bound to find out more."

"It's a bad idea, Hope. Armstrong could have you snuffed out like a candle with just a word."

"No, he won't. Like I said, Ben and I are friends."

"Friends? Look, Hope you don't make friends with a snake. This guy is planning to overthrow the United States Government. To him, you're nothing but a speed bump on the highway to perdition. You've got to get out of there."

"Clive, I know what I'm doing."

"Maybe Jack can talk some sense into you."

"You leave Jack out of this."

"Dammit, at least talk to Tina. I'll get her on the line."

"No, wait." Hope heard a series of beeps and clicks.

"Hello, Clive?" It was Tina.

"Hi," said Clive. "I've got you on the line with Hope."

"What's shakin' girl?"

"I'm fine, Tina," said Hope.

"She's not fine," said Clive. "She's getting too close to Armstrong. The guy's nothing but trouble. I'm afraid for her life. She's already been threatened by his lackey, that Lattimore character. Help me talk her out of staying any longer."

"Is this true, Hope?"

Hope sighed. "Yeah, Lattimore threatened me. But Ben's going to have a talk with him."

"Whose Ben?" asked Tina.

"It's General Armstrong. Apparently, they're on a first-name basis now," said Clive, his voice gushing with sarcasm.

"Clive, that was kinda uncalled for," said Tina.

"Thanks, Tina," said Hope. "At least I've got somebody on my side."

"Look, girlfriend, I'm not taking sides in this." Tina's voice was stern. "And, Clive, I understand that you're concerned. But Hope is a big girl. She can take care of herself."

"Thank you, Tina," said Hope. Her mouth widened into a grin at her friend's rebuke of Clive.

"Now, Hope, has this Lattimore done any more than talk about hurting you?" asked Tina.

"Er, no."

"Cause you know that Big Reggie and I are just a couple of blocks away. We can be there in five minutes."

"It's OK, Tina. He hasn't done anything but talk."

"OK," said Tina. "Clive, I promise, Big Reggie and I will keep a close eye on Hope. So, don't worry. We haven't lost a client yet. And…"

Hope's thoughts began drifting back to Ben alone in his room. She worried that tonight might present a nightmare or flashback. A mental picture of his cluttered room flashed to the fore. The laptops. The dry-erase board. And all those stacks of papers.

"...so, like I said, we've got you, Hope. OK?" said Tina.

That was it—the papers. They had to be the key to the location of the Ides of March, thought Hope.

"Hope? Hope?" said Tina. "You there?"

"Er...yeah. Hey, Clive, I think I know how to find the time and location of the attack."

"What are you talking about, Hope?" Clive sounded even more worried.

"Ben has these piles of papers in his room. There's gotta be some information about the attack within those stacks. I need a little time to go through them."

"No, Hope. You can't go rooting around Armstrong's room. If he catches you, he won't hesitate to kill you," said Clive.

"Hope," said Tina. "I gotta agree with your man on this one. It does sound too dangerous."

Hope shook her head. "You don't understand. Ben trusts me. I spent the night with him the other night, and..."

"No!" yelled Clive.

"Let me explain," said Hope. "He was having a flashback. I helped to calm him down, and then I just sat by his bedside while he slept. There was no contact, no kissing, and everyone was fully clothed. Geeze, Clive, I'm disappointed you'd think so little of me."

In a trembling voice, Clive said, "Sorry, Hope."

"Gotta admit, girl," said Tina, "you had me going too for a second."

"Both of you just settle down. I've got this," said Hope.

"But, what about this Lattimore dude?" asked Tina.

"He's all talk," said Hope. "Look, Tina, if I need you, I've got your number. And, Clive, I love you. Get some sleep, and don't worry."

Before either of them could protest, Hope ended the call and began formulating the plan: Sit with Ben while he sleeps like the other night, and while he is in the midst of REM sleep, find his blueprint for overthrowing the President of the United States.

She began to pace as she concocted a convincing enough lie that Ben would let her sit by his bed again while he slept.

By the third lap, there was a knock on the door. Hope gazed through the peephole. All she saw was a tuft of hair. Whoever was outside was either bent over or very short.

"Who is it?" she asked, leaning against the door.

In a strange southern drawl came the reply: "Er... room service, complements of General Armstrong."

Elated that Ben saved her the chore of devising a lie to go to his room, she turned the deadbolt and removed the door's chain.

Hope opened the door, confident that she could later pop over to thank him for the late-night treat.

Before she could react, he slammed his fist into her chest with the force of a bolt of lightning.

Stumbling backward and falling on her rear, Hope was disoriented.

Dazed, she looked up. He stood over her, cruel, vicious like a ravenous beast.

She uttered one word: "Lattimore!"

CHAPTER 28

The radio shock-jock reached back, slammed the door, and engaged the deadbolt.

He ran a hand through his unruly mop of hair and sneered. "This is gonna be fun."

Hope turned on her stomach and tried to crawl away.

Lattimore dropped onto her lower back before she could move more than a few inches, straddling her. He grabbed a tuft of her hair with his right hand and slammed her head into the floor.

Despite cushioning by the wall-to-wall carpet, her head began to ache from Lattimore's rhythmic pounding of her skull.

Hope screamed.

"Go ahead, scream," shouted Lattimore. "Nobody's gonna hear you. I made sure the occupants of the rooms surrounding yours would be out on the town. And your precious Ben? I told him he needed to rest tonight and gave him a sleeping pill. He's knocking out the zzzs by now. So he can't save you like the time I put that carfentanil-laced paper in your bathroom."

Realizing she would soon be unconscious if she didn't act, Hope reached back and gripped his right wrist. She dug her thumbnails into his radial nerve. Lattimore howled and released his grip on her hair.

Feline quick, Hope shimmied from beneath the shock-jock and got to her feet. Facing her adversary, she said, "Why are you doing this?"

Lattimore stood and, shaking his numb right hand, said, "You don't get it, do you?"

Hope bent in a crouch, awaiting his next assault. "Get the hell out of my room," she shouted.

He continued to stand between her and the door. "I can't let you ruin everything we've worked for."

"What are you talking about?"

"Conchrane is finished. You can't change that."

"Just get out!"

"No." Lattimore began opening and closing his right hand as he approached Hope.

She moved to the side. But he sidled his steps to keep his body between her and the door.

Hope knew it was only a matter of time before the feeling fully returned to his hand. Then Lattimore would pounce.

She scanned the room for something she could use as a weapon. Maybe the desk phone. She slowly stepped in that direction.

With the swiftness of a demon on steroids, Lattimore shot to the desk, grabbed the phone, and yanked the cord from the wall. He threw the desk set against the door. "Nice try," he said.

"What do you want?" yelled Hope.

"I want you to go away. I won't let you stop the General. We've worked too hard for this moment."

"What moment?"

Lattimore grinned. "Ides of March."

"Ben said that was just a term for when President Conchrane would likely be impeached."

"Oh, is that what he told you?"

"Get out!" yelled Hope. "Regardless of whatever it means, you're going to prison."

Lattimore stopped working his right hand. "I'm not going anywhere." He inched closer.

Panicked now, Hope realized he'd maneuvered her into a corner of the room.

Dizziness from Lattimore's continuous pounding of her head was beginning to overtake her. Hope started seeing double. Her body was weakening. *Buy time, Hope*, she told herself.

Raising her hands in a defensive posture, Hope said, "OK, OK, what if I just left? Or…or…what if I convinced Ben to ramp up his rhetoric again? Maybe put that cross back on stage?"

Lattimore seemed to relax for a moment as if considering her proposals.

"I…I could maybe speak out during my presentation on how masking, vaccines, and social distancing were not appropriate during that pandemic."

"You'd do that?"

"Yes. Yes, I would. And I promise I won't press charges against you. Just leave now. It'll be like this never happened. And…and…whatever you and Ben have planned, I'll go along with it, one hundred percent."

"Really?" Lattimore looked like he was buying it.

"Yeah. Why don't we sit down for a moment, and you can fill me in on everything." Hope stumbled and placed a hand on the wall to steady herself.

Lattimore smirked. "Good try, Allerd. But I like my plan better." Balling his hand into a fist, he swung.

Hope parried his punch with her forearm. The collision sent her tumbling to the floor.

For a moment, she lost sight of Lattimore. Unnerved, she quickly scanned the room for him, only worsening her dizziness.

She spied him at the desk, holding the table lamp over his head. He took deliberate steps and closed the distance, intent on delivering the death blow.

Hope tried to get to her feet but tottered, falling back to the floor.

He came on. A foot closer.

She found herself on her back, unable to rise. Her adrenaline-soaked mind recalled times when she'd pushed herself to exhaustion during a long swim. *Just one more kick*, she'd told herself to keep going.

He was now standing over her, the boyish face a mask of pure malevolence.

Lattimore's muscles twitched as he slammed the metal lamp downward.

In a split second, her skull would splinter.

CHAPTER 29

Just one more kick. Hope pressed her right leg upwards, heel striking Lattimore's groin.

The lamp crashed against the carpet millimeters from her head.

The shock jock emitted a high pitched yelp, staggered, holding his crotch, and fell backward.

Still unsteady, Hope got to her feet, unlocked the door, and dashed from the hotel room. Using the wall to steady herself, she ran to the nearest exit and, gripping the railing to hold herself upright, descended the stairs, footfalls echoing through the stairwell.

She exited the stairwell at the lobby level and stumbled to the front desk.

Breathless, she said, "Call the police. I've been assaulted."

The panicked look on the young female hotel clerk's face assured Hope that she had an ally. The woman immediately began dialing the desk phone.

Hope shakily stepped over to a nearby fabric chair and sat, head in hand. Two other female clerks who saw the commotion came over. One of them asked her if she needed water and an ambulance, and the other gently rubbed her back as a gesture of support.

Two patrol officers arrived and took Hope's statement. It took a few moments for them to understand that she was accusing Eric Lattimore, the radio shock-jock and presidential candidate, of assaulting her.

Paramedics came and assessed her. Not needing to be hospitalized, she rode the elevator with the police officers and a detective to her room. There, she repeated her account of the attack, pointing out what happened in detail. However, the lamp and desk phone were missing. It was no surprise to Hope as they bore Lattimore's fingerprints.

Since the room was now a crime scene, Hope had to find another. She was allowed to pack her suitcase. In the lobby again, she checked at the front desk. The hotel was full. After all, it was the holiday season.

On the verge of tears from the assault and the recounting of it to the police, Hope stepped away from the desk and walked into...

"Ben." She looked up at the General. Dressed in a wrinkled blue suit, he stood with arms extended.

"Hope, are you all right? I heard that you were attacked." He looked genuinely concerned.

She nodded. Tears came as she drifted into his outstretched arms. He smelled of sandalwood and sweat. Hope nuzzled her face against his warm, sturdy chest and bawled her eyes out.

A moment later, she pulled back from the embrace. "I'm sorry," she said.

"No. No. I'm sorry," said Armstrong. "I heard that Eric attacked you."

She nodded.

"I have my people scouring the city for him at this very moment. He won't get away with this. I saw you at the desk and guessed the police probably cordoned off your room. Do you need a place to stay?"

"Yes," she said, brushing his tear-stained shirt.

"You'll have my room. I'll bunk with one of my...er assistants."

"But..."

"No 'buts'. I insist. And I'll station a guard outside the room."

"Thank you, Ben. It's very kind of you. I...I don't know how to repay..."

"After what you've been through, it's the least I can do. Let me take you upstairs."

He carried her suitcase as she accompanied Ben up the elevator to his room. It was already cleared out and made up for her. He left her inside. Stopping at the door, he said, "Get some rest."

Hope tried to sleep. But she was awake for most of the night, and when she did drift off, she was plagued with nightmares of Lattimore breaking the door down and clubbing her with that metal lamp.

◆ ◆ ◆

Bleary-eyed, Hope took her usual seat on the bus. They were bound for Dallas. It was to be a two-day event. Armstrong sat down next to her and placed a cup of coffee on the table in front of her.

She looked up at him. "Thanks."

He placed packets of sugar, artificial sweetener, and cream beside the cup. "I didn't know how you like your coffee."

As she poured cream into the cup and stirred, she said, "Cream with no sugar."

"I take it you didn't sleep well last night," said Armstrong.

"Very little."

"I swear we will find Lattimore. He's got to pay for what he did to you. I'm just glad you weren't injured."

Hope nodded. Something occurred to her as she sat sipping her coffee and watching the cityscape pass. During Lattimore's assault, he'd referred to the Ides of March as a "moment." And he'd responded to her statement that the Ides of March was about the time President Conchrane would be impeached by saying, "Oh, is that what he told you?"

As the bus pulled onto the interstate, Hope realized that either Ben or Lattimore was lying about the Ides of March. And knowing that Lattimore had spoken to her as someone to whom he had no reason to lie as he'd been sure she'd be dead in a few minutes, Hope was inclined to believe the shock jock over Ben.

She looked at Ben and wondered if she should bring it up. He turned, smiled at her, then squeezed her hand.

No, thought Hope, *don't say a word*.

She returned his smile and nodded. Closing her eyes, she devised a plan to reenter his room and peruse that sheaf of papers. It was there, she was sure, that she'd find the meaning of the Ides of March and Armstrong's plan to overthrow Conchrane.

◆ ◆ ◆

The first Dallas rally went off as usual. Hope spoke of her fight against the recent pandemic, followed by Armstrong's spirited oration. The crowd seemed more enthusiastic than in some of the previous cities. And predictably, there were riots after the rally.

Back in her room, Hope called Clive.

"Where are you, Dallas?" he asked.

"Yeah. How did you know?"

"A riot broke out there. It was on the evening news."

"It's just an unfortunate occurrence. I guess some people don't like what General Armstrong is saying."

"Hope, have you been paying attention to what's happening nationally?"

"What do you mean?" She had to admit she had not read a paper or watched a newscast besides the occasional late-evening programs of the cities she was in that highlighted the local riots.

"Hope, riots have been ongoing in every city you stopped in. Riots are also occurring in West Coast cities like Los Angeles, San Francisco, and Seattle. The whole country appears to be in a state of anarchy."

"What about President Conchrane?"

"She's been calling for calm. But it isn't working. Cities have been calling out—what's the name? —the National Guard to try and restore peace, but to no avail. Some people in your Congress have been calling for Conchrane to be impeached."

"OK, Clive. Look, I'm safe if you're worried about that." She momentarily considered recounting Lattimore's attack but decided it would only worry him more.

"Hope," he said, voice sounding strained, "are you going to tell me about the assault?"

"What?"

"Eric Lattimore. It's all over the news. He's wanted by the Oklahoma City police for assaulting you."

"Oh, yeah." It was stupid of her to try to hide the assault charge against Lattimore. *Of course,* she thought, *it would be a newsworthy item picked up by national news outlets.* "Clive, I just didn't want to worry you."

Clive said nothing.

"Clive, you still there?"

A jagged breath was followed by, "Yeah, I'm here."

"Clive, I'm sorry. I didn't want you to worry about me."

"I'm afraid it doesn't work like that, Hope."

"What do you mean?"

"Keeping secrets."

"Look, you're right. I should have told you."

"After I read the newspaper account, I was heartsick."

"Like I said, I just didn't want you worrying about me."

"So, is this how it's going to go from now on? You decide what I should or should not know?"

"Er, no."

"You not trusting me enough to tell me things?"

"No."

"With every dark turn of your countenance, are you going to cause me to agonize over some secret you may be harboring?"

"Clive, you know I wouldn't do that."

"Hope, it just makes me wonder."

"Wonder what?"

"Wonder if this whole engagement thing is a good idea."

"Clive, no!"

"Look, Hope, I don't think I can live this way."

From the cell phone, Hope heard a distant utterance in the background—a woman's voice speaking in a foreign language over a PA system.

"I've got to go," said Clive.

Hope heard the *click*. Heartbroken, she continued holding her cell to her ear.

Finally, she put the burner phone away and sat in the dark contemplating the unthinkable—a life without Clive Andrew.

CHAPTER 30

When she arose the next morning after a fitful rest, Hope felt that Clive just needed some time to come to his senses over her not telling him about the assault. She'd wait and call him in the evening after the second Dallas rally. Meanwhile, she'd spend the morning focusing on what had been happening politically since Armstrong's tour began.

After a quick breakfast of eggs and toast at the hotel's dining room, she retired to her room and began channel surfing.

She settled on an all-day news station that appeared biased toward President Conchrane. The pundit, a middle-aged, attractive black woman with short brown curly hair, was pontificating about Armstrong. "...and, you know," she said, "the General has been doing a speaking tour through the midwest during this holiday season. Or, should I say, a scorched earth tour? Because in each city he's visited, violent riots have broken out. And they have continued days after the tour has moved on. So far, ten people have died as a result. You know, folks, he's not some savior on a white horse. He's nothing but an anarchist. Armstrong wants to burn this country down. Joining me today is Samuel Akers of the Country First Institute. Sam, what's your take on our famous General?"

A sixty-ish balding man in a three-piece suit sat across from the pundit and smirked at the camera. He leaned forward and said, "Thank you, Violet. Look, Benjamin Armstrong is nothing more than an autocrat wannabe. He's done nothing but incite violence and discontent throughout the nation since President Conchrane's reelection. Maybe he's just a sore loser since the guy he backed, Eric Lattimore, lost the election. But I think he's more than that. I think he's a danger to our democracy."

"How so, Sam?" asked Violet.

"He's basically running the Hitler playbook. During those rallies, he inflames the audience's grievances, fear, and feelings of victimhood. It's all against the 'other'. And who's the 'other'? It's anyone who doesn't fit the mold. The immigrant, the poor, basically anyone who doesn't think like Armstrong."

"So, what's his next move, Sam?" asked a grinning Violet.

Sam shrugged. "Hitler burned down the Reichstag. Look, I really don't know what Armstrong will do next. All I know is that he doesn't stand for anything. He's nothing but a swindler. A huckster in a uniform."

Hope glowered at Sam. The guy was too smarmy for her tastes, and Violet was too phony. She picked up the remote and started channel surfing again until she found another all-day news station. This one was pro-Armstrong. The anchor, a pleasant-looking man in a blue suit with pristinely quaffed blonde hair, flashed one of those made-for-TV grins. He then pinched his face into an I'm-very-serious-now mien.

In a melodious baritone voice, he said, "Folks, it is patently clear that Martha Conchrane is just not working out. She has just been elected for a second term, and her poll numbers are already in the crapper. She has been and will continue to be the worst President the Country has ever had. And frankly, she needs to go. The stock market is down to an all-time five-year low, and we're in the grips of inflation. Ben

Armstrong has been on the right side of things for quite a while. Just listen to this clip."

On-screen, a video of Armstrong walking down a corridor flanked by his entourage appeared. Suddenly, a gaggle of reporters approached, shouting questions. One bellowed over the rest, "General Armstrong, what do you think of President Conchrane?"

Armstrong stopped, flashed that engaging smile, and said, "She's a third-rate President. We need better leadership for the times, and she needs to go."

"What are you saying? Should she be impeached?" asked the reporter.

"I think Thomas Jefferson said it best: '...a little rebellion now and then is a good thing, and as necessary in the political world as storms in the physical.' And, he also said, 'The tree of liberty must be refreshed from time to time with the blood of patriots and tyrants.'"

Geeze, Ben, thought Hope, *can all you do is quote Jefferson?*

The anchor was back on screen. He leaned forward slightly and, with brows furled, said, "Is General Armstrong correct? Is it time for rebellion? Gaging by the demonstrations occurring after his rallies, it certainly seems so. I don't know about you folks, but I'm beginning to think that maybe a little rebellion right now would be a good thing."

Hope found this guy too theatrical and maybe even a little dangerous. She pressed the power button on the remote and sat staring at the blank screen for a moment. Each side predicted only crisis and conflict proceeding from the other.

But, Hope reasoned, if Ben was about to foment a rebellion in advance of staging a coup, it had to be wrong, despite what Jefferson said. Regardless of how poor a president Martha Conchrane was, she was the duly elected leader of the

Nation. And using carfentanil to commit mass murder to press home his cause was, at best, misguided and, at worst, savage and immoral. There was no doubt about it. Ben Armstrong had to be stopped and by any means necessary.

◆ ◆ ◆

Hope decided she needed to clear her head and get out of that hotel for a while. She opened her room door and told her guard, a tall woman in the khaki and blue blazer uniform, that she was going to take a short walk outside, just around the hotel property.

"I wouldn't advise that, ma'am," said her guard. "Bad people are roaming the streets."

Yeah, thanks to what we've been saying at those rallies, thought Hope. She nodded and said to the young woman, "Look, I'll be careful and stay within a block or two of the hotel. I have my cell phone. I promise I won't be long. I just need some alone time outside of this hotel to, you know, clear my head."

Not waiting for a reply, Hope headed down the corridor. When the woman didn't pursue her, Hope took it as a sign of acquiescence and traipsed past the elevator to the exit door.

In the stairwell, she called Tina as she bound down the fifteen floors. "Hey, Tina, it's Hope. Can you guys pick me up? I'll be on the corner a block east of the hotel in about five minutes."

"Hope, good to hear from you. Look, sorry about the assault. Big Reggie and I feel really bad that we couldn't have been there to help you."

"Don't worry about it. The guy just came out of nowhere. Couldn't be helped. Can you make it?"

"Sure thing."

The call ended as Hope bound down the final flight of

stairs and opened the door to the lobby. She wandered toward the rear of the building and found a side door. On the street, she tried to blend in with the myriad of pedestrians slogging along the sidewalk.

She worked her way to a spot a block east of the hotel and stood in front of a bookstore. Within five minutes, a black Escalade stopped in front of her.

The window rolled down. Tina's familiar face appeared. "Hop in," she said.

Hope opened the SUV's rear door, sat, and fastened her seatbelt. Big Reggie, at the wheel, turned and nodded. "Hey, Miss Hope." He fiddled with this black cylindrical object mounted on the Escalade's dashboard.

In the front passenger's seat, Tina turned and said, "I swear, he's always messing with that dashcam."

"Never know when some video might come in handy," said Big Reggie.

Tina just shook her head. "Where to, girl?" she asked.

Hope wasn't sure at first. Then it came to her. She'd spent the morning listening to the pontifications of TV pundits. She now needed to hear from the real people. "Take me to where the riots took place."

Big Reggie drove through the downtown streets, passing high-rise apartments and office buildings with the familiar facades of chain stores in between.

A few blocks ahead, Hope could see it. Black smoke rose from the burnt-out shells of stores and offices ahead. The street was littered with debris and the charred frames of automobiles.

As Big Reggie weaved his way through the section of downtown Dallas hit by the rioting, Hope saw a tiny man in jeans wearing a faded white apron wielding a push broom as he shoved mounds of broken glass from in front of a fire-damaged deli.

"Stop here," shouted Hope.

Reggie pulled to a stop. Hope rolled down the window and called to the little man, "Sir, may I ask you a question?"

Appearing to be relieved by Hope's interruption, he stopped sweeping and walked over to the SUV. "Yes, can I help you?" he said in a foreign accent Hope didn't recognize.

"Sorry to disturb you," said Hope, "but I was wondering how you felt about the people who did all of this."

"Did this?" he asked, looking back at his charred-out store. "I don't know who did this. Maybe backers of Conchrane, maybe backers of Armstrong. I don't care. You know what I care about?"

Hope shook her head.

"I care about mothers raising their babies. I care about students learning so that they can grow up to be good citizens. I care about old people like me who want to live their last days in peace. I came to this country for a better life. And this is what I get. I don't get into politics. I just want to make the best sandwiches for all the people. My satisfaction comes from the smile on a customer's face when they bite into my pastrami on rye."

The man went back to his pushbroom.

Hope sat back in her seat and rolled up the window. She'd seen and heard enough. The deli owner likely summed up the hearts of everyone along this section of downtown who'd lost their businesses to the riots.

"Where to next, Miss Hope?" asked Big Reggie.

"Take me back to the hotel." It was becoming decidedly evident to her that there was a third side to this fight: the people who wished for a quiet existence free of political strife and extremism—those with a live-and-let-live attitude. They were content to sail through life, spreading acts of kindness when they could and forgiving their fellow human beings when they stumbled.

As she closed her eyes, Hope wondered if, when the dust settled from the coming battle with Armstrong, if she survived, she could one day be numbered among that third cluster.

CHAPTER 31

The second Dallas rally started like all the others. A raucous crowd packed the arena. The preliminary program went off flawlessly. Hope gave her talk about fighting the pandemic in her usual dispassionate manner.

However, when it came time for the man of the hour, things went awry.

Ben arose to give his usual ardent firebrand diatribe, and it happened. Hope was the first to notice it when she turned to look at him during his introduction. Armstrong had the face of a slack-jawed, hollowed-out shell of a man. His movements were forced as if he'd completed a marathon and was now asked to scale a mountain peak.

As he spoke, his delivery was slow and halting. He was not himself.

Hope turned to him when he sat and placed her hand on his shoulder. "Ben, are you all right?"

"Er, I'm fine. Just feeling a little tired."

She nodded. But deep inside, she was sure his expressionless elocution and apathetic gesticulations were related to his PTSD.

Later that evening, the second Dallas rally was followed predictably by the city's second riot. Hope, back in her hotel room, decided to call Clive. Surely, by now, he'd have had enough time to cool off from his little rant about trust.

Taking her burner phone, Hope entered his number. After several rings, she got the standard "the caller is not available" message. After repeating the call to his number three more times and getting the same messages, she decided to call Jack.

"Hey, Sis," answered Jack on the third ring.

"Hi, I've been calling Clive, but he's not answering his phone. Is everything all right?"

The line went quiet for a moment.

"Jack, you there?"

"Uh, yeah, Sis. Er, look, I don't know how to say this any other way, so I'll just come out and say it."

"Oh, my God, Jack, what is it?"

"Clive. He's been seeing Marta. I think they spent Christmas Day together."

The news hit like an anvil dropped from a second-story window. Devastated by the information, Hope replied with a pitiable, "Oh."

"Sorry, Hope. I tried to talk to him, but he ranted on about you not trusting him enough to tell him about being assaulted by that Lattimore guy. Kept saying he had to find out about it on the news. By the way, are you OK?"

"I'm…I'm fine. He got the worst of it. I don't think he'll be back anytime soon." Recalling Sophie, Clive's daughter, she said, "You said he spent Christmas Day with Marta?"

"Yeah, I think so."

"Uh, could be he was there to spend time with his daughter, Sophie. It has been a while since he's seen her."

"I dunno."

"I mean, that could explain it." Hope realized she was attempting to put a positive spin on a rotten situation. And it wasn't working.

"I guess, Sis. Hey, where are you now?"

"I'm in Dallas."

"When are you coming back to D.C.?"

"Er, we're going to seven more cities: Jackson, Birmingham, Charlotte, Nashville, Louisville, Columbus, and Detroit. We'll be back on January fifth."

"It'll be good to see you again."

"Yeah, I miss you too. Look, if you see Clive, ask him to call me."

"Will do. But when I last spoke with him, he said he had to fly to Europe. You gonna be OK?"

"Uh, sure. You know, I'm your resilient big sister."

"Call me if you need anything."

"Will do, Jack." Hope ended the call and collapsed on her bed in a storm of tears.

Thirty minutes later, Hope was in the bathroom splashing cold water on her tear-stained face. Red eyes stared back at her from the mirror.

She felt the angry, vengeful Hope emerging. If Clive was going to call off their engagement to sleep with Marta, she wasn't going to sit in this room pining away like some miserable little storybook princess. *Two can play at this game*, she told herself.

She dried her face with a hand towel and applied just the right smattering of makeup.

She exited her room on a twofold mission: to exact revenge on Clive Andrew by comforting someone who needed succor and glean that vial scintilla of intelligence—the real meaning of the Ides of March.

A short stroll down the hotel's corridor brought her to her objective.

Hope knocked on Ben's door.

◆ ◆ ◆

The door opened. Hope stood at the threshold facing a washed-out, broken Ben Armstrong.

"Ben," she said, "I was concerned. You didn't look well at the rally."

He stepped back and opened the door wider. She took it as an invitation to enter and strolled into the room. The surroundings were the same as her last visit: two open laptops on his desk, the dry-erase board covered with figures propped in a corner, and the papers on his bed. The TV was off.

Armstrong, hands jammed in his robe pockets, said, "Hello, Hope."

Looking around, Hope gave him her snap diagnosis: "You're working too hard."

"I'll be fine. I just…just need…." He sat on an unoccupied corner of the bed, staring at nothing in particular.

"You need to rest," said Hope. She began clearing the papers from his bed.

"Do you think they are with us?" asked Armstrong.

"Who?"

"Tonight's attendees. Are they on our side?"

"Ben, I'm sure they are. They adore you."

"I sure hope so. We're gonna need everyone we can get. How about you?"

"What?"

"Are you with me?"

"I've done all of these rallies, haven't I?" She sat down beside him.

Ben smiled gently. "But you've never told me how you really feel about the cause. And…and about me."

Hope sighed. Here it was. The opening she'd wished for. A chance to stick it to traitor Clive. *Just tell him you're falling for him*, she thought.

"I think you're a powerful, talented, and driven man. I feel lucky to be working with you, and I've certainly learned a lot."

Ben nodded. "Yeah, but what do you really think of me? As a person?"

"Well, I'd be lying if I said I wasn't attracted to you. Is that what you wanted to hear?"

"Something like that." Ben caressed her cheek and gave her a peck on the lips. "I trust I'm not being too forward. But I've come to care for you. Deeply."

"Oh," said Hope, "I uh…"

"Look, things are moving fast. In about a week, everything's going to change. For the better. I'd like you by my side when that happens."

"What's going to happen?"

"You'll see. Anyway…." He yawned. "Man, I do feel tired."

"Like I said, you've been working too hard. You need to get some rest. We can talk about this later."

He yawned again. "Yeah, you're probably right."

Recalling their last encounter when Hope touched his cheek, she asked, "Ben, may I remove your robe?"

He nodded.

She unfastened the ties and slipped the robe from his shoulders. Pulling the covers back, she assisted him as he lay down.

Closing his eyes, he said, "It's gonna be big."

"What?" asked Hope.

"Ides of March. The whole shebang. You'll see."

"You get some rest," said Hope as she tucked the comforter around his shoulders.

Deciding not to press him for information as he drifted off, Hope pulled up a chair next to the bed, extinguished the lights, and sat. She had the whole night. There would be plenty of time to rifle through those stacks of papers.

She was sure the key to the Ides of March rested between the pages heaped on the floor.

CHAPTER 32

It was nearly eight a.m. local time as Clive entered the small Catholic church in the center of a snow-covered village on the outskirts of Chisinau, Moldova. Sitting on a back pew in a black cassock was the thin middle-aged man he came to meet. Father Albot rose from the pew and extended his hand.

Clive shook hands with the cleric, smiled, and said, "Thank you for meeting me on such short notice."

"When I told my good friend Father Mazur about the man who came to seek asylum in my church, he informed me of your crusade," said Father Albot in a thick Moldavian accent, "I thought you two needed to meet as expeditiously as possible."

Clive scanned the chapel for the man and, on seeing no one else there, asked, "Where is he?"

"Sergei has gone through a great deal since coming here. He wanted me to—What's the word?—screen you first."

"Screen me? I'm not a policeman if that's what he's worried about."

The priest glanced at the ceiling momentarily, then said, "He wants to know why you are interested in his role in this tragedy."

"Ah, yes," said Clive. "I'm an investigative reporter. My main interest is in discovering the identity of the man who purchased a weapon of mass destruction from his boss, Lev Petrov. It's urgent that I find him before he deploys it somewhere in the United States."

Father Albot nodded. "I see. And how can Sergei help?"

"Any information he can provide could help me discover the identity of this…this terrorist before he strikes."

Albot nodded again. "Laudable. I think Sergei, as part of his penitence, should fully cooperate with you. Follow me."

Clive followed the priest to a small room behind the chapel. Albot knocked on the door and called, "Sergei, it's Father Albot and the man I told you about, Mr. Clive Andrew."

After a moment, the door opened a crack. The sliver of a face appeared out of the shadows within the room. "Has he come to arrest me?" asked the man within the room.

"No, my son. Mr. Andrew is a reporter seeking the identity of a terrorist. He thinks you may be able to help. I urge you to cooperate with him as part of your penitence."

The door opened wider. Clive saw a hulking man dressed in a tattered black jacket and trousers. He stood at least six four with a balding head and a face out of some horror movie. He limped toward the center of the small room as Clive and Father Albot entered. The priest flicked a switch on the wall, turning on the overhead light. The room was sparsely furnished with a double bed, chair, and table.

Sergei sat on his bed and then promptly arose. "May I sit, Father?" he asked.

"Yes, my son."

He sat back down. "Please, Mr. Andrew," he said, pointing to the one chair in the room.

Clive sat as he watched Father Albot close the door and lean against it with arms crossed.

"What do you want to know?" asked Sergei, avoiding eye contact with Clive.

"Father Albot told me that you kidnapped multiple young

women from the streets of several cities in Moldova, Belarus, and Slovakia."

"Yes, yes. And I'm so, so sorry. I promise I will never do it again. I will never abuse a woman again."

"Yes, well, I'd like to know why you did it."

"My boss, Lev Petrov, wanted them. And he said it was OK to have my way with them. You know, sexually. And I'm sorry."

"Did he say why he wanted them?"

"For a demonstration."

"What kind of demonstration?"

"I don't know."

"Where did you take these women?"

Sergei arose from the bed and walked over to Clive. The reporter flinched as the giant of a man leaned over the desk, took a pencil and notepad, and began to write. He put the pencil down, handed Clive the paper, and returned to the bed.

Perusing the writing, Clive was initially puzzled. Sergei had written two rows of numbers. Then it dawned on him. The figures were a longitude and latitude.

"This is the location?" asked Clive.

"Yes. It is just a barn in a field. I used my smartphone to pinpoint the place so I could return without searching. I went back and forth so many times that I memorized the location."

"And you kept the women in this barn."

"Yes. I'm so sorry."

"How did you keep them from escaping?"

"Chained their ankles to the baseboard."

Despite his repeated utterances of regret, Clive no longer saw a man sitting on the bed but a heartless monster.

He had one final question for Sergei. "Did you ever see the man to whom Petrov demonstrated the weapon? Or learn his name?"

"No. But Petrov said he was American. Called him John Wayne because he said he looked like the actor." With that final answer, Sergei seemed to shrink a few inches.

Clive arose from the chair and walked out of the church. At the entrance, he stopped and pulled his coat collar high about his neck against the freezing wind.

"Go with God, my son." Father Albot appeared beside him in the cold.

Turning to the cleric, Clive asked, "How can you shelter that thing in there?"

"Everyone deserves God's grace."

Clive shook his head. "Not everyone."

As he descended the church's stairs, Clive heard Father Albot say, "When you report him to the police, please ask them to be merciful when they come to arrest him."

CHAPTER 33

Clive drove his rented Range Rover slowly over the snow-covered road past a monotonous Belarusian landscape. He periodically checked the GPS signal on his cell phone as he progressed along the path past fields and hills covered with white powder.

The numbers on the phone's GPS suddenly matched the ones on the paper Sergei had given him, and he halted along a nondescript patch of snow-blanketed pasture. In the distance were charred timbers in the rough rectangular outline of a building.

Clive got out and removed an entrenching tool he'd bought at an army surplus store from the back of the Range Rover.

He trudged through the snow to the burned-out structure. Once within the periphery of the structure, he removed his cell phone and began taking photos. Next, Clive kneeled and, taking the entrenching tool, scraped away snow until he saw charred earth. He then gently raked the blackened frozen dirt until he found them.

Lifting scorched slivers of bone up to the sunlight, Clive, knowing that hundreds of similar bits of human tissue were within that fire-spent barn, felt his eyes moisten. He deposited the shards of bone in an envelope he'd brought with him and started for the Range Rover.

Halfway along the walk back to the road, Clive, overcome

with the enormity of his find, dropped to his knees, and openly wept for those who had no one else to mourn their passing.

◆ ◆ ◆

As she sat in the dark watching Ben softly snore, Hope began to feel a pang of guilt well up from within. Was this cheating? After all, he kissed her. And the only thing she did was admit an attraction for him. It wasn't like she'd confessed her undying love or anything like that.

And what had old Clive done with Marta in her apartment? Was he sleeping with her at this moment? Making passionate love between the sheets?

Come on, Hope, she told herself, *stop it. You don't know that Clive's done anything wrong. So, he spent Christmas Day with his daughter and her mother. Was there really anything wrong with that?*

Ben rolled over and coughed, returning her thoughts to the task at hand. She had to admit she was attracted to the handsome General, but she also knew he was toxic. Toxic for her and the country. Despite the attraction, she had to quash his ambitions of what, for all practical purposes, was a bid for absolute power.

Her greatest dilemma now came to the fore. She saw no way to stop him short of killing him.

She waited thirty minutes more. Leaning forward in the chair, she could now see his eyes moving back and forth beneath his lids by the ambient light. REM sleep. It was time.

Removing her burner phone from her pocket and flicking on the LED light on the back, Hope walked over to the stack of papers at the foot of the bed. She kneeled and began rifling through the sheets.

Uncertain of what she was searching for other than a

reference to the Ides of March, she went through the stacks page by page.

The first and second stacks revealed nothing about the Ides of March. Taking a deep breath, Hope started through the third and final stack of papers. Halfway along, she heard a rustling. Looking up, she came face to face with Ben, sitting up in bed.

"What are you doing?" he asked with eyes wide open.

Hope froze.

◆ ◆ ◆

Ben blinked a couple of times. "Hope?" he said, "Is that you?"

"Er, yeah. I was just, er…fixing your stack of papers. They were about to fall over, and I…"

"Thanks, you didn't have to do that."

"It was no problem. Can't you sleep?"

"Guess not." He shrugged.

"Didn't you have some sleeping pills?" She arose from the foot of the bed and walked over to his night table. Opening the drawer a few inches, she saw a pill bottle and removed it. There was something else in the drawer—metallic and shiny. Daring not to open it any further and risk suffering Ben's ire, Hope closed the drawer.

She read the bottle's label aloud: "Triazolam."

"Oh, yeah. Eric got them for me."

Hope removed one from the bottle, retrieved a glass of water from the bathroom, and offered it to him. Ben downed the tablet, followed by a gulp of water.

As Ben settled under the covers, Hope sat and waited.

A half-hour later, he snored in a drug-induced sleep. She arose and opened the table drawer wider this time, revealing a loaded nickel-plated revolver. She fingered the cool metallic cylinder.

Here was her chance. She could end it all right now. Just take the gun out, aim for the head, and pull the trigger. Ben wouldn't feel a thing. One shot, and it would all be over. She would save the nation, no, the world, from a vicious would-be dictator. The mathematics was irrefutable: redeeming countless lives by just taking one.

She took the revolver from the drawer by its grip and put her finger through the trigger guard. Aiming for his head, she touched the trigger and closed her eyes.

One shot, and it would all be over.

She pressed her index finger against the trigger.

But one restraining thought rang through her consciousness: thou shalt not murder.

Hope let the weapon fall to her side.

Ben Armstrong was guilty of only one thing, as far as she could see—planning a coup. He hadn't carried it out, killed anyone, or toppled the government. After all, despite the carfentanil, what if this whole thing was just some jingoistic tirade to impeach Conchrane?

Kill someone for committing mass murder in some possible future scenario? It was risky at best. And there was no guarantee that some champion wouldn't take up the mantle of a martyred Ben Armstrong to carry out the plan of mass murder and American dictatorship while she rotted away in some dank prison cell.

Hope put the gun back into the drawer on top of a folder she hadn't noticed before. It contained black and red lettering. The red letters caught her attention, and she slid it from beneath the weapon.

The bold red text at the top and bottom read: TOP SECRET.

She removed the contents of the folder. There were five sheets of paper inside. They were all marked, top and bottom, with the TOP SECRET moniker.

As she read, Hope was initially dismayed. It was written in some military jargon she couldn't begin to decipher. But one line informed her she was on the right track. It read:

OPERATION PLAN/ORDER 0001 IDES OF MARCH TOP SECRET.

This was the first reference to Ides of March in all the papers she'd examined. Excited, she removed her burner phone from her pocket and photographed each sheet. Maybe Jack could use his computer skills to interpret the army mumbo-jumbo.

After carefully returning the folder to the drawer beneath the revolver, Hope sat back down in the chair and closed her eyes.

She eventually fell asleep beside the man she both admired and hated, secure in the knowledge she now had the evidence to thwart his nefarious plans and save America.

CHAPTER 34

Over the next two days, they visited Jackson, Mississippi, and Birmingham, Alabama. The rallies went off as usual with enthusiastic crowds and, to Hope's dismay, riots in the streets afterward.

Hope said nothing to Ben about the revolver or the orders she'd photographed. However, he seemed to act more on edge with each passing day. Snapping at his subordinates. Forgetting items like dates and times. And on occasion, appearing in a fog.

Just before the Birmingham rally, he'd left his speaking notes in his room. When he yelled at one of the young assistants, blaming the soldier for the oversight, Hope asked him, "Ben, are you all right?"

"Huh, oh uh, yes, yes, I'm fine."

"I dunno, you just seem distracted."

"I'm fine, Hope. You just do your job, and I'll do mine." He stalked off behind the stage.

Nonplused, Hope stood frozen at the stage's edge. This was the first time Ben had been short with her. *Despite the sleeping pill, had he seen me remove the gun from his table drawer and point it at him?* she wondered.

As a precaution, she decided to make herself scarce for the remainder of the evening after the rally.

As the rally began, she took her usual seat beside Ben

and watched him on stage from the corner of her eye. Since Lattimore had left a few days back, one of his assistants, a gregarious man with graying hair and a swollen waistline, took over the master of ceremonies duty.

In typical carnival huckster fashion, the guy revved up the audience to a frenzy.

He then introduced Hope. She gave her usual talk without fanfare or hyperbole.

When she concluded her remarks and sat, Ben leaned over to her and, in a tight-lipped whisper, said, "You could have been more enthusiastic, you know."

Hope was again taken aback. This was the first time he'd criticized her presentation in the eight days of rallies. "Sorry," she replied, "I'll do better tomorrow."

The MC then introduced Ben. He arose and began his usual patter. But, halfway through, he seemed confused and stopped several times as if lost in thought before continuing. By the end, he was rambling. The MC bolted to the microphone and ended the presentation with a fiery conclusion castigating Conchrane.

Hope cut out for her room as soon as the MC concluded his remarks. She didn't want to be anywhere near Ben.

When she got to her room, Hope was concerned that Ben would pound on her door at any moment, demanding to be let in. She decided to make herself scarce for the evening and called Tina.

Using the same ruse on the guard outside her door the last time she left the hotel, Hope escaped to find herself on a street corner two blocks away. The familiar black Escalade pulled up, and Tina's familiar face appeared as the tinted window rolled down.

"Need a lift?" she said.

Hope got in the back seat. She noticed the dashcam's red light blinking, indicating it was recording.

At the wheel, Big Reggie said, "Hey, Miss Hope. Where to?"

"I dunno. Just drive around."

"What's been happening?" asked Tina.

"Ben, er, General Armstrong has been acting kinda strange. I just had to get away."

"Strange? How so?" asked Tina.

"Well, he's been forgetting small things. He lost his train of thought several times during his speech tonight. And he was short with me."

"Humm," said Tina. "Not a good sign."

"Don't sound like the General Armstrong I knew," said Big Reggie.

"That's right. You served under him while in the Army," said Hope.

"Yeah. He was always in charge. Never knew him to act like you said he did." Big Reggie turned a corner and drove up the on-ramp to the interstate. He floored it once on the highway. The big Cadillac SUV moved through the night as smoothly as water on glass.

"You wanna pull out?" asked Tina. "We can just keep driving."

"Er, no," answered Hope.

"Hey," said Big Reggie, "There was this one time."

"Yeah?" said Hope.

"I remember General Armstrong did act squirrely. It was back when we were going through this training exercise. All the big brass was there. Know what I mean? Kinda one of those make-or-break moments. All during that time, he ran around like a chicken with his head cut off."

"So," said Tina. "It looks as if Armstrong gets really stressed just before some big event."

"Like this Ides of March thing," said Hope. "Must mean one thing. It's about to happen any day now, and we're no closer to knowing the when or where."

"Tough," said Big Reggie.

Hope sat reviewing what she'd learned so far. Then it hit her. "Big Reggie, you know how to read military orders, right?"

"Yes, ma'am."

"OK, pull over."

He stopped on the side of the road and switched places with Tina. As she took off and headed back to downtown Birmingham, Hope found the photos she took of the TOP SECRET orders from Ben's drawer on her phone. She gave the device to Big Reggie.

He perused the text over the next twenty minutes, only occasionally emitting a "Hum."

Anxious to finally know what Ides of March meant, Hope leaned forward and said, "Well?"

Big Reggie turned in his seat, a pained expression on his face. "Sorry, Miss Hope. I can tell you the time of day of this operation, that it involves a battalion-sized unit and consists of rendezvouses and transportation to various locations. But I can't tell you what Ides of March means. I know the orders refer to it, but there's no definition. Likely means General Armstrong and each unit commander are the only ones who know that. The same goes for the location. They are just grid coordinates. You need the maps to know that; this just refers to maps by their serial numbers."

"And only Armstrong and his commanders would have

those," said Hope.

"Yes, ma'am."

"OK, what specifically can you tell from those orders?"

"Uh, let's see. Well, the operation starts at ten a.m. when Company A intercepts ODALIK and transports it to a grid location. Then, at noon, Company B enters SERALGIO, captures KIZLAR, and takes it to the same grid location while Company C and D form a perimeter around SERALGIO. Precisely one hour after Company B moves, the Ides of March takes place."

"So, what's ODALIK, KIZLAR, and SERALGIO?"

"Thems codenames. The first two are for people, you know, the enemy, and the last is a specific location like a house or base."

"And only Armstrong and his commanders know the codenames," said Hope dryly.

"Yes, ma'am."

"So, we're back to square one."

"No, ma'am. We know some things. We know exactly what time this Ides of March is gonna take place. We know the movements of each company involved and their times. I mean, that's something."

"I don't get it," said Tina. "What's the big deal about this Ides of March?"

"If I'm right, and I'm pretty sure I am, this Ides of March thing is going to involve mass murder on an industrial scale. And the clock is ticking."

"Sorry, Miss Hope," said Big Reggie.

"No, you've done well. You've given me the time and a general idea of what's going to happen. And that's important. Now I need to know what maps are being used and the date and location of the Ides of March. There's one other source I need to consult. Better take me back."

CHAPTER 35

Back in her hotel room, Hope sat at her desk and punched in the numbers on her burner phone for Jack. During the downtime in Jackson, she'd sent him the photos of the orders. She could just as easily have called him while in the SUV, but she wanted complete privacy for the second part of her impending phone conversation with her brother.

Jack answered on the fifth ring.

"Hey, Sis," said Jack in a sleep-slurred tone.

"Sorry to wake you, but I need to know what you found out about those orders I sent you."

"Uh, not much."

"Let me guess, you couldn't find a date, map coordinates, or meanings for those codenames."

"If you knew all that, you could have just let me sleep."

"I talked to Big Reggie. He was in the Army, you know. And he told me about the time the Ides of March would happen and about all those Company movements. But we need locations, the definitions of the codenames, and the actual date. Otherwise, a lot of people are gonna die."

"Gee, no pressure here."

"Sorry, Jack. But I feel like we're so close."

"Well, I did find something."

"What's that?"

"Those codenames. They're Turkish. Ol' Armstrong's got a sick sense of humor."

"What do you mean?"

"Those codenames are terms related to a harem."

"You mean like a house of prostitution?"

"Yep, but not quite how we think of a harem today. The harem could mean just a dwelling place for females in a family or mistresses. SERALGIO means a palace or a harem. ODALIK is a term for a female attendant in the harem or a concubine. KIZLAR is a eunuch."

"Oh, wow."

"And just so you don't think I've been sleeping on the job, I've got a program running to find the maps Armstrong is using. Do you know how many maps the Government has and how hard it is to hack into the DOD system?"

"Sorry, Jack. I should know better than to doubt your abilities."

"As soon as I have something, I'll text or call."

"Thanks. Uh, there is one more thing I want to ask you about."

"Let me guess. You want to know about Clive."

"I've tried to call him, but he isn't answering his phone."

"Look, I haven't heard from him since Christmas. Sorry, Hope. But I don't know where he is. Like I told you before, he said he was going to Europe."

"You think he's still with...."

"With Marta? Geez, I just don't know."

"Could you do me a favor, Jack? Could you go by her apartment and check? I mean, if he's still there, then...."

"OK, Sis, I'll do my best to track him down. In the meantime, why don't you get some rest?"

"Thanks, Jack." Hope ended the call and ended her expectation that Clive would return to her.

◆ ◆ ◆

The blue panel truck sporting the fresh paint job of a sunrise breaking over a lake and the logo: New Capitol HVAC Services cruised through the downtown D.C. streets with Brad Trett at the wheel. He wore a gray uniform with a patch over the left breast pocket with the same logo that graced the truck's side panels. Over the right pocket was an embroidered script proclaiming his name as "Sam."

In the distance, he saw the U.S. Capitol appear—the objective for the day. Brad's heartbeat surged as he approached the area.

He glanced at the clipboard on the passenger seat. Clipped to it was the official-looking work order and inspection paperwork clearing him to enter the Capitol grounds.

The Capitol Police's off-site inspection had gone off like clockwork, and now he just had to install the device and set the timer. It was going to be a lot easier than he thought.

He pulled up to the gate and presented his driver's license, company ID, and the inspection form. Of course, the driver's license and company ID were fakes proclaiming him as Sam Ellison.

Once on the Capitol grounds, he stopped in a space near the loading docks. According to the detailed blueprints he'd been given, this was the ideal location. An air duct leading from the Capitol powerplant, an off-site location, to the floor of the House Chamber ran through the ceiling of the loading area.

Brad exited the vehicle, walked to the back, and opened

the double doors. He removed a hand truck, positioned it on the blacktop, and began the difficult job of wresting the device from the truck's rear.

Its dimensions were four feet high and two feet square. It weighed two hundred pounds. As Brad crouched on the truck's bed and slowly lowered it from the back onto the pavement, he heard a voice: "Need some help?"

Looking past the dark gray bulky item, Brad saw a Capitol Policeman, a burly black man with an inviting round face and a short beard. He smiled and said, "Just looks pretty heavy."

"Oh, yeah," said Brad, wondering if the guy was going to cause trouble.

Putting his hands on the device to steady its trip to the pavement, the officer said, "I'm your escort."

"Escort?"

"Yeah. Every vendor has to have a police escort. New rules." He steadied the device as it settled on the concrete. "Hey, what is this thing?"

Brad hopped from the rear of the truck, leaving the doors open. "Air purifier. The 2317. Latest model. Filters out impurities down to a virus."

"Really?" The officer pursed his lips and nodded. "Guess nothing's too good for our folks in Congress."

"Guess not." Brad slid the hand truck's nose plate beneath the device.

"Ramp's right over here," said the officer, pointing to a concrete ramp on the far side of the loading dock. Several vans were parked against the elevated dock, and two sets of stairs ran up to it. The cavernous interior with cinderblock walls was populated with large garbage bins, cellophane-wrapped parcels on wooden pallets, old desks, swivel chairs, and credenzas. Overhead were dozens of light fixtures and a dizzying array of piping running in a multitude of directions.

Once on the loading dock, Brad stopped and removed a set of blueprints from his back pocket. After perusing the interior momentarily, he rolled the device next to a concrete pillar. Checking the ductwork above, he was finally satisfied he had the correct location.

The officer standing behind him said, "Know something?"

"What's that?"

"Never had anybody come to the loading docks to install any kind of HVAC equipment before."

Brad tried to hide his exasperated look. "Like I said, the latest equipment."

He made several trips back to the truck to retrieve a ladder, tools, and ducting hoses. He then connected the ducting hoses to the device and cut a hole in the ductwork above to install the hoses.

The officer stood at the foot of the ladder, head craned upward to watch the installation process. "I recall," he said, "a feller having to install some HVAC equipment a year or so ago, and it went into the off-site power plant."

"Yeah, so?" Brad couldn't conceal the irritation in his voice.

"Just sayin'."

"Look, officer er...."

"Orville." He pointed to his name badge. "John Orville. You can call me John."

"Look, John, I just install the equipment, and according to the specs, it goes right here. Care to review them?"

John raised his hands, palms up. "Naw, naw, I was just

making conversation."

Brad scanned the area. Vendors were coming and going with deliveries. *Too many witnesses*, he thought, *to off this busybody cop out here. But maybe there was another way.*

He climbed down from his ladder and gathered his tools and the surplus hoses. He turned to the officer. "Look, John, the cooled or heated air comes from the power plant, goes into the 2317, is filtered, and then sent back up the ductwork to the vents in the floor of the House Chamber. Got it?"

John flashed a sympathetic smile and said, "Got it."

At the truck, Brad placed the tools and hoses against the side, leaving the bed clear. Next, he removed a foot-long razor-sharp stiletto from a sheath in the toolbox and placed it at the edge of the bed near the rear doors. He reviewed what he needed to do as he returned to the device in the loading docks. *Quick, short moves,* he told himself.

When he returned to the device, Brad saw John squatting before it, fiddling with the front panel as if trying to open it.

"Gonna need this," said Brad, pulling a small T wrench from his pocket.

John stood and stepped aside. "Oh, yeah. I was just looking at it."

"Sure." Brad squatted in front of the device and removed the panel's four screws with the T wrench. Placing the rectangular metal shell to the side, he pressed a button. A digital timer came to life. Using his cell phone as a guide, he set it for the appropriate moment. The moment when the maximum number of people would populate the House Chamber. And when the device would do maximum damage.

As Brad replaced the panel and secured the screws, he could feel John behind him, eyeing every move. *Yeah, this busybody's gotta disappear*, thought Brad.

On getting to his feet and turning, Brad stood almost nose-to-nose with the policeman.

John pointed over Brad's shoulder at the panel and said, "I don't get it. That looked like a timer."

Brad nodded. "Yeah. The 2317's fan runs periodically. The digital device indicates the next time it engages."

John nodded and grinned as if impressed.

"John, I'd like to show you something."

"Yeah?"

"In my truck. Since you're interested in HVAC equipment, I'm sure you'll love this. Follow me."

John fell in line behind Brad as he made his way to the panel truck. Once there, Brad opened one of the rear doors, scooped up the stiletto, hiding it against his hip, and stepped onto the clear bed.

"It's right here," said Brad, turning and beckoning John to get in.

As the policeman hefted himself onto the bed of the panel truck, Brad swung the door closed, and with the speed and viciousness of a raptor, he plunged the blade into John's gut over a dozen times.

After covering the dying man with a tarp, Brad slid into the driver's seat and motored off the Capitol grounds and into late afternoon traffic.

CHAPTER 36

With the morning came a new dread. As Hope boarded the bus for Charlotte, she wondered about Ben's mood. Would he act short with her like he did on the previous evening?

She took her usual seat and braced for the worst. Five minutes later, she saw Ben in slacks and a jacket climbing the bus's steps. He looked preoccupied as he sat next to her.

"Over halfway through," said Hope, attempting to channel the conversation along a light track.

Ben nodded. "Yeah. From now on, we'd better bring our A-game."

"I'm on it," she said, trying to sound enthusiastic.

Ben was quiet for a moment. He then turned to her with a look so intense that Hope thought he might begin to pummel her into a coma. "Hope, I need to know something," he said.

"Sure, anything."

"I need to know if you're truly with me on this."

"One hundred percent."

"No kidding. No appeasing. I need a partner. Someone to walk side-by-side with me into this. Someone willing to go through the fire. Is that you, Hope?"

"Er, yes, Ben. I'm right beside you." She stared into those blazing brown eyes and tried to look as sincere as possible, all the while wondering, *Hope, what are you getting yourself into?*

"Are you a patriot or a plotter?"

"Er, a patriot, of course." To emphasize her agreement, she gently squeezed his hand.

He smiled and took her hand in both of his. "Good," he said and closed his eyes. For the nearly six-hour bus ride to Charlotte, North Carolina, Ben slept holding onto Hope's hand as if she were his talisman.

As she watched the scenery pass from her seat on the luxury bus, Hope thought back to Martha Conchrane's warning about Ben: "...if Armstrong explodes, he'll take you down with him."

Was the fuse to that human bomb now lit?

◆ ◆ ◆

Martha Conchrane sat behind the Resolute desk in the Oval Office and scowled at the schedule typed on official White House stationary.

"Really, Sam, is this trip necessary?"

Sam Withers, the White House Chief of Staff, shifted his lanky frame on the couch and, with a narrow-eyed stare, said, "Madame President, your education platform was one of the things that got you reelected. An early gesture of support for elementary education, particularly in a rural county, would go a long way in showing that you're keeping your campaign promise."

She shook her head. "I don't know."

"I promise it will be short and sweet. We drive—"

"Drive? Why can't I take Marine One?"

"To show you're fulfilling another campaign promise:

frugality. A short drive will be less expensive than taking that helicopter."

"I don't know. The Beast is pretty costly."

"That's the beauty of it. You won't need the presidential limousine. It'll be such a quick trip that an SUV will suffice. The state police of Virginia and West Virginia will have the roads clear."

"You said, 'We.' Are you accompanying me?"

"If you'd like. But I need to stay here to coordinate your cabinet meeting. It's set to start the moment you return."

"And just what am I supposed to do in this grade school?"

"It's called Evans County Elementary. You'll meet the principal, schmooze with a few teachers, talk about your bill to fund education to the gathered press, and, oh, I dunno, maybe read to the kiddos. It'll make a great photo op for the evening news programs."

"But shouldn't I stay in Washington? With Congress meeting in joint—"

"Why? It's just a cut-and-dry session. Nothing to be concerned about." Sam leaned back, pursed his thin lips, and then suddenly shot forward like a cobra about to strike. "Madame President, Martha, one of the reasons you brought me on board was to keep your polling numbers up. And that's just what I'm working to do."

President Conchrane looked down at the schedule once more, then up at Sam Withers curled snakelike on that couch and wondered, just for a moment, if she'd appointed an actual viper as Chief of Staff.

❖ ❖ ❖

The Charlotte rally was explosive. Hope, mindful of

her early morning bus conversation with Ben, spoke with a passion that even surprised him based on the enthusiastic hug he gave her at her conclusion. And Ben. Well, Ben was the most fiery she'd ever seen him during the tour. The crowd was so worked up that Hope thought they were going to rush the stage, carry Ben all the way to Washington, and demand he be appointed President then and there.

Unfortunately, the crowd's enthusiasm continued into the streets after the rally. Upon encountering a group of protesters waving signs and shouting across the street from the arena, they overpowered the police separating them and descended upon the dissenters like a ravenous pride of lions attacking a herd of antelope.

The carnage continued well into the night. Hope could see buildings and cars burning in the distance from her tenth-story hotel window. The late evening news reported ten dead.

Dismayed by the scene from her window, Hope was about to dress for bed when she was startled by a staccato knock on her room door. She spied through the peephole. It was one of the assistants.

Hope opened the door a crack. "Yes?" she said in an irritated tone.

"Ma'am," gushed the young man, "you weren't about to go to bed, were you?"

"If it's any business of yours, yes."

"But it's New Year's Eve. General Armstrong sent me to be sure you knew we're having a party in the hotel's ballroom. He'd be very disappointed if you didn't attend."

Hope had utterly forgotten that it was the thirty-first. And, since she seemed to be in Ben's good graces, she didn't want to rock the boat. "OK," she said to the young man. "I'll be down in a few minutes."

◆ ◆ ◆

Hope strolled into the hotel ballroom in a mid-calf-length red chiffon number with a V-neck and matching heels that she had packed on the off chance she'd attend a New Year's party with Clive. Heads turned, and eyes dilated.

The area was packed. The room was decorated with colorful balloons and streamers overhead. Men wore basic black tuxes, and most of the women wore some variation of a miniskirt. Hope assumed they were Armstrong's assistants finally allowed just to be happy young adults for a change. An open bar was along one wall, and a buffet occupied the opposite side.

Revelers danced in the center of the room to a live band. After getting a glass of white wine from the bar, Hope found a spot along the wall and observed the revelry nodding to the funky beat.

The band took a break. Hope scanned the room for Armstrong. Despite the pulsating music, her cozy wine-driven mood, and the warm vibe of the party, Hope was still troubled by the riot she'd seen from her window and the reports of continuous nightly riots in the cities they'd visited. The death toll was rising, and it had to stop.

Commanding in his dress uniform replete with a chest full of medals, Armstrong was a demigod among mere mortals as he held forth before a small crowd of partyers across the room.

With glass in hand, Hope walked over. She stood at the periphery of the colleagues gathered about him. She caught his eye with a cloying smile and nod.

Stopping his recitation mid-sentence, Armstrong said, "Excuse me," to the group and sauntered over to Hope. "Glad you could make it," he said.

"I came at your request."

He stepped back and said, "You look marvelous."

"Thank you. Er, I was wondering if I could speak with you. Alone."

Armstrong flashed his thousand-watt grin and nodded. "Let's go outside."

With a hand on her bare back, he escorted her to the glass wall at the far end of the building, where she could see the red and green city lights. They stepped out onto the balcony. Hope felt the sting of the cold on her bare shoulders and began rubbing her upper arms. With a sweeping gesture, Armstrong removed his woolen jacket and draped it around Hope.

Looking up into those hypnotic brown eyes, Hope said, "Thank you."

"What did you want to talk about?"

Hope turned her attention to the distant landscape, which flickered a flaming red from burning buildings and cars. "There," she pointed.

"Oh yes," said Armstrong, gazing at the devastation. "Isn't it marvelous?"

"No, it's not. People are being injured and killed. Property is being damaged and destroyed. You've got to call it off. Look, there are four more cities on the tour. Just tone down the rhetoric. Tell the audience to protest but to do it peacefully."

Armstrong laughed. "Hope you don't understand."

Suddenly, those enticing eyes turned frosty. His face became waxy, like he'd morphed into a stone statue.

"Ben, please," said Hope.

"See the zeal building out there? That's not a riot. It's America calling me."

"Calling you?"

"Calling me to fulfill my destiny, calling me to ascend the throne, calling me to usher in our Country's new dynasty."

With that, he ripped his jacket from around Hope's shoulder, put it on, and walked back into the New Year's party with hands lifted as if receiving the adulation of some unseen acolytes.

She watched from the balcony as he returned to his small group of followers to speak and gesticulate as before. From that point on, Hope realized that Armstrong was operating beyond reason. He had soared into some fantasy world where he was the god-king of all he beheld.

Feeling a fresh chill, Hope returned to the party, gazing one last time at the riot in the distance, thinking Armstrong was fueling the fires of America's demise.

CHAPTER 37

Clive Andrew leaned back in his chair. He faced Ivan Donici, the Chief of the General Police Inspectorate of Moldova, the man in charge of eight thousand police officers in the tiny Eastern European country. They sat in Donici's office in Chisinau.

The Chief, a thin, athletic man with a two-day-old stubble who looked younger than his forty-five years, ran his hand through his thick mop of hair and squinted at the papers on his desk. His brown eyes seemed to move machine-like over the information, especially the photos of the burned-out barn and shards of bone in that Belarussian field.

"Do you suppose the lab can obtain DNA from the bone fragments?" asked Donici.

"I think they are analyzing them as we speak," said Clive.

"Good. We are working on several missing persons cases involving young women. Along with Sergei Bukin's confessions, that information might provide closure for some grieving families."

Clive nodded.

"By the way, you have my gratitude for tipping us off on Bukin's whereabouts."

"It was the least I could do."

"He seemed genuinely remorseful when we came to arrest him."

"You can thank Father Albot for that."

Donici steepled his hands beneath his chin. "And this brings us to the big fish."

"Lev Petrov," whispered Clive.

"Yes. Interpol has had a Red Notice out on him for some time."

"And no police force has been able to apprehend him yet."

"Catching an illegal arms trader is difficult if he is good. And Petrov is good."

"But a charge of murder…."

Donici smiled. "With the evidence and witness you are providing and his confession, I think we can arrest him for murder and make the charge stick. Mr. Andrew, we do appreciate your willingness to cooperate in this matter."

"As I said, it's the least I can do."

"You do realize we cannot fully guarantee your safety. Petrov has been known to wield a knife at close range with the skill of a sleight of hand magician. We know of at least two people he's killed who sat across from him in a restaurant. Apparently, he suddenly stands, places his coat over his knife hand, and slices open the victim's abdomen as he walks past. In each case, he was long gone before the waiter found the dead man sitting slumped in his chair."

"So, you're saying if Petrov suddenly stands during dinner and drapes his coat over his arm, I am a dead man."

Donici tried to smile. "Something like that. You know you don't have to do this."

Clive sighed. "I visited the burned-out barn, saw those scorched bones, and cried for those murdered young women who didn't have a chance. How can I let this monster go free?"

Donici pursed his lips. "I understand. So, let's review. Three days from now in the evening at ten p.m., you will meet Petrov in the Oliva Restaurant. You'll wear a wire. Talk to him about his arms dealing. Say perhaps that you want to write an article about his day-to-day activities, but you won't use his name. Tell him he is a fascinating character and that your article will be flattering, making him sound like a hero. But, also say you'll discuss his work as if it is completely legal despite several nations wanting to arrest him. He is misunderstood. A saint."

Clive grinned at the recommendation.

"Then," continued Donici, "ask him about the recent sale to the American. Say casually that there was some sort of… demonstration of the product. Tell him you understand that is usual. You buy assault rifles, and you want to fire off some rounds into targets. You buy RPGs, and you want to blow up a vehicle. You buy a deadly aerosolized narcotic, and you—"

"You murder a couple of dozen kidnapped women," said Clive.

"Well, perhaps not in those words."

"I think I can make him talk about killing those women. I think he wants to brag about it. To show how resourceful he is."

"Good. Once he's admitted it, we will close in. We've arranged with the restaurant manager to close it to patrons. Everyone inside will be undercover police officers. If you feel things are going wrong and you are in danger, an officer posing as your waiter will come to your table and demand you immediately see the manager about an unpaid bill. He will whisk you to the back and drive you to police headquarters."

"How will he know?"

"Say, 'I think it will snow tomorrow.' That will be our

signal."

"I think it will snow tomorrow," repeated Clive.

"You'll come to police headquarters at six p.m. that evening to let us fit you with the wire," said the Chief.

As he left Donici's office, Clive began to wonder if he'd live to find out if, indeed, it would snow four days from now.

◆ ◆ ◆

The next stop on the tour was Nashville. On the six-hour bus ride, Hope made it a point to sit in the rear beside the young woman who had stood guard outside her door during the hotel stays after Lattimore's attack. During the rally, Hope gave her usual canned talk on her role in the recent pandemic. However, Armstrong continued to stare into the clouds as if communing with some higher power. His speech was more passionate than ever. And, predictably, the riot following the rally was near epic in its scope and destruction. Twelve people were killed.

Over the next two days, during stops in Louisville, Kentucky, and Columbus, Ohio, Armstrong behaved the same, and his talks were just as charged, leading to riots in both cities.

Hope wearily trudged back to her hotel room at the end of the Columbus rally. Feeling depressed about Armstrong's inflammatory rhetoric and the crowd taking to the streets to riot in response, she just wanted to get a warm bath and then sleep for a month.

Opening her room door, she noticed an envelope on the floor. Likely shoved under the door. Picking it up, Hope opened it. Inside was a single sheet of paper with a one-sentence handwritten note that said: "Meet me at the north end of the third level of the hotel parking garage at midnight to learn the solution to your conundrum."

Too tired and miserable to play guessing games with some unknown prankster, she tossed the note on the desk and went into the bathroom to draw a bath.

Sitting on the side of the tub, listening to the water run, Hope let her mind drift in tune with the flow of the warming bath water.

Her thoughts meandered back to that cryptic letter. What conundrum did she have? Nothing was puzzling her, except the Ides of March mystery.

She turned off the water, exited the bathroom, and picked up the letter on the desk. Scanning it a second time, she wondered if, against all odds, some unknown ally was attempting to come to her aid.

Looking at her watch, Hope noted it was eleven forty-four. Putting the letter back down, she walked to the floor-to-ceiling window overlooking downtown Columbus. As in every other city they'd visited, she could see the flames of burning buildings in the distance—the detritus of Columbus's Armstrong-fueled riot.

Grabbing her coat, Hope exited her room. This all had to cease, and if there was the faintest of possibilities that someone possessed the key to the Ides of March riddle and thus a way to stop Armstrong, she had to investigate.

◆ ◆ ◆

The third level of the parking garage was half full and smelled of exhaust and dirty motor oil. Overhead lighting glowed with the flare of LED bulbs in some areas, contrasting in a random pattern with pitch-dark rows of cars under burned-out lamps.

Hope took tentative steps towards the north end,

footfalls echoing in the mammoth concrete and steel structure punctuated by the occasional distant slam of a car door and the rev of an engine on other floors. Scanning her surroundings, she saw no one on her level.

As she approached a pillar shrouded in shadows, she thought she saw something move in the murkiness ahead.

Stopping, Hope called, "Hello? Is anyone there?"

"Over here," a hoarsely whispered voice called from behind her.

Hope wheeled around. Standing in gloominess between two cars was a figure. It took a step. Hope could make out the shape of a man, medium build in a tattered trench coat, hands in pockets. He had a beard and unruly hair.

He moved from between the cars. It was him!

"Agee," whispered Hope.

He grinned, and the familiar grimy, red-bearded face brightened a bit.

"As always, it's good to see you, Dr. Allerd."

"I should call the police."

"Don't bother. By the time they arrive, I'll be long gone. Besides,"—he scanned the area— "the reception here is spotty at best."

"What do you want?"

He took a step forward. Hope reacted by backing up.

"Don't worry," he said. "I shan't harm you."

"Oh, really, like that time in Dr. Hyde's home?" Hope referred to the confrontation she had with Agee several months back on discovering he was a serial murderer and tricking him into confessing his malfeasance.

"Secretly recording my confession. That was well played.

I've been a fugitive ever since." He stroked his beard. "Hence, my continued use of the disguise."

"You were at Father Mazur's church with those homeless people the other night. Why?"

"Part of my disguise. Also, I wanted to see how you were doing."

"Why?"

"Hope, twelve million dollars is a lot of money. There are people who want to see you, your brother, and your fiancé dead because of your theft of EQV's funds. Particularly your brother. His computer hacking is, to say the least, galling."

"It couldn't be helped. He did it to save my life."

"Now, now, Hope. 'Thou shalt not steal.'"

"And 'thou shalt not kill.'"

"Touché. But, like your theft, I committed those murders for a just cause."

"Oh, really? Whose life were you trying to save?"

"Not life, lives. Tens of thousands of lives."

"What are you talking about?"

"I can protect you, your brother, and your fiancé for just so long. Eventually, EQV will want their pound of flesh. Unless...."

"Unless what?"

The enigmatic grin was back.

"What are you talking about?" asked Hope.

"You're a smart woman, Dr. Allerd. But, as they say, you're 'barking up the wrong tree.'"

"I don't understand."

"Ides of March," said the priest.

"Yeah? Wait, how do you know about that?"

"I'm here to help you. There's not much time. Get it right, and maybe things will go well for you and your compatriots."

"Get what, right?"

"Ides of March. It's not a date, but it points to what you seek."

"I don't understand."

"Hope, 'they frameth mischief by a law.'"

A tire screeched. Agee turned.

An engine roared. The priest bolted for the exit door on the far wall.

Blinded by approaching headlights, Hope shielded her eyes and ducked into the shadows.

A muffled *pop, pop* erupted, then footsteps, followed by a door slamming shut.

Hope gazed from the cover of a sedan's hood in time to see the rear brake lights of a dark SUV disappear around the corner and down the exit ramp.

She emerged from behind the car and called, "Father Agee." Her voice echoed in the canyon-like enclosure. He was nowhere to be seen.

She walked over to the exit door he had sprinted to, intending to go through and take the stairs in search of Agee. But she was stopped short by something on the concrete floor a few feet from the door.

She squatted and examined the surface using her cell phone's LED light.

Fresh blood sat in a circular puddle on the concrete floor. Drops of blood led from the dark red pool towards a spot where that SUV had likely stopped.

Hope stood and exited the garage. It was no use in searching any further.

She knew that Agee was now dead—his lifeless body inside that black SUV.

Descending the adjacent stairs to the street, she hoped to glimpse the SUV's rear license tag. But the vehicle was long gone. She pulled her coat collar tighter around her neck against a building wind and pondered Agee's final words: "... they frameth mischief by a law."

CHAPTER 38

Hope picked up a morning newspaper from the Columbus hotel's front desk as she walked through the lobby to board the bus bound for their last stop. The headline blared a sickening: "Riots Continue Throughout Country." Front-page articles detailed the carnage not only in Columbus but throughout the nation.

America continued to burn as Armstrong espoused an ever-increasing rhetoric of revenge and destruction targeted at President Cochrane. For Hope, it was becoming intolerable to see city after city set ablaze by his expressed dystopian viewpoint of the country.

◆ ◆ ◆

The tape holding the tiny microphone to his chest itched as Clive crossed the street in front of the Oliva Restaurant. He scanned the area for police. None could be seen, at least none he'd recognize as law enforcement officers.

He pulled his coat collar around his neck against the dropping temperature and waited. Petrov promised he'd meet him in front of the restaurant. Clive checked his watch. It was nine fifty-five.

Fifteen minutes later, Clive saw the fat Russian approach. In a black wool coat and fur hat, Petrov waddled up to the reporter and asked, "Been waiting long?"

Clive shook his head. "Let's go in," he said, extending his

hand.

Inside, Clive gave his name to the maitre d' who escorted them to a table in a quiet corner of the half-full establishment. Men and women sitting at tables and the bar filled the room with a buzz of conversations over a local band on stage playing Moldavian folk songs.

Petrov took the seat against the wall, allowing him a view of the entire restaurant. He'd refused to check his coat and hat and draped his coat over his chair.

A waiter brought them menus. To Clive, he seemed to let his eyes linger a bit too long over Petrov.

Scanning his menu, Petrov asked, "I take it you've eaten here before. What is good?"

Clive shrugged. "Try the sarmale."

"OK, I try. Now, tell me, what is so important that I must see great reporter at this hour?"

"I'm only in Moldova for a short time, and it occurred to me that I've never done an in-depth story on you."

"And you never will."

"I know what you're thinking. But hear me out."

Petrov's eyes narrowed. "OK."

"I'd like to do a story on you as an anonymous arms dealer. No names, nothing that would identify you, and from the perspective of the good you do."

"Good I do?"

"Yes. What about all of the freedom fighters you help equip? Without you, oppressed people all over the world would continue to suffer untold hardship under brutal regimes. Your arms help free these people, giving them a better life. You are a saint to freedom-loving people all over this planet, and your story needs to be told."

Petrov's thick lips widened a bit. "You think so?"

"I know so. I just want to tell your side of the story. The story of a man who provides a badly needed service to the world. A service that aids downtrodden people everywhere."

"And you will not use my name?"

"I'll make sure no one can identify you. And, of course, you'll have the right to disapprove any part of the story you don't like."

Petrov was quiet for a moment. "All right. I do it."

As Clive removed a pen and notepad from his inside jacket pocket, the waiter came to take their orders. This time, he seemed to glare at Clive just before leaving with their orders.

Petrov looked from the egressing waiter to Clive. "You know him?"

"Er, no." Clive began to feel the first fruits of anxiety well up from within. Despite the police being in the restaurant, Clive knew that the arms dealer was a man to be feared and, based on Donici's description, would not hesitate to slit his abdomen at the slightest provocation right where they sat.

Looking around, the Russian said, "Strange."

Clive looked behind him at what appeared to be regular activity in the restaurant and asked, "How so?"

"No children. This is family establishment. But no children."

Beads of sweat formed on Clive's forehead. "Er, well, it's late. They're likely all abed."

The Russian huffed. "Another thing."

Clive wondered if he should speak the safe sentence and

get out of there.

"Funny, but everyone looks to be same age."

Clive turned around again. He had to admit the place was populated with what appeared to be twenty- and thirty-something fit adults—the correct age and build for police officers. Donici didn't think this through.

As Clive turned back around, Petrov was out of his chair. "Very strange here. I leave."

The sign Donici mentioned, thought Clive. *If he takes his coat, I'm a dead man.*

"Something very wrong."

"No. No. Wait," said Clive, raising his hands to calm the arms dealer. "Er, er...."

"Yes?" Petrov took his coat from the chair back.

That was it. Clive's gut tightened, awaiting the penetration of cold steel.

He tried to say the safe phrase, but memory failed him.

The Russian, coat over his forearm, took a step toward Clive.

Petrov stirred like the angel of death. Clive, life flashing before him, shut his eyes against the approaching doom.

Then...a final chance?

◆ ◆ ◆

"Er, I forgot," said Clive in an excited voice. "When I made the reservations, the maitre d' said that a company had rented out the restaurant for a private party but that he would allow us in."

"What company?"

"Some, some software company. I don't recall the name."

Petrov scanned the room again and nodded. "Computer geniuses all young and rich." He returned his coat to the chair back and sat down.

Relieved, Clive opened his notepad and said, "Shall we begin?"

For the next ten minutes, Petrov talked about his start in dealing arms. He related how, as a soldier in the Russian army stationed in Chechnya, he stumbled across a cache of AK-47s. Strapped for cash, he stole the weapons, traveled to Africa, and sold them to some rebels. Somewhere during the story, the waiter brought them their meals along with a bottle of wine. Petrov had insisted on wine.

Clive began to relax as he asked guiding questions, and Petrov answered them with some embellishments. As the wine flowed and the savory food enticed their palates, the reporter realized that Petrov seemed to unwind more with every answer.

It was time, decided Clive. He went for the jugular, as it were. "When you make your sales, I suppose you provide some sort of demonstration of your product," he said in an effort to guide Petrov into that needed admission.

"I let them take samples if they want. Discharge rounds. Fire RPG into passing automobile. Shoot down plane with Stinger even."

Red-faced and grinning, Petrov was now ripe for the critical question.

"Yes," said Clive. "How did you demonstrate that weapon we discussed a few weeks ago?"

"Ides of March thing?"

"Yes."

Petrov drained his glass of wine and poured another from the third bottle on the table. "I had Sergei gather women. Waifs, orphans, prostitutes. They would not be missed. Put them in barn. Released the weapon. Let us say only I and buyer left barn."

Chilled by the admission, Clive dropped his pen. Resisting the urge to turn around or bound from his chair, he leaned back, taking in the egregiousness of Petrov's statement.

"What is wrong?" asked Petrov.

With a calm like the air before a tornado, Clive gazed out of a window to his left and said, "I think it will snow tomorrow."

"What?" said Petrov, looking behind him for a moment.

The waiter appeared. He looked incensed. "Mr. Andrew?" he said.

Startled, Clive looked up. "Yes?"

"You must come with me immediately."

"What? Why?"

"You were here last week and paid with counterfeit bills. The manager remembers you and wants to see you. Now!"

Petrov guffawed. "Andrew, you didn't pay your bill?" He turned to the waiter. "How much? I will pay it."

"Now, Mr. Andrew," shouted the waiter. Heads turned toward their table as Clive rose and hurried away with the waiter behind the bar and through a door.

After that, everything was a blur to Clive. He recalled congratulatory handshakes from policemen and women in the backroom. He was able to peek through the door behind the bar in time to see four burly officers escorting Petrov, who cursed and vowed to dismember Clive, out of the restaurant in handcuffs.

At some point, Donici appeared and said, "Thanks to you, we got him."

Then it happened. Clive began to shake uncontrollably. He didn't feel composed until his flight reached its overwater leg back to the States.

The fight attendant brought him a scotch on the rocks. He sipped the malty-flavored drink in celebration. Not only had he brought that arms dealer Petrov to justice, but he'd secured a lead on the weapon's buyer.

He now just had to return to Washington, D.C., and identify this "John Wayne" before he unleashed hell on America.

CHAPTER 39

Jack rolled to his hotel room door to answer after the third knock. He opened the door the length of its security chain and saw Clive standing in the corridor.

"Where have you been?" asked Jack after disengaging the chain and opening the door wider.

Clive stepped in. "Eastern Europe. Is Hope back?"

"No. She's still on that speaking tour with Armstrong. Should be back tomorrow."

Clive closed his eyes and shook his head.

"Dude," said Jack, "you've got some explaining to do."

"What do you mean?"

"Hope knows you spent the night with that Marta woman."

"It was late. I couldn't get a taxi, and nothing happened. I slept in her guest room. I swear."

Jack scowled and pounded his fists against his chair's armrests. "I'm not the one you have to convince. Of course, if I could get out of this chair, I'd beat the stuffing out of you."

Clive sat in the room's desk chair and buried his face in his hands. "Jack, I've never lied to you, and I'm not lying now. The day after Christmas, I took a flight to Moldova."

"Moldova? What for?"

"I was trying to find out who bought the carfentanil from

that arms dealer Petrov. A priest I know, Father Mazur, received a tip from a colleague in Moldova. He put me onto a Sergei Bukin, one of Petrov's flunkies. He said Petrov told him the buyer looked like that American movie star, John Wayne."

"Not much to go on."

"But it's a start. Petrov had Bukin kidnap several young women to use in a demonstration of the carfentanil's potency in an aerosolized form. I found their remains. I couldn't leave things like that, so I helped the Moldavian police arrest Petrov and Bukin for murder."

"Good for you. So, how do we catch this John Wayne guy?" asked Jack.

Clive shrugged. "How would you deploy aerosolized carfentanil?"

Jack sat quietly for a moment. "Maybe in the HVAC system?"

"Perhaps a new HVAC company would—"

"I'm on it," said Jack, wheeling over to his laptop. He began clacking away on the keyboard. Twenty minutes later, he said, "OK, three new HVAC companies applied for business licenses in the D.C. area over the last six months. I went over their records. Two contracted with auto body shops to paint their new trucks. One didn't. Blue Skies HVAC."

"What does that mean?" asked Clive.

"The one that didn't have a truck painted looks suspicious."

"I suppose checking who the companies serviced might help."

Jack hacked further into the records. "Looks like the first two did routine stuff. Residences, some commercial buildings, but nothing at any sensitive locations. Got nothing for the third one."

"Got an address for Blue Skies HVAC?"

"Yeah," said Jack. He hit some keys, and an address appeared on the screen. Clive removed his notebook and pen from his jacket pocket and wrote it down. "Might be worth paying them a visit."

Jack nodded and continued to clack away. "Hello," he said, "Take a look at this."

On-screen was a newspaper article about an unsolved murder of the owner of an auto body and paint shop. Clive began to read it. "Do you think that third HVAC company and this auto body shop are somehow related?"

Jack shrugged. "Could be. Maybe they did work on the truck off the books."

"It's a bit of a long shot, but I'll check it out." Clive recorded the address. He returned his notebook to his jacket pocket and started for the door.

"Where're you going?" asked Jack.

"Might as well go to both places. I'll stop at the auto body shop first."

"Be careful," said Jack with a wry grin. "If that Blue Skies is involved, John Wayne may be inclined to shoot first and ask questions later."

◆ ◆ ◆

Clive parked his rental in front of Ralph's Paint and Body Shop and exited. He walked into the open garage area and was immediately assailed by the acrid odor of spray paint, the whine of pneumatic drills, hammering, and the occasional ringing of a phone. A half dozen cars were being serviced on the floor. Two were on hydraulic jacks.

"Can I help you?" shouted a middle-aged man in a dark green oil-stained uniform sitting on a stool behind a tall wooden desk.

"Yes," said Clive. I was wondering if you could give me some information about the murder that occurred here."

"You a cop?"

"No. A reporter."

"We already had reporters crawling around here up to our eyeballs. Don't need anymore." His desk phone rang. He picked up the receiver. "Ralph's Paint and Body Shop. How can I help you?" There was a pause, then he pressed a button on the console and spoke into the receiver, "Tommy, line three." His words were picked up over a loudspeaker. Turning back to Clive, he said, "You still here?"

"Look, I don't mean to be a burden, but it's vitally important that I ask just a few questions."

The guy at the desk frowned, his bushy eyebrows coming together like two caterpillars kissing. "OK, one question."

"The owner, Ralph Marone, was shot and killed. The police don't have a lead."

"Yeah, so?"

"I think he may have been doing a paint job, er, off the books as they say, for a man that looks like the actor John Wayne."

"OK. I don't know anything about that, but it sounds like you need to talk to the police."

"I know, and I will, but the paint job was for a Blue Skies HVAC company van. Would anyone recall seeing such a vehicle?"

The guy shook his head, then picked up the phone and dialed a single number. "Hey, send Kurt up here," he said into the receiver.

Two minutes later, a short man with thick curly hair in white coveralls and a spray-painting respirator around his neck walked up.

"Hey, Kurt," said the man at the desk, "you were working late the night the boss was killed, right?"

"Yeah, so what?" said Kurt.

"Well, this reporter here wants to ask you a question."

"Hello Kurt, my name is Clive Andrew. On the evening of Ralph Marone's murder, did you see a van with a new paint job from Blue Skies HVAC? Or maybe a client who looked like the actor John Wayne?"

Kurt dropped his head. "Er, Mr. Marone said not to say anything."

The desk guy glared at Kurt. "Hey, Ralph's dead. He sure ain't gonna fire you."

"OK, OK. I was leaving when I saw Mr. Marone pullin' a tarp off this van over in the corner. Had a new paint job. I think it did have lettering that said, 'Blue Skies.' Mr. Marone saw me and told me not to say anything about it, so I left. On my way out, I saw this tall guy coming in. And yeah, he kinda looked like John Wayne."

Clive nodded and said, "Thank you, Kurt."

Armed with this new information, he put the address of Blue Skies HVAC into his phone's GPS and drove into evening D.C. traffic.

Thirty minutes later, he found himself in a familiar area. It was the warehouse district where he and Hope had witnessed Armstrong's initiation by EQV. The address took him to a garage sandwiched between two large warehouses. It was dark and looked abandoned.

Clive parked on the street and got out. Using his phone's LED light, he looked into a window. Sitting alone in the rubble-strewn space was the van: The side was painted with a sunrise scene and the logo, 'Blue Skies HVAC.'

He tried a side door with a half window—it was locked. Looking around, Clive saw no one in the murky street. Taking a deep breath, he removed his jacket and wrapped it around his hand and forearm. He slammed his covered fist against the door's half window, shattering the glass. Reaching in, he disengaged the handle's lock and opened the door.

Inside now, Clive walked over the concrete floor to the van, crunching bits of broken glass and debris under his shoes. He tried the driver's door. It was unlocked. Looking inside, he noticed something in the rear. It was an irregular shape about six feet long, covered by a tarp. A foul stench wafted from the area.

He walked to the rear, opened the double doors, and stepped in beside the large object. Holding his breath, Clive pulled the tarp back.

Lying in a pool of dried blood was the nude, bloated body of a black man. He snapped a photo of the face and then raced out of the garage.

Slammed with a surge of nausea, he sat sideways, facing the open door of his rental car, head in hand. Finally, Clive vomited onto the street before driving off.

◆ ◆ ◆

"Geez, Clive," said Jack, looking at the photo the reporter had taken of the dead man, "how am I supposed to use facial rec on this? The guy's bloated like a balloon."

Still feeling queasy, Clive paced back and forth in Jack's room. "I don't know. Maybe use your computer magic to morph the face back to its original shape."

Jack glared at the reporter. "Yeah, right. I'll just snap my fingers and…."

"What is it?" asked Clive.

"Maybe there is a way. I've got some software that can change the face in a photo. Maybe I could alter the swelling to get the guy's original face and run it through the FBI's facial rec software. Anyway, it's worth a shot."

Clive stopped pacing. "And maybe we should call the police."

"Yeah, right. And risk EQV finding out, tracking us down, and putting two bullets apiece in our heads. No thanks."

"But the police should know about the body."

"Alright, alright. I'll create a false email address and location. Maybe some twenty-something guy from, let's say, Maryland, and send an email to the D.C. police."

"Thanks, Jack. Now we know the who and how of this impending crime."

"Yeah," said Jack, "but we still need the when and where."

CHAPTER 40

On arrival in Detroit, the final city on the tour, Hope had had enough. In her hotel room overlooking the downtown area, she paced. She had to put an end to this. Wishing she'd now pulled the trigger of the gun she'd held several days ago while Armstrong slept to end all of this chaos and decimation, Hope formulated a plan. It was tenuous at best, but it was all she had at her disposal.

As the rally started, she took her seat on stage and glanced at Armstrong. He looked straight ahead as if he could neither see nor hear.

Hope took a deep breath and said, "I'm not going to let you start another riot. It all has to stop now."

Armstrong maintained his statue-like posture.

Thinking he didn't hear her, she repeated, "I'm not going to let you start another riot."

As the professional MC, a beanpole of a man with salt and pepper hair and a velvety smooth voice, brought in to cover for Lattimore, started his spiel, Armstrong slowly turned to Hope and, in a chilling voice, said, "You can't stop me. No one can."

When it came to her turn to speak, Hope presented the usual dispassionate discussion of her role in the pandemic. But, as she concluded, she began to adlib a postscript—her plan.

Looking over the raucous audience, she smiled and said, "Everyone here is important, just like everyone outside this arena. We are all Americans. We live in a unique nation where we elect our leaders. And if we don't like what they do, we vote them out of office. There are countries where that doesn't happen. Countries where strongmen rule with iron fists, jailing or murdering the opposition. Countries where ordinary citizens are mere pawns in some epic drama of power and authority. Where people like you and I are trampled upon and disposed of like so much excess cloth in a seamstress shop. We cannot let this happen to our country. And that is why we can no longer listen to this man!" Hope pointed to Armstrong.

A murmur erupted throughout the audience, growing into a crescendo of shouts and boos.

"And I beg you," continued Hope, "Don't listen to him. Treat your fellow American with kindness and dignity. Leave this place with charity in your hearts and—"

Hope felt an iron-hard grip around her waist and a bear claw of a hand over her mouth. She was yanked unceremoniously from the stage by two powerfully built assistants.

Held fast just off stage, Hope watched the MC return and discredit everything she'd just said by claiming she had been drinking. He then asked, "Are you ready for the man of the hour?"

The audience began to yell and cheer.

"Without further adieu, I present your next leader, General Benjamin Armstrong."

Armstrong arose from his chair and took the podium. He spoke for an hour, spouting what could only be described as verbal dynamite, whipping the audience into a frenzy of hatred and retribution.

At the conclusion of his speech, he shouted, "Follow me, follow me as we take back America from Conchrane and her ilk."

What happened next was beyond astonishing. Armstrong bound down from the stage and into the audience. Beckoning, he continued to shout, "Follow me!" as he charged toward the arena's entrance. The fevered crowd, roaring with fists in the air, followed like minions.

"Let me go," yelled Hope, still in the clutches of the blue-jacketed assistants. The MC, now standing off stage, nodded, and they let her go.

Turning to the MC, Hope asked, "Why did you stop me?"

The angular man just smiled. "It's too late."

Hope dashed for the entrance behind the exiting crowd. As she ran into the snow-covered streets, she witnessed Armstrong kicking down a police barrier separating protestors across the boulevard from the arena. He turned to the following crowd and yelled, "Follow me and take back your Country! The tree of liberty must be refreshed with the blood of tyrants!"

His followers surged forward, trampling the police line despite them swinging their batons. They collided with the sign-holding protestors like a tsunami hammering a coastal town. The melee surged. It was a running battle for three blocks. And at the center, Armstrong kicked and punched his way along the thoroughfare.

Hope burst into the crowd of supporters attempting to get to Armstrong. She shoved her way to the middle and, seeing Armstrong ten feet ahead, rushed to his side.

Grabbing his jacket lapels, she shouted, "You've got to stop this! People are going to die!"

"Isn't it wonderful?" he yelled above the roar.

"Stop it. Stop it now!"

Armstrong's face suddenly hardened. In a flash, he drew back his fist and swung, striking Hope's cheek.

She reeled from the blow, released his jacket, and staggered backward. Her cheek throbbed, and her head spun as consciousness ebbed.

The last thing she recalled was grabbing a rotund bearded man's arm before dropping to the pavement.

◆ ◆ ◆

The throbbing pain in her swollen cheek gradually changed into a frozen numbness from the bag of ice she held against her face. Hope sat in the rear seat of Big Reggie's Escalade as they motored through the early morning gloom out of downtown Detroit.

She'd awakened in the street at the rear of the riot that had moved through downtown Detroit, leaving brutalized and dying protestors and burning storefronts and cars in its wake. Her head had throbbed as she shuffled away from the fracas to sit on a quiet curb. She'd called Tina asking for a ride. When Big Reggie's massive SUV arrived, Hope told them she'd had enough of the tour and wanted to return to D.C. After a brief stop at her hotel room to pack, they drove out of the city.

As they motored their way along Interstate 75, Big Reggie said, "Miss Hope, how you doin' back there?"

"I'll survive."

"Ain't no man should be hittin' no woman," said Big Reggie. "I swear, insubordinate or not, for two cents, I will kick Armstrong's narrow ass for you."

CHAPTER 41

After being dropped off at her hotel in Washington, D.C., Hope entered the lobby and took the elevator to her room, happy that she'd not officially checked out. Exhausted, she lay on the bed after calling Jack to tell him she was back.

Moments later, someone knocked on the door.

Hope, with narrowed eyes and a scowl, arose and opened the door. Standing in the hallway was her fiancé, Clive. He gazed at her with that lost puppy dog look—the expression he always had when he'd done something he knew had angered Hope.

"Well?" said Hope.

"Well, what?" Clive looked truly surprised by her attitude.

"Jack told me. You spent Christmas night with Marta."

"Oh, uh, nothing happened."

"Right." Hope crossed her arms over her chest.

"It was late. Marta said it would be impossible to get a cab at that time of night and suggested I stay over. I slept in the guest room. Alone."

"And you expect me to believe that?"

"It's the truth. I left early the next morning."

"Sure."

"If you don't believe me, you can ask Marta."

"Right. Like she'd say you two slept together."

"I'm sorry, Hope, but I had to go. I had to see Sophie. I thought you'd understand that."

Hope began to pace, anger burning like a flare.

"I hadn't seen my daughter in over a year. And the way this investigation of ours is going, I don't know when I'll get to see her again."

Hope stopped her pacing to stand face-to-face with Clive. Glaring up at his face, her nose nearly touching his chin, she said, "Why are you always doing things to gall me? Every time I need you around, you disappear or do something to rip us apart. I swear, Clive, it's like sometimes you plan to piss me off."

"What was I supposed to do?"

"I don't know. Maybe take your daughter out to dinner or out Christmas shopping. Maybe meet them at some neutral site. Anything but spend the night with your old girlfriend." Hope turned on her heels and stepped deeper into the room.

"Wait," said Clive. "Don't you want to know where I've been?"

She strode up to the threshold and grasped the door handle. "Do you really think I give a damn right now?"

"But I have a lead on the guy who bought the carfentanil."

"Talk to Jack." She slammed the door.

◆ ◆ ◆

Hope fought back tears as she walked to the window overlooking the evening streets some ten stories below. Cars, trucks, and buses inched along, painting the blacktop in streaks of red and white.

Clive was an idiot. There was no debating that point.

Yet....

Hope didn't want to think about their argument anymore. She turned to the television and pressed the remote to turn it on. *Find some dull news program,* she thought, *take your mind off your relationship or, as it looks at the present, the remnants of the relationship.*

She sat on the bed and channel-surfed, finally deciding on some news magazine program called *Democracy in Action*. The two talking heads droned on about some fine points in federal law. Enough to make her eyes want to glaze over.

Hope noticed one thing that stood out as she listened to the boring discussion. The moderator would ask a question, and the guest would respond most of the time by citing some statute in the U.S. Code. It went something like this:

"Now you say..."

"Yes, as I stated before, if you look at Ten U.S. Code twenty-seven, you'll notice..."

It was always a number followed by "U.S. Code," then another number.

Bored out of her mind, Hope began to mock the broadcast in an exaggerated attempt to imitate the guest's New England accent. She shouted random numbers at the TV: "Seven, U.S. Code eighty-nine. Six, U.S. Code twenty-two. Three U.S. Code fifteen."

Wait a sec, thought Hope. *Three U.S. Code fifteen. Three fifteen. Could it be that easy?* She hit the remote to silence the TV.

In that late-night parking garage encounter with Father Agee, he'd said the Ides of March was not a date but pointed to "what you seek." Then he said something else.

She pulled her laptop from its case and opened it on the desk. Sitting, she Googled his exact quote: "...they frameth mischief by a law." The result was Psalms 94:20: "Shall the throne of iniquity have fellowship with thee, which frameth mischief by a law?"

Was that it? she wondered. *Was Armstrong's Ides of March mantra a law that pointed to a date? A date that would mark the end of the United States as we know it?*

With trembling hands, she entered "three U.S. Code fifteen" in the Google search bar.

She read the statute:

Congress shall be in session on the sixth day of January succeeding every meeting of the electors. The Senate and House of Representatives shall meet in the Hall of the House of Representatives at the hour of 1 o'clock in the afternoon on that day, and the President of the Senate shall be their presiding officer.

There it was, the date, time, and location of the act that would kill hundreds of people and bring down the United States of America.

On wobbly legs, Hope arose. She had to tell Jack, Tina, Big Reggie, and, yes, even Clive. They had only one day to stop the most significant insurrection against the United States since the Civil War.

Hope heard a wood-on-wood sliding sound behind her as she approached the room door. It was the opening of her room closet. Startled, she whirled around.

Standing just inside the open closet with a sardonic grin on his face was...

"Lattimore!" breathed Hope.

CHAPTER 42

The talk show host brandished a small semiautomatic pistol. He stepped out of the closet and scanned Hope's computer screen. "So, you figured it out," he said.

"What are you doing here?" she demanded.

"I'm here to stop you from making a big mistake."

"The only mistake is you and Armstrong trying to take over the country."

"You actually don't get it."

"Get what?"

"We're not trying to take over the country; we're trying to save it. From people like Conchrane, like you. Like all the bleeding hearts out there. People too stupid to see what's happening. It's all slipping away, Hope. Slipping away right before your eyes. My instincts were right from the beginning. You're not on our side. You were never on our side. Who put you up to infiltrating our crusade? Was it Conchrane?"

"Nobody put me up to anything."

"Well, too bad you won't see the glorious new government we are going to institute. A splendid new America that will last ten thousand years."

Glancing at the gun in Lattimore's hand, Hope asked, "What are you going to do? Shoot me?"

"If you don't do exactly as I say, yes, I will shoot you. Get your coat. We're going for a ride."

Careful to keep the pistol trained on Hope by switching it from hand to hand, Lattimore removed his coat and slid it over his arm to cover the weapon.

When Hope had her coat on, he said, "Let's go."

Now, in the corridor, they walked toward the elevator. Hope was in front, and Lattimore was just behind her with the coat-draped pistol pressed against her back.

"Press 'down'," said Lattimore when they arrived at the bank of elevators.

Hope complied.

While waiting, both looked up at the display indicating the floor locations of each car.

There was a ding, and the elevator doors opened. Lattimore gently shoved Hope into the car, which was half filled with patrons staring up at the floor indicator.

Just as Lattimore leaned against her to push the "Lobby" button, the doors closed, and Hope could have sworn she heard someone call her name.

◆ ◆ ◆

Clive, overcome with guilt and angst, paced in his room. *How could I have let this happen?* he agonized as he played the conversation with Hope in his head.

No, he thought, *it won't end this way. We are destined to be together for all time. I must fight for her. I must get her back.*

Clive darted from his room. As he raced down the corridor, he spied a bizarre occurrence maybe twenty-five yards ahead. A man and woman marched in a stilted lockstep, she in front and him behind; he held a coat over his arm that seemed pressed against her back.

As Clive arrived at Hope's room and began knocking, he noticed they were at the elevator. It was then he realized the woman was Hope.

Sprinting toward the open elevator, Clive yelled, "Hope!" just as they entered the car and the door closed.

He got to the elevator and pressed the "Down" button repeatedly. The car made its way to the lower floors. *Lobby*, he thought, and bolted for the exit door next to the bank of elevators.

Clive took the stairs, descending floor by floor in a mad dash, hoping to catch them before they could exit the hotel and disappear in the early evening foot traffic.

Winded, he opened the exit door onto a lobby packed with hotel patrons checking in and checking out. Starting at the bank of elevators to his left, he scanned the crowd, looking for Hope and the man with the coat over his arm. It was impossible. He'd never find them in this horde.

Then it hit him. What if they didn't stop in the lobby? He ducked back into the stairwell and bound up to the second floor and the hotel's parking deck entrance.

◆ ◆ ◆

"You won't get away with this," said Hope as she marched ahead of Lattimore through the cavernous parking deck. Lighting was spotty at best, and he seemed to guide her along a shadowy path of extinguished overhead bulbs.

They stopped at the rear of a cream-colored sedan. Lattimore pressed his remote, opening the trunk.

Hope looked down at the spacious compartment. She knew the rule: never let a kidnapper put you in the trunk. She then turned to Lattimore.

"Get in," he said.

Hope shook her head and then scoured the garage from where she stood, praying another soul was exiting their car. To her chagrin, the space looked bereft of other people.

"Scream, and I will kill you right here. Now get into the trunk." Lattimore shoved the pistol's barrel into her back for emphasis.

A car door slammed. Hope turned to the sound.

Before she could open her mouth, a sharp metallic blow struck the back of her head.

Knees buckled, and consciousness teetered as she tumbled face-first into the trunk.

◆ ◆ ◆

Unbelievable, thought Clive as he witnessed what looked like a body collapse into the trunk of an off-white sedan in a murky section of the parking garage. A man slammed the trunk lid shut, got in, started the engine, and took off, tires squealing along the concrete ramp.

It had to be Hope. He sprinted after the vehicle, red brake lights extinguishing as it accelerated toward the downward turn.

Too exhausted to run further, Clive did the only other thing he could think of. Removing his cell phone from his inside jacket pocket, he snapped a photo of the rear of the escaping sedan.

Standing in the center of the ramp, he prayed his hand hadn't shaken when he hit the "photo" icon button. Bringing up the picture and expanding it with two fingers, he saw it, blurry but readable.

Finding a section of the garage that allowed a signal, Clive punched in Jack's number.

"Hey, Clive, what's up?" said Jack.

"It's Hope. She's been kidnapped."

"What?" screamed Jack. Terror laced his voice.

"She's in the trunk of an off-white late-model sedan. I'm sending you a photo of the rear. Can you use the car's GPS or something to track it?"

Clive heard the clacking of computer keys. "I'm…I'm on it," stammered Jack.

Clive found his rental in the garage and started the engine. He drove out of the enclosure into early evening traffic, praying Jack would lead him to Hope before her abductor could do something unspeakable.

CHAPTER 43

Clive drove, bumper to bumper, through rush hour traffic. He could not see the off-white sedan with Hope in the trunk. His chest ached as he imagined what could happen to her if he didn't catch up with the fleeing car.

He called Jack on his burner phone.

"OK, I've got his tracker," said Jack. "He's on Interstate 66. Just get on, and I'll tell you when he takes an exit."

"Thanks, Jack."

Clive drove onto the interstate as the sun began to set. He lowered the visor against the glare of dying daylight. Traffic began to flow smoother. But still no sign of the sedan.

You'll just have to trust Jack and his technology, old boy, he thought.

A little over half an hour later, he got a call from Jack. The sedan had taken a series of turns, bringing it onto State Route 48. Clive followed Jack's instructions to get him onto the same road just as night fell.

Another hour brought him across the state line from Virginia to West Virginia.

Twenty minutes later, Jack called again.

"Looks like he's taken a right onto a service road."

"Service road?" said Clive.

"Yeah. It's a two-lane road just parallel to Route 48."

"But I don't see any signs."

"Trust me, Clive. I've got your tracker on my computer, also. I'll tell you when to turn. He's about two miles ahead of you."

Clive made the turn onto a two-lane blacktop and slowed his speed. Tall oaks and pine trees grew on either side, and further back were dense woodlands. He still didn't see the sedan.

Five miles into the forested area, Jack called again.

"OK, he made a left turn onto what might be a dirt road and has stopped. Slow down, and I'll tell you when to turn."

"Right, Jack." Clive cut his speed, thankful that no other cars were on this stretch of road.

"OK, now," said Jack.

Clive scoured the evening twilight to his left for a break in the trees. Seeing the gap, he turned onto a dirt road. Proceeding at a crawl along the winding narrow path, he felt that gut-crunching sensation again.

What if, he thought, *they have cameras out here?* He cut the lights, pulled over onto a grassy patch behind an oak, and proceeded on foot.

He called Jack.

"I'm going on foot," he said.

"OK, the sedan is about a hundred yards from your car. Be careful."

Using the trees as cover, Clive stepped along a zigzag path until he came upon a massive two-story log cabin with a wraparound porch in a clearing. The lights were on inside, and the off-white sedan sat in front.

Walking in a crouch, he sidled up to the car's rear and

checked the tag. It was the one. He rapped on the trunk and whispered, "Hope, you in there?"

Receiving no answer, he surveyed the property. There were security cameras at both corners of the facade, and his route to the car looked to be a blind spot.

Clive decided to return to the woods the way he came. He then walked a semicircular trek to the rear of the cabin, staying hidden by the trees and foliage.

There was a deck in the rear with a large glass double door. Lights were on inside, and he could see some of the interior. It was an open floor plan. A large mahogany dining table was just beyond the double doors, and a kitchen area lay just past the table.

Sitting in one of the straight-back dining chairs at the table was someone who appeared to be bound and gagged. It was Hope!

Clive took a few steps to his left and, peering through windows beside the door, noticed two men sitting on brown leather chairs in a living room area.

It would be two against one if he tried to enter now. *As long as Hope remains within sight, better to wait until one or both men retire and then break in*, he told himself.

Clive scoured the ground for a weapon. On finding a rock, he hefted in his left hand. Now, it was wait and watch.

◆ ◆ ◆

Lattimore leaned forward in the brown leather chair and grinned. "Just think," he said, "Tomorrow we will take back our country from those pansy liberals for good."

Brad Trett shifted in his chair and turned to look at their prisoner. Hope, still in the coat she'd put on at the hotel, with a gag in her mouth, sat tied to the dining chair. "What do we do with her?" he asked.

"Talked with the General. He wants her alive to interrogate when he arrives. She somehow found out about the Ides of March, and he wants to know if there was a leak somewhere."

Brad shook his head. "Hate to be the one who told her."

Lattimore chuckled.

Rising from his chair, Brad walked over to face Hope, who glared at the conspirator. He then sidled up to the rear doors and peered into the dark. He took in a deep breath and slowly exhaled. "You know, ever since I was in Eastern Europe to make that buy, I've had a bad feeling about this whole operation."

"What do you mean?" Lattimore arose from his chair.

"I don't know. Maybe it's just my conscious tugging at me. That SOB Russian arms dealer, Petrov, had these young, half-naked women chained in this barn for what he called a demonstration of the gas."

"Yeah, but they were foreigners. They don't count."

"One of them was American. She begged me to help her. And I didn't do a damned thing. Still have nightmares about that."

"Couldn't be helped. It was for the greater good."

"Yeah. Guess so." Brad walked back into the living room area.

"Look, Brad, when the General comes into power, he won't forget you. You can write your own ticket."

"Yeah, suppose so."

"Why don't you get some sleep? Tomorrow is going to be a busy day. A contingent of Unit-458 will bring her here by early afternoon."

"Who?"

"Conchrane, of course. They're gonna bring her entire cabinet here, also. You got that basement conference room ready?"

"Yeah. I spent the morning cleaning up. What's Armstrong going to do with them once they're here?"

"You don't want to know. Go get some rest, Brad. You've earned it." Lattimore sat at the head of the dining room table, removed his pistol from his pants pocket, and placed it on the tabletop.

Brad yawned. "I'll try. What about her?" He pointed to Hope.

"Don't worry. I'll stay up and watch our little prisoner here. As soon as the General arrives and finishes his interrogation of Hope Allerd, I'm sure she'll join Conchrane and the rest of them in hell."

CHAPTER 44

The interior lights went out in the cabin. Clive could still make out Hope's form in the chair from his location behind a tree. There seemed to be no activity inside. *The two men have likely gone to bed*, he surmised. He waited an hour.

Time to act. He picked up the rock and, moving in a crouch to avoid being picked up by the cameras, made his way onto the deck and to the rear door.

Just as he drew back to strike the glass door with the rock, the deck lit up like high noon. It was a motion-sensitive light.

Clive struck the door with the rock, shattering the glass into thousands of shards. A high-pitched wail slashed through the cool night air.

He reached inside, unlocked the door, opened it, and charged into the dining area. Hope, wide-eyed, looked in his direction.

As he reached her, Clive saw a form burst from the darkness holding a handgun.

Before he could get within arm's length, three shots rang out, shattering the glass of the other door, missing him by inches.

The man adjusted his aim, stepped closer, and pulled the trigger. Simultaneous with his action, Hope rocked her chair, slamming the chair back and her body into his chest. The round hit the ceiling just as they both tumbled to the floor.

The gun flew from the man's hand and clattered across the room. Clive dove for the weapon just as the man shoved Hope and the chair from his chest and groped for the gun.

Clive was faster. Picking up the small pistol, he yelled, "Get back!"

The man raised his hands and grinned. "You won't get away," he said.

Just then, another man appeared from around a corner, cloaked in shadows. Taller and aiming a shotgun, he shouted, "Drop it."

Clive squinted and quickly sifted his aim toward the new intruder. There was something familiar about him. Clive yelled out over the wail of the alarm, "John Wayne."

"What?" said the man holding the shotgun.

"You're the man who bought the carfentanil from Petrov," said Clive. "The man who watched as that sadistic arms dealer tortured and killed all those young women. Tell me, you son of a bitch, did you enjoy seeing them squirm and gasp for their final breath?"

The man's expression softened. He lowered the shotgun. For a second, Clive could swear he saw remorse in the man's eyes.

But just as quickly, his face hardened as he re-aimed the shotgun and pressed his finger against the trigger.

CHAPTER 45

A deafening *pop-pop-pop* reverberated through the air.

Clive had squeezed off three rounds into the man's chest before he could fire the shotgun. He dropped where he stood.

The smaller man, now trembling, shouted, "Please, don't shoot me."

"Untie her," commanded Clive.

He righted the chair, removed the gag in Hope's mouth, and untied the rope binding her to the chair back.

Hope bound from the chair. "Boy, am I glad to see you," she said. "What do we do with Lattimore here?"

"What's good for the goose—"

"—is good for the gander," said Hope, finishing Clive's sentence. She glared at Lattimore and kicked the chair toward him. "Sit down!"

She tied him to the chair back. As she was about to stuff the cloth gag into his mouth, the shock-jock said, "You won't get far."

"What are you talking about?" asked Hope.

Lattimore grinned again. "Before your friend broke in, I received a phone call. A contingent of Unit-458 should be arriving at any moment."

Hope grasped his jaw and jammed the rag into his mouth.

A stab of light suddenly pierced the front windows, followed by the purr of engines.

"We'd better go," said Clive.

They ran out onto the deck, down the stairs, and toward the safety of the night-cloaked woods.

At the tree line, Clive suddenly turned.

"What is it?" asked Hope.

"I should have taken the shotgun."

"Too late now. Let's go."

As they became engulfed by the foliage, Clive developed a sinking feeling.

He was confident that, before the night ended, they'd regret not taking that shotgun.

◆ ◆ ◆

After trekking about a hundred yards, Hope turned to Clive. "Just where are we going?" she asked.

"Away from that cabin."

"Yeah, but shouldn't we try calling Jack or Tina?"

Clive stopped, pulled his burner phone from his pocket, and raised it above his head. Looking at the display, he said, "No service. And the compass app won't work, either. We'd better keep going. If that guy in the cabin was right, those Unit-458 goons are probably out here searching for us. We've got to reach higher ground."

They continued trudging through the snowy woods.

About a mile into their trek, Hope stopped and said, "Frostbite."

"What?" asked Clive.

"I can't feel my feet. I think I'm getting frostbite."

He looked down at her soaked canvas sneakers and his leather loafers, turned around, and bent his knees. "Hop on."

Hope climbed onto his back, wrapping her arms around his upper chest. He secured her legs in his arms and started walking again.

After a few yards, Hope asked, "How did you know that guy was the carfentanil buyer?"

"Like I said, I flew back to Moldova after Christmas to investigate. I located the man who kidnapped women for Petrov. He described the guy. Later, I found the barn where that arms dealer held these young women. He released carfentanil to demonstrate its effectiveness on them, then burned the barn down with their dead bodies inside. I held their bone shards in my hand. Afterward, I participated in a sting operation with the local police to put Petrov behind bars. When I returned, Jack and I tracked down the van our guy used to place the device. It had the logo of a made-up company: New Capitol HVAC Services. There was a dead body inside the van. Likely a Capitol Policeman."

"So, the device is in play," said Hope.

"Yeah."

"That means we have less than twenty-four hours to find it and disarm it."

"How do you know?"

"You're not the only one doing detective work. I deciphered the Ides of March thing."

"What does it mean?"

"Three-fifteen. It refers to a law. Three U.S. Code fifteen. It lays out the time and place for counting the electoral votes. It's tomorrow at one p.m. in the U.S. House Chamber. Members of the House and Senate will gather there. And that device will release the carfentanil, killing the entire Congress."

"Who have you told?"

"You're the first. Lattimore kidnapped me before I could warn anyone. We just have to locate it."

"It's in the air conditioning system," said Clive. "Like I said, the guy's van had a paint job: New Capitol HVAC Services."

"Try the phone again."

Clive stopped and turned on the burner phone. "Still no service," he said, holding it above his head. "Let's keep going. How are your feet?"

"I can feel them burning a little."

"Is that a good sign?"

"Kinda, yeah."

He continued trudging through the forest with Hope on his back for several more hours. He found a patch of higher ground and began an ascent. Halfway up, he slowed, puffing like a mistimed engine.

"Stop," said Hope. "Rest."

Clive staggered a bit.

"There's a tree stump over there. Set me down on it," said Hope.

Clive walked over to the stump and lowered Hope down. She immediately removed her sneakers and began rubbing her feet. "I just need to warm them up."

Clive opened his coat and jacket and then unbuttoned his shirt. He kneeled in the snow before Hope, taking both her feet in his hands and pressing the soles against his bare chest.

Seeing the pained look on his face, Hope said, "Clive, you don't...."

"You need to warm them up," he said, teeth chattering.

After ten minutes, her feet felt red-hot. "I think it's working."

"Good." He continued to kneel statue-still, holding her feet to his chest.

"Clive," she said, "did you sleep with her?"

"Who?"

"Marta, you idiot."

"No. I went to her apartment to spend Christmas with Sophie. I stayed the night because getting a cab in the evening would be impossible. I slept in the guest bedroom. In the morning, I left for Moldova. I'm sorry that I didn't tell you."

"And I'm sorry I didn't believe you." She pulled her feet away from his chest, put on the sneakers, and grinned. "The feeling is returning."

"Is that why you're grinning?"

"No. This whole incident: you breaking into that cabin to rescue me, me knocking Lattimore over before he could shoot you, and you killing that shotgun-wielding guy. It reminded me of something."

"What's that?"

"Why we're good for each other."

"Why?"

"We save each other."

◆ ◆ ◆

"It should be sunup soon," said Hope, glancing at her watch as she bounced along on Clive's back to the crest of the prominence. On reaching the top, she said, "Put me down."

Clive let her down and checked the phone again. "Got a signal." When Hope did not respond, he said, "Did you hear me? I've got bars."

He turned to see Hope staring at the ground below. There were half a dozen beams of light moving in a back-and-forth fashion. As if searching.

"It's Unit-458," said Clive. "We'd better keep going."

They scrambled into the thicket ahead of them. After five minutes of trekking through the dense woods, they came to a clearing.

Brought up short by something strange ahead, they stood fast, staring at what appeared to be a pair of eyes shining from the abyss ahead.

"What is it?" whispered Hope.

Clive just shook his head.

Looking back, she could see the beams of sweeping lights grow larger.

In front of them, the eyes grew closer until they could see...

...a bear appearing. Massive with menacing claws, it reared on its hind legs. Ten feet or more in height. It came down on all fours, pounding the ground with its paws. It then made a bone-rattling huffing sound, pinned its ears forward, and galloped towards them like a runaway freight train.

"Shoot it!" screamed Hope.

Clive, wide-eyed, just stood there.

"Shoot it!"

Clive removed the pistol from his pocket, aimed, and pulled the trigger.

Click.

He pulled the trigger three more times:

Click-click-click.

The bear steadily closed the distance.

Hope jumped between Clive and the bear, leaped up and down, waved her arms, and shouted a guttural, "Ahhh!"

Clive, jarred out of his inaction, immediately joined Hope in jumping and shouting.

It came on—a massive ball of fury.

Ten feet.

Five feet.

Hope smelled her fear.

CHAPTER 46

Coming to within a claw's swipe, the bear suddenly veered off into the woods.

Seconds later, a staccato burst of gunfire erupted from behind them.

The bear emitted a plaintive growl.

Then all was silent.

"This way," whispered Clive, moving perpendicular to the oncoming soldiers. Hope followed.

Hope moved swiftly along the right-angle path that Clive created through the thick foliage. After about one hundred yards, Clive stopped and turned. "Hop on," he said, and they continued for another hundred with Hope on his back. Looking behind them, they could see the lights moving past and disappearing into the dense forest.

"Try the phone," said Hope.

Clive stopped and took out his burner phone. He had bars. "Who should I call?"

"Jack."

As he dialed, the first rays of sunrise filtered through the dense trees.

Jack answered on the tenth ring. "Clive," he said, "did you find Hope?"

"She's here with me."

"And just where are you?"

"Er, good question. Somewhere in West Virginia, I think."

Hope reached over his shoulder and took the phone. "Jack, we're lost."

"Hope? You alright?"

"Other than a little headache and almost frostbit feet, I'm fine. Look, Jack, can you—what's the word? —vector us out of here by tracking the phone's signal?"

"Sure, Sis."

"Also, and this is important, can you call the Capitol Police and warn them to evacuate the House Chamber before one p.m. today? We've figured out that's where and when that carfentanil will be released into the air conditioning system."

"Yeah, no problem. But I don't think they'll believe me."

"Well, do it anyway. And send Tina and Big Reggie to pick us up."

"Will do. And I'm coming with them."

Following Jack's directions and walking for five hours, with five-minute breaks, Clive made slow progress through the snow-covered forest with Hope on his back.

It was nearly eleven a.m. when they reached a two-lane road. Now they waited for Big Reggie's Escalade. Hope, standing on a patch of dry ground, paced. Jack had called, stating that his warning to the Capitol Police was received as a prank. He even had Tina call with the same results.

Hope called Jack again. "I need a cell number," she said.

"Sure Sis."

"A Senator Eddie Edelstein. We met at the Medal Ceremony."

"OK, I'm on it."

Turning to Clive, she said, "He's got to listen to me and cancel that joint session of Congress."

On receiving the number from Jack, she dialed. It rang. A curt "Hello…?"

"Senator Edelstein, this is Hope Allerd from—"

She heard a *click*. They were disconnected. She called back and got a recording that the person was not available. Trying twice more, she got the same message.

"He blocked the number," she said.

Hope looked at her watch. She knew now the only alternative was to go there in person to stop the release of the deadly narcotic and the murder of over five hundred members of Congress. "How long did it take you to drive to that cabin from Washington, D.C.?" she asked.

"I dunno, maybe a little over two hours."

"I won't make it in time."

CHAPTER 47

The ten-vehicle presidential motorcade wound along the two-lane blacktop West Virginia road returning to the White House. A Cadillac limo motored along in the center of the procession. However, President Conchrane rode in an SUV two cars to the rear. The limo was a decoy. The actual Presidential Limousine, the Beast, was nestled in its garage. It was a cost-saving brainchild of Chief of Staff Withers, which Conchrane loathed.

Flanked by two young White House staffers in the rear of the SUV, Conchrane huffed. The school visit to introduce her new education bill hadn't gone well.

"If I never see another one of those little crayon-eating snot factories again, it'll be too soon," said Conchrane. "And who was that kid that said, 'I wouldn't vote for you if you were the last person on earth?' Leslie, call the IRS and have the little piss ant's parents audited each year until the next millennium."

Leslie Wilson, a rail-thin, fresh-faced blonde, smiled. "Yes, Madame President," he said, writing her demand in the notebook he carried.

"And call the White House florist," continued Conchrane, "and have them send a dozen roses to Withers with the blooms cut off for arranging this fiasco."

"So, just stems and thorns," said Leslie.

"You heard me."

As he wrote Conchrane's order, Leslie said, "Yes, Madame President."

"Leslie, cancel the calls to the IRS and the florist."

"Yes, Madame President." Leslie scratched through his notes.

Leslie and Marjorie, the other staffer, began to chuckle. They enjoyed it when the boss was at what they termed DEFCON 1 angry. She slung more barbs than a standup comic on open mic night.

Conchrane dropped her head as her lips widened into a smile at the drama she'd just created.

A moment later, the motorcade came to a screeching stop.

"What's going on?" said Conchrane.

Her Secret Service driver, Ed Watters, turned around. "I'm checking." He spoke into the mic hidden in his shirt sleeve, and when he received a reply, he said, "There seems to be some sort of roadblock up ahead."

Conchrane's face pinched. "I'm the President of the United States, dammit. Just drive through it."

"Er, I'm afraid it won't be that easy."

"What are you talking about?"

It was then that Conchrane saw soldiers in battle dress holding M4 carbines at the ready materializing from the surrounding woods. Up ahead, another soldier came running towards the SUV. As he drew closer, Conchrane recognized the hawk-faced man as a colonel. He rapped on the driver's window.

Ed opened the window just wide enough to facilitate a conversation.

"Sorry, Madame President," said the colonel, "I'm afraid

you'll have to come with me."

"The hell I will," shouted Conchrane. "Ed, let's go."

"I'm going to have to insist, ma'am," replied the Colonel, waving a hand. The surrounding soldiers aimed their service weapons at the vehicle.

"You don't scare me, Colonel. Those 5.56 NATO rounds can't penetrate the SUV's armor. Ed, let's go."

The Colonel made another gesture, and two more soldiers appeared from the woods, aiming what looked to be some sort of antitank rocket tubes at the SUV.

Ed said, "Madame President, those are Javelins. They can obliterate anything short of an Abrams tank."

As Ed pulled the SUV out of the stopped motorcade and into a clearing beside the road at the Colonel's terse instruction, all along the motorcade, a dozen more soldiers appeared with the Javelin launchers from the woods. They fired point-blank at the SUVs and limo remaining on the road.

Looking back at the carnage from the back seat of her vehicle, Conchrane, eyes wet with tears, cursed Armstrong under her breath.

CHAPTER 48

It was eleven fifteen. The House Chamber began to fill with a few Representatives, mostly younger, fresh-faced first-term Congresspeople who didn't want to be late for the counting of the electoral votes and to get a good seat for what they considered history being made before their eyes. After all, it was likely to be a battle royal between the parties over the electoral votes certifying President Conchrane's reelection.

But they didn't know—what they could never conceive in a million years—that just below them, connected to the air conditioning vents in the floor of the House, was the harbinger of their impending demise.

The device, innocuous in form, sat among pallets of supplies, old furniture, and garbage bins, quietly awaiting its singular task.

Buried within the workings of coiled pipes, circuit boards, and fans that periodically ran was a small tank under pressure.

The tank, the heart of the device, and its raison d'etre contained enough carfentanil to kill a basketball arena full of people.

The release valve was held in a closed position by a plunger connected by a spring to a solenoid. The carfentanil remained confined as long as no electric current passed through the solenoid.

But, a battery, its flow of electricity controlled by one of

Trett's surrogates, awaited the close of the solenoid circuit and a flow of electricity that would open the spring that would release the valve, allowing the deadly narcotic to flow up into the House Chamber.

A digital timer counted down the seconds…

… 1:45:00… 1:44:59… 1:44:58…

The seconds until oblivion.

◆ ◆ ◆

Tina and Big Reggie arrived in their SUV at eleven seventeen, and a minute later, Jack pulled up in his wheelchair van. Hope grinned on seeing them.

As Tina and Big Reggie exited the Escalade, Hope said, "I'm glad to see you two. We don't have much time."

"Sorry, Hope, I called everyone I know at FBI Headquarters. No one would believe that the Capitol is going to be attacked," said Tina.

"So, I've got to go there and try to stop that joint session. Otherwise, they'll all die."

Jack called from the driver's seat of his van, "Hey, Sis, I finally broke that code regarding Armstrong's map."

Hope and Clive walked over to the van.

"ODALIK is President Conchrane," said Jack, "KIZLAR is the Cabinet, and SERALGIO is the White House. And the grid coordinate in the order is a cabin somewhere here in West Virginia." Jack produced a Google Map satellite view of the cabin.

"That's the cabin we were in," said Clive.

"If I remember right," said Big Reggie, "that order read something like: the operation starts at ten a.m. Soon after,

Company A intercepts ODALIK and transports it to that grid location. Then, at noon, Company B enters SERALGIO, captures KIZLAR, and takes it to the same grid location while Company C and D form a perimeter around SERALGIO. The Ides of March takes place precisely one hour after Company B moves."

Hope nodded and said, "So that's it. Armstrong has kidnapped President Conchrane by now. He'll also round up her Cabinet from the White House, and they'll all be in that cabin with the President guarded by elements of Unit-458. And for the piece de resistance, he's going to kill every member of Congress by one o'clock today, effectively decapitating the government."

"So, what do we do?" asked Tina.

Hope paced for a moment. "OK, OK," she said, "Big Reggie and I will drive to the Capitol to try and stop that gas attack on Congress. Tina, you and Clive ride with Jack. Go to FBI Headquarters and talk to your colleagues in person. Do whatever you have to in order to convince them that the President and her Cabinet are being held in that cabin. If you don't, I'm certain Armstrong will eliminate them all by the end of the day. Let's go."

As she climbed into the Escalade, Hope checked her watch. It was now eleven twenty-one.

CHAPTER 49

Secretary of State Marion Keppler gazed at her watch. It was nearly noon. The diminutive gray-haired head of the State Department then leaned back in her brown leather executive chair and yawned. Looking to her left at the empty chair, Secretary Keppler wondered why President Conchrane had called an emergency cabinet meeting and failed to show.

The other cabinet members sat patiently around the expansive mahogany table, engaging in animated conversation.

Now in a huff, Keppler rotated her chair a complete one-eighty and glared at Chief of Staff Withers sitting against the wall. She tapped her watch and whispered, "Where's President Conchrane?"

With a sheepish grin, Withers shrugged, arose from his chair, and walked over to Keppler. Leaning close, he said, "I'll see what's holding her up." He then exited the cabinet room.

Five more minutes ticked by. Now livid, Keppler turned to Secretary of Defense Samuel Corman, sitting on the other side of Conchrane's empty chair, and said, "Something strange is going on here."

The stocky fifty-something Secretary ran his hand over his balding head and furled his bushy eyebrows. "Yeah, I don't like it," he proclaimed in his booming Alabama accent.

Just as Corman arose to step into the corridor, General Armstrong strode in. Everyone in the room gasped. Instead of his service uniform, Armstrong was decked out in battle dress: camo fatigues, combat boots, a Kevlar helmet, a flack vest, and a sidearm. His four-star rank insignia was prominently displayed over the vest.

"What's going on, General?" asked Corman.

Armstrong smiled briefly, raising his gloved hands to bring calm to the situation. "Ladies and gentlemen," he began, "I'm sorry to disturb the meeting, but there has been a terrorist breach of the White House."

A flurry of strained voices arose from within the room, uttering disbelief and angst.

Armstrong continued, "We have managed to secure a section of the building and—"

"We need to go to the Situation Room at once," shouted Corman.

"I'm sorry, Mr. Secretary, but that part of the White House is still in the terrorists' hands. If you'll just—"

"We haven't heard any gunfire or shouting sounds, "Agriculture Secretary Keene interrupted.

As if on cue, the staccato report of rifle fire filled the hallway, sending everyone except Armstrong scurrying under the table.

"Please," said Armstrong, "if you just follow me, I've arranged for buses to take everyone to a safe, undisclosed location."

Slowly, the cabinet members and their staff began to rise and file out of the cabinet room into the corridor, which was filled with armed soldiers scurrying back and forth. Armstrong led the procession onto the White House grounds, where two luxury buses sat with engines running and doors open. Three up-armored Humvees with manned .50 caliber machine guns mounted on the tops were parked in the front of the buses and three in the rear.

Once inside and seated, the bus doors closed, and they drove off escorted by the half dozen Army Humvees. Armstrong stood on the curb and waved. His mouth widened into a smirk as the buses turned onto Pennsylvania Avenue.

CHAPTER 50

Hope allowed herself to smile as the warm air from the heater in Big Reggie's Escalade bathed her freezing bare feet. She sat in the passenger seat as the beefy security guard motored along the rural West Virginia two-lane road toward the Capitol at twenty miles per hour above the posted speed limit.

After putting on her dried-out sneakers, Hope looked at the big security guard and asked, "Can't you go any faster?"

"Could, Miss Hope, but I'm afraid if we go any faster, a state trooper's gonna pull us over, and we'll never make it in time."

♦ ♦ ♦

His footsteps echoed within the Capitol Rotunda as Vice President Will Cranston strode across the polished marble floor. The lean blonde man glanced up at the fresco in the Rotunda's dome, *The Apotheosis of Washington,* and grinned. The painting purported to show a deified President Washington in the heavens. Cranston always thought the work was a bit overblown.

He strode ahead of members of the United States Senate who followed in groups of twos and threes on their way to the House Chamber to carry out their solemn but routine duty to count the electoral votes that reelected Martha Conchrane as President.

At the door of the House Chamber, Cranston and his

entourage stopped as tellers—official counters—assembled ahead of them holding large mahogany boxes sealed with leather straps containing the official electoral votes from each state.

The congressmen and women sat or milled about within the House Chamber amid a swirl of diverse conversations in the massive room.

Cranston acknowledged Speaker of the House Mark Savage standing at the podium holding the oversized gavel, with a nod and grin. Like him, Savage was relatively young and new to the job.

The Sergeant at Arms, a tall, craggy septuagenarian who looked to Cranston as if he'd been at the job since Washington was President, stepped into the center aisle. He strode toward the podium, stopped, and intoned: "Mr. Speaker: the Vice President and the United States Senate."

Taking the cue, Cranston marched solemnly down the aisle, slowing to recognize a few members of the House with a nod or a handshake. The senators followed, taking seats at the front of the Chamber as Cranston mounted stairs to the podium beside Savage.

Behind the two men, a burst of warm air wafted from a vent in the floor.

Feeling the agreeable flow of air to his rear, Cranston briefly glanced behind at the grated aperture.

If Cranston could have somehow looked down past the grating and within the ductwork leading down to the invisible death angel awaiting them below the Chamber, he would have seen the digital display tick down their final seconds of life...

...00:09:47 ...00:09:46 ...00:09:45 ...

CHAPTER 51

Big Reggie dropped Hope off at the Capitol Visitors Center. She walked up to a winding queue leading into the cavernous room. Men, women, and a smattering of children in jackets and windbreakers stood within an area cordoned off by stanchions and ropes as they slowly made their way to a long desk staffed by half a dozen men and women in red blazers in front of computer consoles. Above the desk was a massive picture of the Capitol building in relief.

Just below the picture of the Capitol was a clock—the time: twelve forty-four. Hope had to act.

She ducked under the rope and made a beeline for the desk. A man behind her yelled, "Hey!"

"Ma'am, ma'am," shouted a Capitol employee standing at the beginning of the queue. He took off after Hope.

She got to the desk and climbed on top, facing the line of tourists. "Everyone," she shouted, "listen to me. You're all in danger. You need to get out immediately."

Two men behind the desk grabbed her coat, pulling her to her knees. A woman lifted a desk phone receiver to her ear and dialed. Several people in the crowd walked towards the exit.

"No," said Hope. "You don't understand. There's a terrorist threat in the House Chamber."

The two men pulled her to the floor just as two Capitol Policemen arrived and cuffed her.

"She jumped on the desk yelling something about danger," said one of the red-jacketed men.

Pulling her to a standing position, the two burly policemen flanking her gripped her upper arms.

One of the jacketed employees raised his hands and said, "It's OK, folks. We've got things under control." Just then, five other Capitol Police Officers came running through the doorway near the desk toward the crowd of tourists. One of them shouted, "Everyone will need to leave immediately. The Capitol is on lockdown," as they began rushing the tourists out of the Visitors Center.

The two policemen holding Hope stopped for a moment. One asked her, "What do you know about this?"

"There's a device under the building set to release a powerful narcotic gas into the House Chamber at one p.m. We need to somehow disarm it."

"Yeah, right," replied the policeman.

They took her to a small room deeper into the building, where a set of bars occupied half the space, and deposited her in the makeshift cell.

"Hey, hey," yelled Hope. "You've got to listen to me. People are going to die. We've got to get everyone out of the House Chamber."

◆ ◆ ◆

Will Cranston glanced at the boxes of electoral votes sitting on the lower tier of the House podium as the tellers began unfastening the leather straps.

The House Parliamentarian, a short, plump woman wearing a pair of glasses on a chain around her neck on the tier just below Cranston, handed him a sheaf of papers.

He recognized them as the official text to open the joint session of Congress. Nodding, he perused the writing as Speaker Savage rapped the gavel on the wooden sound block and said, "The House will come to order."

As the whir of conversations died down, Cranston took the gavel and brought it down onto the sound block. He then read: "Mr. Speaker, members of Congress, pursuant to the Constitution and the laws of the United States, the Senate and House of Representatives are meeting in joint session to verify the—"

A commotion erupted behind him. Looking back, Cranston saw four men in suits, part of his Secret Service detail, scramble up to the podium and surround him. More than a dozen plainclothes and uniformed Capitol Police Officers charged down the aisles of the House Chamber, covering all the doors amid shouts of, "What's going on?" and "How dare—," erupting from the floor. Uniformed officers cleared the gallery above.

A plainclothes policeman whispered something into Speaker Savage's ear. The young congressman listened with a wide-eyed look of disbelief on his face. After the message was passed, he shouted in a shaky voice over the diverse murmuring by Representatives on the House floor: "I've just been informed that the President has gone missing along with her cabinet. We are now on lockdown. Er, the situation is very fluid and...."

Cranston huddled in a corner near the podium as his Secret Service detail stood around him with sidearms drawn.

...00:06:14 ...00:06:13 ...00:06:12 ...

CHAPTER 52

Hope glanced at the clock on the wall from behind the bars. She had less than six minutes. "You've got to believe me," she said to the lone uniformed officer sitting at a desk in the corner of the room. He stared at the computer terminal on his desk, ignoring her pleas.

The door opened, and in walked a towering woman with dark hair pulled back into a short ponytail. Her pock-marked face was gaunt like she'd just been handed the worst news of her life. She wore dark trousers and a dark long-sleeved shirt. When she turned her back, Hope saw "FBI BOMB TECH" stenciled on the shirt. Two men dressed similarly and wearing vests with various tools in their pockets stood in the doorway.

Presenting a set of credentials to the policeman at the desk, she said, "I'm Special Agent Laura Hargrove. I need to speak to your prisoner."

Taken aback, the Capitol Policeman arose and nodded. Laura walked over to Hope. "Dr. Allerd, tell me everything you know about this so-called bomb you say is under the building."

Hope gripped the bars. "It's not a bomb, perse. It's more of a device to disperse a gas, carfentanil. Did Tina DeLuca send you?"

Laura nodded and then turned to the policeman. "Call your supervisor and tell him they need to start evacuating everyone in the House Chamber immediately."

Using the radio attached to his uniform, the policeman

made the call, saying the FBI was there, and the agent ordered an immediate evacuation of the House Chamber.

"Wait one," was the response.

"Release her," said Laura. The policeman opened the cell and removed Hope's handcuffs.

Hope glanced at the clock on the wall. It was twelve fifty-five.

"That's a negative," said the supervisor's voice. "Orders from the top are to continue to shelter in place."

Turning to Hope, Laura asked, "How much time?"

"Five minutes."

"Where's the device?"

Hope hesitated. She realized she had no idea where the thing would be.

"You don't know where it is?" said Laura, voice rife with irritation.

Think, Hope, think, she told herself. Recalling what Clive had said about finding that van, she pointed to the computer terminal. "Can you pull up recent vendors who made deliveries to the Capitol on that?" she asked the policemen.

"Sure," he said, sat and began typing. "Who are you looking for?"

"Er, a New Capitol HVAC Services."

"Here we are. They delivered and installed a piece of HVAC equipment a few days ago."

"Where?" asked Hope.

"Loading docks."

"Let's go," said Laura.

Hope and Laura, led by the policeman, sprinted for the

loading docks. The other two Special Agents followed.

It was twelve fifty-six.

◆ ◆ ◆

Two minutes later, they arrived at the cavernous space filled with garbage bins, pallets, and old furniture.

"Where is it?" asked Laura.

Hope turned to the policeman. He shook his head.

"OK," said Laura, "spread out. Look for something resembling HVAC equipment. Something that looks new."

Everyone fanned out, scanning the area for the device. Hope wandered in a zig-zag pattern, examining the various items within the loading docks. As she turned to make another pass, she heard a thump and the whir of a fan. Drawn to the sound, she stepped over a shiny blue rectangular device against one of the pillars. Raised lettering on it proclaimed: "2317". Looking from the top of the device up to the ceiling, Hope saw what looked like tubing from the device going into the ductwork above.

"I think I found it!" yelled Hope.

She was immediately surrounded by Laura, the policeman, and the two other bomb tech/Special Agents.

"There's a plug on the side," said one of the bomb techs as the other kneeled, removed a T wrench from his vest, and began unscrewing the bolts that secured the front panel.

"Wait," said Laura, "the panel's almost off."

The agent made the final turns on the last of four bolts with the T wrench and removed the thin metal panel. Inside was a dizzying array of wires, vents, and a whirring fan. Sitting dead center was a digital timer that flashed in red numerals: 00:01:23 ...00:01:22 ... 00:01:21 ...

"That shouldn't be there," said Laura as she ran her hand over the wires. "OK, pull the plug."

The agent yanked the plug from the outlet in the pillar. The fan stopped, but the timer continued its countdown: 00:00:53 ...00:00:52 ...00:00:51 ...

Turning to the policeman, Laura said, "Don't they have some sort of emergency equipment with gas masks inside the House Chamber?"

The policeman nodded.

"Tell them they need to put on their gas masks immediately."

He made the call to his supervisor.

Taking a pair of wire cutters, Laura gripped a red wire running from the timer with her left hand and snipped it. The timer continued. "Damn," she muttered under her breath.

She traced another wire and cut it. The unrelenting timer persisted in its countdown.

"I don't understand," said Laura.

Hope turned to the policeman. "You need to have your supervisor contact D.C. EMS and tell them there's a mass casualty situation at the Capitol. And that they'll need all the Narcan they can find."

The timer ticked down: 00:00:03 ...00:00:02 ...00:00:01 ...

At 00:00:00, all of them braced for the inevitable. Several seconds went by, but nothing happened.

"A dud?" said one of the bomb techs.

"Maybe," replied Laura, still examining the device.

Then...

A cell phone rang from within the device.

"No, no, no!" implored Laura.

A faint *click* and a *hiss*…

CHAPTER 53

Speaker Savage remained at the podium to relay information from the plainclothes Capitol Policeman in touch by phone with Secret Service Agents and members of the military at the White House. He'd passed along the order to put on escape hoods—transparent plastic hoods with HEPA filters—to the members of Congress sitting in the House Chamber, along with about a dozen other relayed announcements. Taking the command as more of a suggestion, a mere one-third complied. It didn't help that Savage didn't take his own advice.

Carfentanil molecules, by the trillions, wafted up from the tank in the loading docks through the duct system and the vent in the House Chamber.

Savage, being closest to the vent, was the first to feel an onset of drowsiness. The Capitol Policeman beside him became a fuzzy mold of blues and ivory. Sweat dripped from his forehead onto the podium as he swayed like a reed in the wind.

Savage dropped to the floor, followed by the policeman. As the gas drifted through the Chamber, members of the House and Senate who hadn't put on their escape hoods inhaled the deadly narcotic.

A member of Cranston's Secret Service detail found an emergency kit, removed the escape hood, and placed it on the Vice President's head before succumbing to the carfentanil himself.

Men and women nearest the podium began to fall where they stood or sat while people further back began to panic and rush for the exits at the room's rear. Some donned escape hoods from under their seats before charging to the back. Capitol Police, seeing the rush for the doors amid raised fists, screams, and shouting, barred the exits. This led to a clash of bodies pressed against the doors. And against the single-minded police as they pushed back, carrying out their last order—at all costs, keep the Congress sheltered in the House Chamber.

◆ ◆ ◆

"What happened?" demanded Hope.

Laura, stricken with terror, said, "It's too late. The device was triggered by a hidden cell phone. The timer was a decoy."

Hope looked from face to face as the Special Agents, crushed by the apathy of utter failure, stood frozen in place.

"We've got to get them out then," said Hope. "What's the quickest way to the House Chamber?"

Led by the Capitol Policeman, the makeshift team barreled for the doors.

Laura, using her credentials and intimating that they needed to search for a bomb, got them to the House Chamber. They found hundreds of people huddled around the entrance as they opened the doors. Those wearing escape hoods stepped over fallen colleagues and clambered for the exits leading to the Capitol steps. Others, succumbing to the carfentanil, staggered like drunkards for the exits and the succor of outside air. There remained in the Chamber over one hundred members of the House and Senate as well as police officers, tellers, and clerks lying on the floor, sitting in seats, or draped over desks comatose.

Taking in the enormity of the mounting disaster and formulating a plan, Hope said to the policeman, "Have all your colleagues don those hoods and begin to bring everyone out. I'm going outside to start triaging the victims."

Hope made her way to the Capitol grounds via the stairs from the House Chamber. As she descended the long staircase, she was followed by hundreds of people wearing escape hoods and wrapped in foil Mylar emergency blankets against the cold.

Within the outdoor space, Hope began to organize the victims into three groups as they walked or were carried out: those who likely had minimal or no exposure, those who could walk but were intoxicated by the carfentanil, and those who were unconscious or near comatose.

As she started directing people to their assigned locations, ambulances by the dozen began arriving at the Capitol in response to the mass casualty broadcast. She helped administer Narcan via nasal spray or injection provided by the EMS personnel to the affected members of Congress and others. She also aided in the resuscitation of several people who required intubation before ambulances whisked them to hospital ICUs.

Hope made rounds back and forth among the three groups of victims, quickly examining the men and women for any changes that could take them from one group to another. On her third pass among those who were conscious but needed multiple doses of Narcan to stave off the stuporous effects of the carfentanil, she saw him.

Sitting cross-legged between two congresswomen was Vice President Will Cranston. Appearing confused with pinpoint pupils, he held his escape hood under his left arm. Taking a bottle of Narcan nasal spray she carried with her, Hope administered a puff into his nostril. Two minutes later, she repeated the dose. He began to arouse and asked her,

"What happened?"

"Someone released carfentanil, a powerful narcotic gas, into the House Chamber," said Hope.

"Where's President Conchrane?"

"Missing."

Cranston looked around him. "My Secret Service detail?"

Hope recalled, on her first pass through the critical patients, finding several deceased men and women who wore holstered side arms. "I'm afraid they may be dead," she told him.

Eyes now wide with fear, Cranston said, "You've got to help me then."

Hope noticed two men in black suits in the distance walking among the victims and staring into faces. She pointed to them. "Are they Secret Service?"

Cranston shook his head. "No. Never seen them before."

Thinking fast, Hope said, "Put your hood back on." She then stood and made a phone call.

CHAPTER 54

Ben Armstrong made his way to the White House Press Room. It was time to begin the final part of the takeover. He walked through the door that brought him to the podium bearing the Seal of the President of the United States. He surveyed an audience of reporters who sprang from their seats and shouted questions in a cacophonous roar.

Armstrong raised his hands and said, "Quiet down, please. I have an opening statement, and then I'll take questions."

The reporters settled down as pooled TV cameras started, taking the press conference live to all the major networks.

"Beginning on or about ten a.m. this morning," said Armstrong, "a group of very coordinated terrorist attacks occurred in the Washington, D.C. area. The presidential motorcade returning from an event at a local West Virginia elementary school was attacked, and the President is now missing. Her cabinet, en route to a secure location, was also apparently kidnapped. And, as you are all aware by now, the Congress meeting in joint session was subject to a lethal gas attack, leaving dozens dead and most of the members of Congress incapacitated.

"This is a devastating attack on the government of the United States. Presently, the number of terrorists is unknown. All of our intelligence agencies are at work to identify who carried out these attacks, and law enforcement and the military are actively searching for the perpetrators.

"I want to say to our allies around the world that the United States remains strong and stands together with you against terrorism. And to our adversaries, I say beware. This is not the time to test America's resolve. I'll now take questions."

The raucous shouts renewed as reporters jumped from their seats with hands raised, clamoring to be recognized.

Armstrong pointed to a woman in a red dress. She said over the hum of quieting voices around her, "Linda Smallwood of the Washington Daily. Who's in charge of the government right now?"

Armstrong lifted his chin and smirked. "I am," he said as he pointed to another reporter.

An overweight man nodded on being recognized and said, "Yes, uh, Ken Thomas of American News. You mentioned the President going missing. Where is the Vice President?"

Armstrong swallowed. Droplets of sweat blossomed on his forehead. The one potential glitch in his plan surfaced. Despite his men in civilian clothes scouring the Capitol grounds filled with sick and dying members of Congress, they had not located Vice President Cranston.

"Er," began Armstrong, "obviously the Vice President was among the members of Congress in that joint session. He is incapacitated, and, er, his location is secure. If he survives, well...."

After taking two more questions, Armstrong promised to address the Nation from the Oval Office at eleven p.m. and stalked out of the Press Room.

He walked up to a lieutenant colonel standing by in civilian clothing and whispered, "You find that son of a bitch Cranston, and I mean fast. And bring me that Allerd woman. Now!"

❖ ❖ ❖

The effort continued into the late afternoon and early evening. Hope, bathed in fluorescent light from streetlamps on the Capitol grounds, checked the pulse and pupil size of a congresswoman from Illinois before allowing her to leave for home.

In the distance, a large crowd of onlookers had gathered, held back by D.C. police. Reporters from the various networks had wormed their way onto the triage site, now nearly empty of patients but still crammed with law enforcement, EMS personnel gathering used supplies and equipment, and Congressional staff who'd not been in the House Chamber.

Standing at the periphery of the activity, Big Reggie observed Hope with all the care of a mother eagle, watching her chick fly for the first time.

An exhausted Hope had removed her coat to work unencumbered and now donned it again in the dropping temperature. As she buttoned it, a woman approached, pristinely coiffed with a thick application of makeup. She held a microphone. "I'm Carol Jones from New Cable News," she said. "We're about to go live. I'd like to ask you a few questions."

Hope swiped at a film of sweat on her forehead that had formed despite the cold and said, "Uh, OK."

Standing a few feet away, Carol's cameraman turned on the camera's lights, causing Hope to squint. She stuck her microphone under Hope's chin and, turning to the camera, said, "This is Carol Jones coming to you live from the Capitol grounds, the site of a horrific terrorist gas attack on a joint session of Congress as they were about to count the electoral votes. I'm here with Dr. Hope Allerd, who heroically treated stricken House and Senate members. Dr. Allerd, how did you come to be at the site of this attack?"

"I came because I got word of the impending attack and tried to stop it." From the corner of her eye, Hope noticed two burly men in black suits and dark glasses standing just out of camera range.

"I see. And how did you learn of the attack?"

"Well, I—"

The two men swept upon Hope before she could react. Dragging her to a waiting white sedan, they shoved her into the back seat and drove off.

CHAPTER 55

Big Reggie sprinted for the Escalade after noting the physique and relative proportions of Hope's two kidnappers and the make and model of the white car that now contained her. He hopped in and pulled his big SUV into the late afternoon traffic, intent on recovering his charge.

Bumper to bumper with the hundreds of other vehicles leaving the D.C. area, Reggie spotted the white sedan up ahead and checked his dashcam to be sure it was running. Too focused on the escaping sedan, he didn't bother to call Tina, Jack, or Clive as he maneuvered the Escalade through the maze of cars snaking their way for the suburbs. He'd make the call when the traffic eased up.

◆ ◆ ◆

Hope, hands zip-tied behind her back, sat next to General Armstrong in the sedan's back seat.

"I'm disappointed in you, Hope. I thought you were a patriot," he said.

She glared at her captor.

"So, where is he?" he asked.

"Who?"

"Cranston, of course. You were out there on the Capitol grounds treating those people. You must have seen him."

"I honestly don't know where he is."

"We'll find him," said the driver. "We're scouring every hospital within a forty-mile radius of the Capitol."

"You won't get away with this, Ben," said Hope.

"I'm doing well so far. We've put out enough evidence to frame an Arab terrorist group for everything that's happened. And tonight, at eleven p.m., I complete the operation when I address the nation as America's new leader and initiate martial law."

Hope gazed out of the window as the vehicle made its way out of the city. "Where are we going?"

"Just a little side trip. Join me now. Pledge your undying loyalty, and we turn around. Otherwise, I'm afraid you'll have to be eliminated."

Hope bit her lower lip. She blinked back tears as the city lights faded and the darkened landscape became bucolic.

The car turned onto a side road in a wooded area. There appeared to be no other traffic on the two-lane blacktop.

Armstrong took a jagged breath. "You know, I'm really going to hate doing this. But you've had your chance." He removed his SIG Sauer M17 semiautomatic pistol from its holster.

Hope looked down at the brown-tinged gun in Armstrong's hand and then into his eyes. In a quavering voice, she said, "Do the right thing."

"You want to beg for your life? Now's the time."

"Let me tell you a story, Ben," she said. "There was a mother whose son came to her holding a gun and said, 'Mom, I was in a fight. I shot and killed a man.' So, she hid the gun and told the police her son was with her the entire time of the fight and shooting. Over time, as the victim's body rotted in the ground, their memories faded, and they lived a quiet but guilt-plagued life.

"There was another mother whose son came to her holding a gun and said, 'Mom, I was in a fight. I shot and killed a man.' She took the gun to the police and turned her son in. He was arrested, tried, and convicted. He spent the rest of his life in prison, denying he killed the man. The mother visited him regularly and prayed every day for the rest of her life that he would repent and confess his sin. Who was the better mother?"

Armstrong glanced down at the weapon in his right hand. "Look, I'm only defending the principles holding America together."

"You're defending a lie. And you can't go on living a lie. You've got to lay bare the wounds of the past and let them heal. If you want to help America, you must help cleanse her soul. It's the only way the country can move forward. You can't go on defending the indefensible."

Armstrong, near tears, looked at Hope. "Er, well...."

She met his gaze and said, "The most patriotic thing you can do is be the second mother. Do the right thing. Despite what anyone else wants, despite the consequences, do the right thing. I'm not begging for my life, Ben. I'm begging for yours."

They rode in silence for several minutes.

"We're here, General," said the black-suited man behind the wheel. He made a sharp turn and pulled the car off the road onto a clearing in a copse of trees. Beyond it, in the near pitch-black evening, was what looked to be a ravine.

The front passenger seat henchman got out and opened the door on Hope's side. He gripped her arm, yanking her from the car.

Armstrong exited from his side. He pulled the slide back, putting a round in the chamber of the SIG Sauer. He then took Hope's arm, muscling her to the cliff edge.

He put the muzzle against her temple. "Last chance," he said.

"You don't have to do this," replied Hope.

He put his finger on the trigger and slowly squeezed.

CHAPTER 56

The very moment Armstrong felt the give of the trigger, a brilliant light blinded him.

He flinched.

The gun discharged with a loud *pop*, reverberating through the woods. Raising his left arm to shield his eyes, Armstrong saw a black Escalade slowing on the road and then burning rubber as it accelerated from the scene.

Gazing into the ravine for an instant, he was confident he saw Hope's body resting at the bottom at an unnatural angle.

Now, sprinting toward the sedan, Armstrong yelled, "Get him!"

As Armstrong dove into the back seat, the sedan took off in pursuit of the Escalade.

The SUV's red rear lights grew smaller. The sedan's driver floored it. The road became a series of curves. Tires screeched as the driver struggled to stay on the blacktop.

They were getting closer when the Escalade's rear lights flared and winked out.

"Where'd he go?" asked the sedan's driver. As the car continued, Armstrong screamed, "Stop! I think I saw skid marks on the road."

The driver pulled to a stop and then began backing up. "Here," said Armstrong.

Sure enough, wide skid marks covered the road, ending in tracks along the roadside leading to...

"It went over an embankment," said the driver. He pulled onto the shoulder beside the tracks.

The henchman in the passenger seat said, "I'll take care of it." He exited the sedan and walked over to the embankment. Looking down, he saw the Escalade lying upside down in a dry riverbed. The engine was off, likely due to the vehicle's impact sensor tripping the automatic fuel shutoff. Tires slowly turned. The headlights illuminated a foliage-strewn patch of the riverbank.

He found a gentle slope of ground and sidled down to the bottom. Removing his SIG Sauer from his shoulder holster, the henchman traipsed the uneven ground to the SUV. He squatted at the driver-side window, bringing him face to face with the large black man strapped upside down in his seat.

Upon seeing the semiautomatic in the henchman's hand, the black man began furiously fiddling with his seatbelt's latch. Unable to release his belt, he stared wide-eyed at the gunman and slapped his massive hand against the driver-side window.

With all the casualness of a man adjusting his tie, the henchman pumped three rounds into the driver of the crashed SUV, then reached inside and flicked off the SUV's lights.

Back at the sedan, the henchman said, "It's taken care of."

"Good," replied Armstrong. "Take me back to the White House. It's time to inaugurate the Armstrong era of American rule."

CHAPTER 57

"He stopped," said Clive from the passenger seat, staring at Jack's computer resting on his lap.

Jack, at the wheel of his wheelchair van, drove along the two-lane back roads of West Virginia.

They'd just completed the special mission Hope charged them to perform at the Capitol grounds when Big Reggie alerted them that Hope had again been kidnapped and that he was in pursuit of her abductors. After getting the Escalade's specs from the security man, Jack was able to hack into the Escalade's GPS.

The digital map on Jack's laptop now indicated that the Escalade was sitting on a secluded stretch of road in a rural part of the state.

"You think he may be confronting them?" asked Jack.

"I don't know. We've just got to get to Hope."

"It's here just up ahead," said Jack, staring at the screen.

Jack slowed the van as he took a curve. Both men scoured the road and surrounding wooded countryside for the Escalade.

"I don't understand," said Jack.

"It's got to be here," said Clive. "We're right on it, according to the GPS."

Jack's eyes narrowed. "There, skid marks," he said as he

slowed the van further, taking it onto the shoulder as he followed the tire prints in the ground ahead. He stopped.

Clive got out and hiked the soft ground to an embankment and the termination of the tire tracks. He stepped to the edge and looked below. "He's down there."

"Can you see Hope?" asked Jack.

"No, just the Escalade upside down in what looks to be dry riverbed. I'm going down."

Clive found the gentle slope and made his way down to the SUV. Using his phone's LED light, he examined the driver-side through the shattered glass of the window. Big Reggie, upside down in the seat, had three distinct bullet holes in his head. A pool of blood and bits of brain and bone covered the interior of the car's roof.

Clive shined the light at the passenger side and throughout the rear of the vehicle on the off chance that Hope might have been belted in there. He exhaled in relief when he saw no one else inside. But the question remained: Where was Hope?

He was about to go when he saw it.

A faint blinking red light on the dashboard caught his attention. Placing the phone's LED light on the source, he saw the dashcam.

Maybe it held a clue, he thought as he removed the tiny SD card from the device.

On arriving at the van, Clive faced a distraught Jack. "Did you find her?" he asked.

"No."

"Then where's my sister?"

Clive held up the SD card from the dashcam. "Maybe this will help."

Jack plucked it from Clive's hand and inserted it into one of the laptop's slots.

Now back in the van's passenger seat, Clive watched the video along with Jack of what turned out to be the scene Big Reggie observed during his final moments on Earth.

The computer screen revealed the two-lane road illuminated by the Escalade's headlight, as it cruised over the blacktop. It seemed to slow as it came to a sharp curve, and in a clearing, the event walloped Jack like a knife to the heart.

He burst into tears on seeing Armstrong standing on the side of the road with a gun to Hope's head, pulling the trigger, and Hope pitching into the darkness below.

Clive began to tremble as he viewed the scene. "No, it can't be," he muttered.

"That son of a bitch Armstrong killed my sister," shouted Jack.

A quiet moment passed as both men tried to come to grips with what they'd just seen. Finally, Clive said, "We need to get her."

Jack turned the van around and drove while Clive searched for the clearing seen in the video.

"There," he said. Jack pulled onto the side of the road. Clive hopped out and walked to the edge of a ravine. Looking down, he saw what appeared to be a human form lying in the snow below.

There was only a steep drop-off in the immediate vicinity. He hiked along the edge for several yards until he found ground on a gentle incline. He scurried down the path, taking him to the form he saw from above.

As he approached, he could tell it was Hope. "Oh, God," he uttered while kneeling next to her.

Shaking with dread as he reached to feel a pulse on her neck, Clive prayed he would find the sign of life.

The flesh was icy as he inched his fingers over her skin.

Then...

CHAPTER 58

Clive felt a steady throb at the junction of her neck and jaw. "Hope," he whispered as he straightened her limbs and lifted her in his arms from the unforgiving earth.

At the van, with tears in his eyes, Clive said a single word to Jack in a trembling voice: "Alive."

He placed her in one of the van's rear seats behind Jack's wheelchair and plopped into the other. He rubbed her hand and said, "Hope, can you hear me?"

Jack pulled onto the road. "We've got to get her to a hospital."

Jostled on the seat as Jack drove like a maniac, Hope's eyes fluttered then opened.

"Where…am I?" she mumbled.

"In Jack's van with me," said Clive, still holding her hand.

"Wha…what happened?"

"That SOB Armstrong shot you," shouted Jack.

Clive realized for the first time since seeing the video that Hope should have a tremendous head wound and began palpitating her skull.

"What…what are you doing?" said Hope.

"You were shot in the head."

"No. No. He, er, missed."

"What?"

"Yeah. There was...this blinding light. We both turned. He fired, and, uh, he missed."

"He missed?"

"I guess." She put her hand to her forehead. "Concussion? Felt like a sledgehammer. Knocked me out."

"He missed, Jack," said Clive, "Did you hear that?"

"Yeah, thank God."

Hope put her hand to her right ear. "Think I'm deaf in my right ear, though."

Clive shined his phone's LED light over Hope's head. "The gunshot singed your hair."

Hope touched the spot. "Least of our problems. Gotta stop Armstrong."

"What's he doing?" asked Clive.

"He plans to broadcast a speech to the nation at eleven tonight. He will declare martial law throughout the nation and suspend the Constitution. Basically, he's going to announce that he's now in charge of the country."

Clive's eyes narrowed. "How do we stop him?"

Hope shook her head. "I dunno, maybe.... Wait a second. Jack, how did you know Armstrong shot me?"

Jack nodded toward his laptop in the passenger seat. "Big Reggie was following you with his dashcam running. He came upon that stopped sedan just as Armstrong pulled the trigger. That flash of light you saw was his headlights. It's all on video. Old Clive here got the SD card from the dashcam."

"Where's Big Reggie?" asked Hope.

"Afraid he didn't make it," said Clive.

Taking a jagged breath, Hope shut her eyes. When she opened them, Clive had the laptop. He played the video of the shooting for Hope. She winced as she viewed the moment the shot rang out.

Hope shut her eyes again and sat back in her seat. After a moment, she gazed at Clive. "I've got an idea," she said. "Jack, can you hack into a nationwide network broadcast?"

"Uh, yeah, I guess. Just need a satellite dish big enough. And I think there may be one on the roof of the Capitol Hotel."

"Good," said Hope. "And where is our special guest?"

Clive grinned. "He's with Tina in Jack's hotel room."

"I just pray this will work."

CHAPTER 59

In his dress uniform, Armstrong paced back and forth in front of the Resolute desk in the Oval Office of the White House. Several TV and video cameras faced the desk amid a tangle of cables on the floor. A teleprompter and flatscreen monitors stood off-camera. A pooled TV crew wearing headsets worked behind the cameras. Some held boom mics jutting just above the desk. They prepared for the nationwide broadcast that would ordain the General as the sole ruler of the most powerful nation on the planet.

"Five minutes, General," said the director, a stocky man with a pockmarked face wearing a white shirt with rolled-up sleeves who stood in front of the cameras.

Armstrong stopped his pacing and nodded. He looked past the cameras at the far wall. Above the fireplace mantle hung a painting of George Washington in his general's uniform. Armstrong smiled. He felt as if a sacred charge was being passed from Washington to him at this very moment.

The TV studio lights flicked on. "Take your seat, General," said the director. While he sat, a makeup woman with a portable kit began dusting his face with some sort of powder.

As soon as she was done, the director said, "OK, General, the monitor to your right shows what our cameras are picking up. The monitor to your left is now just showing bars. When we go live, it will show what's being broadcast nationwide. Five seconds before we go live, I'll give you a countdown with my fingers. Got it?"

Armstrong's countenance hardened as if he were about to give orders to his troops. He glanced at the teleprompter and noted that his speech was ready. "OK," he said.

The monitor on his left came to life with a logo proclaiming: "Special Report."

The director began the countdown hand signals: five, four, three, two, one, then pointed at Armstrong.

Looking directly at the cameras, the General hesitated, then began reading the teleprompter: "Ladies and gentlemen, I'm General Benjamin Armstrong coming to you from the Oval Office in the White House. As you now may know, a massive, coordinated terrorist attack took place today here in Washington, D.C., with the intent of decapitating the government of the United States. The President, Vice President, members of the Cabinet, and members of Congress have all either been killed or incapacitated. But the attackers failed. I have taken command and, using the prodigious resources of the U.S. Military, have managed to thwart their further efforts. Most, if not all, of them have been killed. However, because of the enormity of their actions, I have found it necessary to proclaim martial law. Beginning immediately, a curfew is in place. Everyone nationwide not involved in essential business will need to shelter at home. I have also federalized the National Guard of all fifty states and placed them under my command. I know..."

From the corner of his eye, Armstrong saw that the left-sided monitor was now displaying static instead of showing him speaking. Uncertain of what to do next, he continued.

"I know that..."

The director stepped up to the desk. "The satellite feed has been disrupted somehow." He turned to face the monitor.

The static suddenly morphed into a rustic nighttime scene of a forest-lined two-lane road illuminated by a vehicle's headlights as it cruised along the asphalt. The vehicle slowed as the headlights came upon a sedan in a clearing at the side of the road. In HD color stood Armstrong holding a semiautomatic pistol to a woman's head. He jerked as the lights framed him in the center of the video and pulled the trigger. The woman's head whipped back as she fell over the edge of a ravine. The scene repeated.

'What's going on," shouted Armstrong.

"I think someone has hacked into the broadcast," said the director.

"Is this going out nationwide?" asked Armstrong.

In a timid voice, the director said, "I'm afraid so."

"Then stop it!"

"We can't."

The screen went blank after a third iteration of the shooting scene played.

Indignant, Armstrong arose from the executive chair, staring at the flat screen.

The monitor went live again. In a rumpled blue suit, hair tousled, with a pasty complexion, Vice President Will Cranston sat in front of a white wall. In a reedy voice that sounded exhausted, he said, "This is Will Cranston, Vice President of the United States. What you have just seen was real. General Benjamin Armstrong shot a woman in cold blood. He also attempted a coup—a blatant attempt to take over the government of the United States. I have ordered the Director of the FBI to immediately place General Armstrong under arrest. As I speak, an FBI hostage rescue team and a Secret Service counter-assault team supported by two battalions from the 29th Infantry Division from Fort Belvoir have surrounded a cabin in West Virginia. Intelligence has revealed that the President and her Cabinet are being held at this site by a rogue army unit loyal to Armstrong. That army unit is presently surrendering to law enforcement and the legitimate military. Order in the nation is being restored...."

A visibly shaken Armstrong looked up from the monitor to see a cadre of men and women approaching from the doorway wearing vests with stenciling proclaiming: "FBI." One of them held up a pair of handcuffs.

CHAPTER 60

Hope, exhausted, sat in the rear seat of a government SUV driven by a Secret Service agent. It had been a day since Armstrong's arrest.

She now gazed out on a somewhat familiar scene as the black vehicle motored into the night along a rural two-lane road flanked by tall shadowy oaks, pines, and ash.

"Can't you tell me anything more?" she asked her driver.

"Sorry, Dr. Allerd. My instructions came from President Conchrane herself. She said to bring you to the designated location. And no more."

Finally, they stopped at a clearing similar to where Armstrong had taken her. A line of black SUVs was parked alongside the road. Two of them faced each other with headlights on, illuminating the bare patch of ground. In the center was the Beast—the Presidential Limousine with the motor running.

Hope's driver got out and opened her door. "We're here," he said.

Hope exited the SUV facing the Beast and waited. The cold air swirled like icy fingers caressing her face.

A short time later, a Secret Service agent exited the limo, walked around, and opened the rear door. Out stepped President Conchrane in a simple pantsuit, trench coat, and black gloves. She smiled at Hope.

"Good evening, Hope," said the President.

"Good evening, Madame President."

"I know you're wondering why I brought you out here. Well, I thought you earned the right to witness this. After all, you and your brother just saved the nation with your bootleg broadcast of Will Cranston last night."

"Witness what?" asked Hope.

Conchrane turned to a Secret Service agent standing near one of the SUVs. "John," she said.

The burly man in a black suit walked over to one of the parked SUVs and opened the rear door. Another agent stood by. Leaning in, he and the other agent seemed to wrestle with something or someone in the darkened backseat. A short time later, they wrenched a handcuffed and gagged Ben Armstrong from the vehicle. The General, still in his dress uniform, twisted and bobbed in protest to being held captive.

The other agent held Armstrong fast while John jerked his service semiautomatic from his shoulder holster, pulled the slide to put a round into the chamber, pressed the gun to Armstrong's temple, and fired one shot.

Hope flinched on hearing the loud report echo through the forested area. She stepped back aghast at the dying General lying on the snowy ground, blood spouting from the entrance wound, a crimson fountain forming an expanding pool around his head.

"But, but...," she stammered.

"Thank you, Hope. We couldn't have ended the coup without your help. I'd love to give you another medal for all of this. But what you just witnessed never happened. By the way, that lech Lattimore and my weasel of a Chief-of-Staff Withers are both in FBI custody," said Conchrane.

Incredulous, Hope watched as two Secret Service agents

put the General's corpse in a black body bag and carried it to one of the SUVs.

Conchrane's mouth widened into a benighted smile.

"You can't get away with this," said Hope.

"Oh, Armstrong's disappearance will be a big thing over the next news cycle. I'll announce that he escaped and have directed the FBI and U.S. Marshals Service to put their best agents on the case. But within a fortnight, the public will have forgotten the good general. Probably be concerned with, I dunno, the changing mortgage interest rates by then."

"But you just had him murdered. He deserved a fair trial," said Hope.

"What? And risk his followers having a martyr to rally around? We'd just go through the same thing in a couple of years. This way, they'll be left with doubt. Maybe he ran off to Europe or South America. Maybe he's hiding out somewhere in Middle America. Or, maybe he's still traipsing through these very woods."

"But what you did was wrong."

"Do you know how hard it is to maintain a democracy in this country? It's like crossing the Grand Canyon on a strand of piano wire without a net. Know what the most important words in the Constitution are, Hope?"

She shook her head.

"It's the first three: 'We the people...'. If Armstrong's followers want a change in government, then they have their candidate run in the next election cycle. Here, in America, the people decide who's President."

"Yeah, but as the first woman President, don't you want your administration to be free of controversy?"

"We women have to stick together." Conchrane jammed

her hand into her coat pocket and pulled out what appeared to be three small booklets: two dark blue and one red. She handed them to Hope.

Looking down at the items, Hope realized that they were passports. Opening them, she saw that the two blue ones were for her and Jack, and the red-covered one was Clive's. "I don't understand," said Hope.

"Just a little token of appreciation from EQV for all your hard work. You won't have to sneak around anymore."

"But…."

"You thought Armstrong was the head of EQV. Cut off the head, and the snake will die, right?"

"He wasn't the head? But I saw him being initiated."

"EQV likes a level playing field. Armstrong tipped it too much in his favor."

"But, but…."

Conchrane chuckled. "Oh, I almost forgot. That little matter of the twelve million you owe EQV. It's forgiven."

"I don't understand," said Hope.

"No need to thank me. You earned it all."

"But if Armstrong wasn't the head of EQV, then…?"

"That's what I like about you, Hope, your delicious naivety. You know, my next four years in the White House are going to be wonderful." Conchrane stepped over to Hope and linked arms.

Hope felt an unnatural chill and began to shiver.

"Oh my," said Conchrane, "you're getting cold. Let's get you in the car before you freeze to death."

As the President started for the Beast, Hope tried to dig in her heels but felt herself being carried along by the current of

Conchrane's iron will.

Up ahead, a Secret Service agent stood by the open rear door. The Beast's shadowy back seat reminded Hope of an open crypt.

As they walked, Conchrane said, "Hope, I want you on my team. You inspire the better angels of my nature."

Speechless, Hope could only look from Conchrane to the SUV containing Armstrong's body and back to the President.

Inside the Beast, Conchrane pated her knee. "You know Hope," she said, "I think this is the beginning of a beautiful friendship."

Despite the soothing warmth of the circulating air and the luxuriant comfort of Corinthian leather seating, Hope had the distinct impression that, as the Secret Service agent shut the massive door, a giant stone had just been rolled over the entrance of her tomb.

*If you enjoyed **Lethal Hope**, read on for a preview of the thrilling sequel: **Fatal Hope** coming soon to Amazon.com*

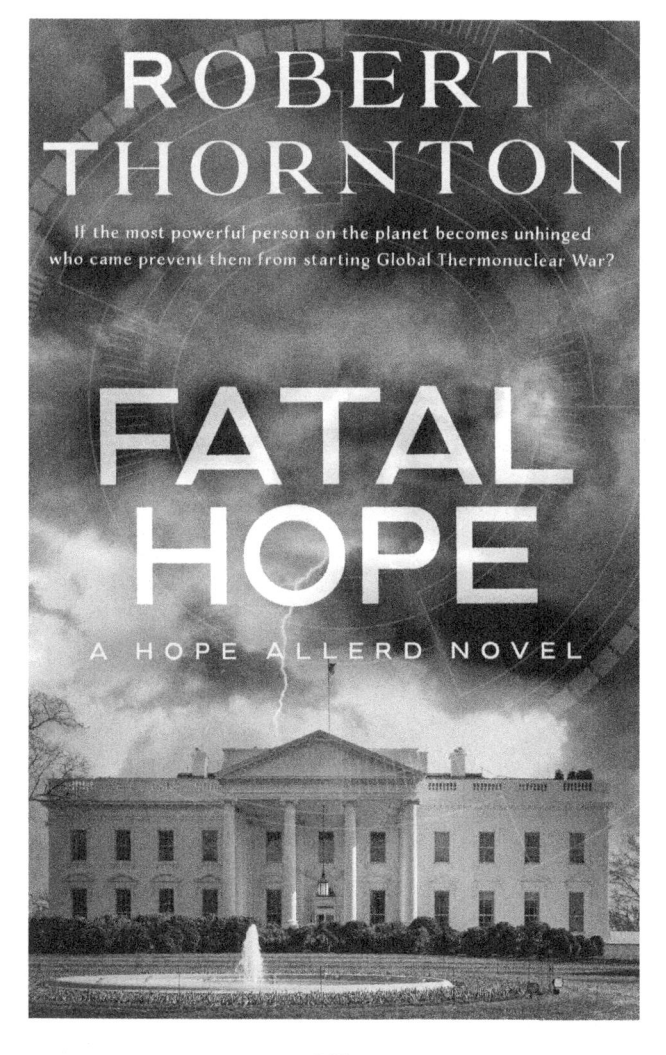

ROBERT THORNTON

If the most powerful person on the planet becomes unhinged who came prevent them from starting Global Thermonuclear War?

FATAL HOPE

A HOPE ALLERD NOVEL

PROLOGUE

In the over two hundred and fifty years that America has been a republic, no president has ever been found to be so mentally incapacitated as to pose an existential threat to the nation or the world.

Until now.

Hope Allerd, M.D., knew this all too well. But she'd chosen to bury the fact deep within her psyche in one of those compartments that everyone possesses. The one reserved for thoughts so painful, so excruciatingly upsetting that conscious contemplation for any length of time would only lead to crippling depression.

Hope also carried with her a shocking corollary: Martha Conchrane, President of the United States, was also a stone-cold killer. And Hope, if truth be told, was an accessory after the fact. Because, at the behest of the most powerful person on the planet, Hope kept the murder of the former Chairman of the Joint Chiefs of Staff, General Benjamin Davis Armstrong, a secret.

A state secret.

There was no doubt that Armstrong had allegedly committed treason. He deserved to be tried by a jury of his peers and, if found guilty, sentenced for his crime. But Conchrane saw things differently. By her peculiar calculus, Armstrong's dangerous influence on America could be erased only through his sudden disappearance.

Witnessing murder and pledging to keep quiet fostered self-reproach within Hope that swirled in her unconscious brain daily like a vortex, only to surface occasionally into her conscious thoughts.

This is why she readily agreed to take a position on President Conchrane's staff as Special Assistant to the Chief of Staff.

It was her penance.

Each day, Hope worked beside the woman whose psyche was a ticking bomb—the woman who called Hope "the angel on my shoulder." And each day, Hope wondered if it would be her last.

Like the governor on a powerful steam engine, she saw her job as a check on Martha Conchrane's foibles, peccadillos, and her one potentially fatal flaw—pathological mental instability.

Without a doubt, Hope was a fish out of water. Her area of expertise was medicine, particularly infectious diseases. And she'd be the first to tell anyone that she was in over her head as a White House staffer to the only President who'd ever ordered the use of a nuclear weapon on a city in the United States.

The bombing was a last-ditch effort to stop the worst worldwide pandemic since the 1918 Spanish flu. Unfortunately, it did little to slow the spread of the disease. It was Hope's epidemiological efforts to find and neutralize patient zero that had brought the pandemic under control. Perhaps it was why Conchrane wanted her on the White House staff. She was the President's good luck charm—the angel on her shoulder.

The disturbing thing that Hope saw in Conchrane was that look in the President's eyes: darkness like a building storm front. Call it intuition or premonition. Whatever it was, Hope knew in her heart of hearts that the genie was out of the bottle. Conchrane, the woman who killed Armstrong without reservation, was also aching to launch another nuclear onslaught, this time on her perceived enemies.

So, she participated in White House staff meetings, negotiations with members of Congress, or ceremonial visits with foreign dignitaries, praying each day that it would not be the day that Conchrane snapped and unleashed nuclear hell on some unsuspecting foreign power.

The incontrovertible truth was that President Conchrane

was the commander-in-chief of the most powerful military on the planet and was the sole arbiter regarding launching nuclear weapons. Her word was the only one necessary to rain down perdition on any and everyone who opposed her.

In short, Hope felt that if she could positively influence President Conchrane, she could alter the character of the woman whose finger hovered over the nuclear trigger.

If not, the planet would soon be doomed to orbit the sun as nothing more than a burned-out cinder.

CHAPTER 1

The expansive terrain was truly unsettling. Endless acres of debris punctuated by the occasional fragmented rebar-enforced concrete wall or twisted scorched metal pole created a desolate and lifeless wasteland against the backdrop of Nevada's craggy red pastel mountains.

This was once Sunset, Nevada, a sleepy burg of five thousand some one hundred miles northwest of Las Vegas. It had been a hamlet of charming family-owned stores, peaceful streets with carefree children playing on well-maintained lawns of split-level homes with picket fences, and front porches where couples spent leisurely evenings beneath clear Western skies. That is until the recent pandemic. Then, a fifteen-kiloton nuclear bomb dropped from an F-15 fighter bomber obliterated this slice of small-town America into nothingness.

"Where's the crater?" whispered Martha Conchrane, President of the United States. She stood a few paces behind the podium with head bowed along with half a dozen local and state dignitaries as Reverend Morrison gave the invocation for the dedication ceremony of the Sunset Memorial.

Behind them, anchored forty feet into the ground, soared a polymimetic grey steel arch some fifty feet above. A crowd of several hundred tourists and locals from Vegas and Rainbow, Nevada, faced the podium behind a line of state police officers. Further back, protestors yelled invectives like, "Conchrane is a murderer," and held signs proclaiming, "Impeach Conchrane!"

Conchrane wiped a thin sheen of perspiration from her nose and mouth. Her bleach-blonde hair began to frizz in the one-hundred degree afternoon. Her age-wrinkled face pruned. As Reverend Morrison said, "Amen," she turned to Hope and whispered again, "Where's the crater?"

In the searing heat, Hope Allerd was thankful she'd kept her goddess braids. What she regretted was imitating her boss by wearing a gray polyester pantsuit. Standing behind and just left of the President, Hope said in a soft voice, "It was an air burst. The explosion was too high up to leave a crater."

"I thought there'd be a crater."

Hope shut her eyes for an instant. "Remember, five thousand people lost their lives here."

"Yeah, yeah, I know. Those protestors ought to be nuked also."

The Lieutenant Governor, a rotund, balding man in a cheap-looking seersucker suit, was now at the podium, introducing President Conchrane.

Hope leaned toward her ear. "Remember, stick to the scripted remarks."

Conchrane scowled at her staffer just before walking to the podium.

Hope held her breath during the first paragraph as the President began reading from the teleprompter. *Would she stay on script?* worried Hope.

This wouldn't be the first time Conchrane committed a gaff during a speech. Hope had seen her boss inappropriately call opposing political party members "rabid dogs" during a speech on free trade not two months ago. This was the conundrum. Hope could see it as clearly as a runaway train bearing down the tracks toward her; Martha Conchrane was slowly and inexorably becoming unhinged.

Hope felt her heart race as Conchrane read the final paragraph.

"Therefore," said the President, "I do hereby dedicate this memorial to the valiant men and women who gave their lives fighting that violent scourge, the megalovirus." She paused, blinked a few times, and continued, "You know, this could have all been prevented if the British government had kept that fool microbiologist, Dr. Zalenski, in check."

No, no, no..., thought Hope as she buried her face in her hand.

"I blame the British Prime Minister. But I digress," said Conchrane. After a short pause, she ended with, "I so dedicate this memorial."

A smattering of applause erupted from the audience, along with quizzical stares and scowls.

Following the program, Conchrane stepped over to a large wreath of white chrysanthemums on a stand held by two officers of the Nevada National Guard. She then touched the blooms as they walked the spray of flowers over to the base of the arch and placed it over an inscribed plaque. The two Guardsmen stepped back and saluted. Conchrane stood facing the flowers with her head down as if in prayer, then crossed herself.

Hope slowly shook her head. Conchrane was Methodist, not Catholic. In a matter of ten minutes, the President of the United States had managed to insult one of the country's closest allies and the Catholic Church.

At the end of the ceremony, Conchrane walked over to Hope. "Well, how did I do?"

Hope winced. "Well, Madame President, you managed to insult the United Kingdom and the Catholic Church."

"Ah, they'll get over it."

Yeah, thought Hope, *they'll get over it after I and about half a dozen other White House staffers work the phones for the next forty-eight hours.*

Conchrane turned to the onlookers. "I'm going to shake some hands. My people deserve to meet their President up close." Looking at her chief Secret Service agent by her side, a tallish, muscular man in a black suit and sunglasses, she said, "John, make it so."

Before Hope could protest, preceded by her Protection Detail, she plunged into the crowd. Flanked by the black-suited agents with dark glasses and the ever-present microphone in their ears on either side, the President clasped hands with a few enthusiastic onlookers.

Hope, dutifully brought up the rear, walked behind Conchrane as she worked the crowd.

With hands out in front, the flanking agents looked for the usual tells from the crowd: hands in pockets, fidgeting, grooming.

Old men with beards and ballcaps, grinning post-adolescents in shorts, mothers with toddlers in tow, and capri-clad middle-aged women jostled behind the barriers to meet the President. Many of them held up cell phones, hoping to capture that precious spontaneous photo op.

Hope slipped on a pair of dark glasses to cut the glare as she looked from face to face.

She spotted the woman. Maybe four or five people down the row of well-wishers. Hope couldn't articulate why a tiny, smirking, wrinkled-faced granny with a beaked nose and grey strands peeking from a shawl on her head caught her eye. Of all the people in the crowd, she was the least likely threat to the protectee. Bent with age and arthritis, she could hardly move as waves of younger and more enthusiastic onlookers seemed to sweep her toward the rear. Yet, Hope continued to track the little old lady.

Conchrane finally reached the geriatric well-wisher. A bony hand extended from the crowd.

It moved as if in slow motion. The pale white, age-spotted, blue vein-streaked appendage jutted in front of the President holding a....

"Gun!" shouted Hope.

A snub-nosed revolver appeared.

Two Secret Service agents grabbed for the weapon.

Hope lunged for the shawled woman.

Pop, pop, pop. Three shots rang out.

Then, the impossible happened.

Hope no longer held the assailant.

Amid the confused screams and stampeding crowd, the

little old lady in plain sight of Hope and everyone else had dematerialized.

ABOUT THE AUTHOR

Robert Thornton

Born in Birmingham, Alabama, Robert Thornton has lived in the South all of his life, except for a stint in the U. S. Coast Guard. He is a retired physician who specialized in Family Medicine. He likes to read history and lay books on quantum mechanics. Yeah, he's a nerd. He's an alumnus of the Maui and SEAK Writers Conferences. LETHAL HOPE is his new thriller. He blogs on his website RobertThorntonOnline.com. Don't worry, he doesn't blog about quantum mechanics.

Made in United States
North Haven, CT
18 May 2025